Praise for *USA TODAY* bestselling author
Lori Foster

"Lori Foster delivers the goods."
—*Publishers Weekly*

"Lori Foster is a master at creating likable characters and placing them in situations that tug at the heart and set your pulse racing…"
—Romance Reviews Today

Praise for *USA TODAY* bestselling author
Donna Kauffman

"Donna Kauffman keeps your heart pumping at a fever pitch… Ms. Kauffman is a master at creating riveting romance under high pressure circumstances."
—*Romantic Times*

"Donna Kauffman gives her readers all of the spice and heat they have come to expect—and love…"
—*Under the Covers* reviews

Praise for award-winning author
Jill Shalvis

"Ms. Shalvis draws the reader into her stories immediately and creates a devastatingly tender love story with plenty of action and intrigue. She knows how to deliver."
—*Rendezvous*

"Jill Shalvis. Wonderful romance, wonderful mystery. Always."
—*Affaire de Coeur*

Lori Foster first published in January of 1996 and since has sold over thirty books with six different houses, including categories, novellas, online books, special projects and most recently, single titles. Lori's second book launched the Temptation Blaze miniseries and her twenty-fifth book launched the new Temptation Heat series. Lori has brought a sensitivity and sensibility to erotic romances by combining family values and sizzling, yet tender, love. Though Lori enjoys writing, her first priority will always be her family. Her husband and three sons keep her on her toes.

Donna Kauffman was first published with Bantam's Loveswept line in 1993. After fourteen books, she moved on to write contemporary single titles for Bantam. In 2001, she returned to her category roots and had her first release from Harlequin's Temptation line. *Walk on the Wild Side* was the number-one-selling Temptation title on Amazon.com the week of its release. Donna is also currently writing for Harlequin's Blaze line. She enjoys creating characters that like to push the edge a little! Donna lives in Virginia with her husband and rapidly growing sons. She also has a rapidly growing menagerie of pets. Her two Australian terrors, er, terriers and bare-eyed cockatoo, were recently joined by a baby African Grey parrot named LuLu. Donna's husband is pretty sure it won't end there. Donna's pretty sure he's right.

Jill Shalvis has been making up stories since she could hold a pencil. Now, thankfully, she gets to do it for a living, and doesn't plan to ever stop. She is the bestselling, award-winning author of over two dozen novels. She's hit the Waldenbooks Bestsellers lists, is a 2000 Rita® Award nominee and is a two-time National Reader's Choice Award winner. She was nominated for *Romantic Times'* Career Achievement Award in Romantic Comedy, Best Duets and Best Temptation.

LORI
FOSTER

DONNA   JILL
KAUFFMAN   SHALVIS

MEN OF COURAGE

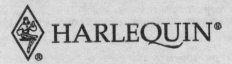

HARLEQUIN®

TORONTO • NEW YORK • LONDON
AMSTERDAM • PARIS • SYDNEY • HAMBURG
STOCKHOLM • ATHENS • TOKYO • MILAN • MADRID
PRAGUE • WARSAW • BUDAPEST • AUCKLAND

ISBN 0-373-83576-0

MEN OF COURAGE

Copyright © 2003 by Harlequin Books S.A.

The publisher acknowledges the copyright holders of the individual works as follows:

TRAPPED!
Copyright © 2003 by Lori Foster

BURIED!
Copyright © 2003 by Donna Jean

STRANDED!
Copyright © 2003 by Jill Shalvis

Visit us at www.eHarlequin.com

Printed in U.S.A.

CONTENTS

TRAPPED!

Lori Foster

CHAPTER ONE

ETHAN WINTERS jerked awake with a start. His heart slammed into his ribs, his head ached, his eyeballs felt gritty and his mouth tasted like sawdust. Still, despite all that, he realized several things at once.

Most noteworthy was the woman in his bed. Yep, that very shapely slim leg draped over his belly was definitely of the feminine variety, not to mention the small, delicate hand resting over his heart. Ethan looked at that hand, but with his eyes so fried, it didn't look like any particular woman's hand. Just a hand. A female hand.

Yeah, okay, so he was in bed with a woman. No big deal. He'd figure that one out soon enough. Since he wore no shoes and no shirt, only slacks that were unsnapped and unzipped— he knew that because he could feel her warm thigh on his skin—it stood to reason that the female was only half-dressed, too. That could mean several things, but likely only meant one thing.

So what? He was thirty years old, single, free to do as he damn well pleased, never mind that he didn't remember what the hell had pleased him.

With the sun so bright through the window, he realized it had to be midmorning. A quick glance at the clock showed it to be eight-forty. What time had he gotten into bed?

The incessant pounding on his front door, now getting louder, had probably awakened him, not the soft woman clinging to him.

Groaning with the effort, Ethan raised his head off the pillow to look at her. All he could see was a luxurious tangle of silvery-brown hair. She had her nose stuck close to his side, practically in his armpit, and she wore his uniform dress shirt—a shirt that didn't quite cover the satiny peach panties stretched over a very fine ass.

He didn't remember giving her his shirt and he sure as hell didn't remember either of them undressing. He reached for her hair, ready to brush aside the heavy mass so he could at least figure out her identity, when the pounding on his front door started again.

The woman stirred, then stretched awake, arching her body into his, raising her hands high above her head. Ethan stirred, too, despite being horribly hungover and in pain. Whoever was at the door could just damn well wait. He smiled down at the woman, anxious to see her, to have the mystery solved.

She rolled onto her back with a sleepy little moan.

Ethan leaped out of bed so fast his head spun and he nearly dropped to his knees. No. Hell, no.

His shaky legs continued to try to give out on him and his heart shot into his throat, making him dangerously close to barfing. He grabbed the footboard for support, swallowed hard, found his voice and shouted, "*What the hell.* Rosie!"

The smile faded off her face. Very slowly she peeked open one smoky-blue eye and groaned. "Shut up, Ethan. My head is splitting."

He sputtered, heard the continued noise at his front door, and nearly panicked. "Get out of my bed."

The look she sent his way wasn't nice. Rather than obey, she rolled onto her stomach and nestled into the pillows. "I need coffee."

Unbound, her hair was glorious, but it wasn't long enough to cover her rump. Ethan stared.

Oh, God. What to do? Rosie. *His* Rosie. His longtime friend, a woman he'd grown up with, his ex-best friend's little sister…

Damn she looked good.

No. No she did not. He squeezed his eyes shut to block out the view of her sprawled in his bed, the sight of her plump bottom turned up for him to see, the long length of those legs. He'd seen her legs before, of course. She wore shorts, even the occasional swimsuit. But he hadn't seen her legs in his bed. Not once. Not ever.

Surely he hadn't… Of course he hadn't. Ethan snorted. What a ridiculous thought. Why, if he'd done anything with Rosie, he'd remember it, and besides, he *wouldn't* do anything with Rosie. She was practically like family. Practically. Not quite, but close enough.

Reassured with his own thoughts, he opened his eyes again—but to be safe he didn't look directly at her. "Stay put."

Rosie grunted but otherwise didn't reply.

Ethan slipped out of the bedroom on unsteady legs and pulled the door shut behind him. Whoever loitered at his front door was making a horrid racket and if he woke up all the neighbors, they'd give Ethan fits.

He crossed the living room, jerked the door open and was met with the sight of Riley Moore, Harris Black and Buck Bosworth. Without being invited, they pushed their way in. Ethan cast a quick glance at the hallway, but all was secure. The very last thing he wanted was for the guys to know Rosie had spent the night.

They wouldn't believe that nothing had happened. Hell, *he* wouldn't have believed it. "What do you guys want? As you can see, you've interrupted my beauty sleep."

Harris snickered. "You'd need to hibernate for a whole winter to improve that mug."

Buck shook his head pityingly. "I knew you were crocked last night, but you must have really fried the old gray matter if you don't remember our fishing day."

Fishing. Oh, hell, he didn't want to fish. Ethan held his splitting head and took two deep breaths. "I've gotta pass today. I can barely stay on my feet."

Riley, the most serious of the three, gave an aggrieved sigh. "I told you last night to quit drinking. I told you to give it up and get over it. But, no, you wouldn't. So now you have to pay the consequences. Go get dressed. We're not leaving without you."

Ethan stiffened. He couldn't credit Riley's nerve, bringing up such a touchy subject. They all knew he didn't want to talk about it. "Go to hell. Me, I'm going back to bed.'' He winced at his own statement. *Rosie was in his bed.*

"Nope.'' Riley sat and propped his big feet on the cluttered coffee table, knocking a newspaper and a Chinese food container to the floor. "I'm sick of you feeling sorry for yourself. It's been well over a year. Enough already.''

Buck and Harris, both silent, both cautious, looked back and forth while following the conversation.

Ethan clenched his teeth. "Drop it, Riley.''

"I will when you do.''

"It's none of your damn business.'' Ethan didn't mean to shout, and, in fact, immediately regretted it when his brain throbbed in pain and his stomach pitched. He rubbed his hands over his face, trying to convince himself he could physically throw Riley out without puking, when a feminine voice suddenly intruded.

"They're your friends, Ethan. Of course it's their business.''

Oh, God.

Riley's feet hit the floor with a thud. Buck's and Harris's chins almost did the same. Ethan groaned. Through his fingers, he looked at Rosie.

Bless the supreme powers that be, she'd had the foresight to at least wrap herself in a sheet.

His shirt covered her upper parts and her lower parts were covered by toga-wrapped linen. Her hair was wild, though, her blue eyes heavy, her cheeks still flushed with sleep.

All three men turned to stare at Ethan. Their expressions ranged from censure to appalled fascination to extreme curiosity.

That was all it took.

"Excuse me a minute, will ya?" Hoping to preserve what little dignity he still possessed, Ethan forced himself to walk to the bathroom, slam the door and lock it. He needed privacy for the next fifteen minutes while he worshiped the porcelain god, praying it was a dream, hoping against hope that when he emerged everyone would be gone—especially Rosie—and his brain could stop pulsing long enough to let him catch his breath.

He was hanging on to the toilet, his head spinning, when he heard footsteps outside the door.

"Ethan?"

He sat back on the cold ceramic-tiled floor and propped himself against the side of the tub, eyes closed. Breathing was a chore, thinking more so. He did not want to talk. "Go away, Rosie."

He expected a sharp comeback, a refusal. Hell, he half expected her to knock the door down.

Through the years he'd known her, Rosie had shown a knack for doing just as she damn well pleased without unnecessary consideration for what anyone else thought. She was headstrong, opinionated, independent—*and she'd been in his bed*.

After a few expectant moments when nothing happened, Ethan tensed with new foreboding. His eyes opened and he stared at the locked door. Rosie hadn't done anything. Had she actually left when he'd asked her to? Or rather, when he'd rudely ordered her to? Had he hurt her feelings?

Had he had sex with her?

His stomach more unsettled than ever, Ethan pushed himself upright and stuck his head out the bathroom door. He didn't hear a single sound. "Riley?"

Ten seconds passed, then, "What?" Riley leaned around the hallway, looked Ethan over, and made a disgusted face.

"Did Rosie leave?"

"She's making breakfast."

"Oh." That figured. If he wasn't so hungover, he'd have remembered that Rosie wasn't a sensitive girly-girl. In fact, she was pretty damn tough…for a female. So of course he hadn't hurt her feelings.

He hadn't slept with her, either.

"It's not what you're thinking," Ethan mumbled to Riley, who continued to look at him as if he was lower than a worm. "Get your mind out of the gutter, will ya?"

Riley crossed his arms over his chest and flattened his mouth. "She said for you to shower and join us."

And Rosie being Rosie, she fully expected to be obeyed. "Yeah, all right."

"She said you have ten minutes."

Annoyed, Ethan slammed the door. He'd take as long as he damn well pleased, and that was that. Hell, the woman didn't own him. Just because she'd awakened in his bed didn't mean she could start thinking about bossing him around.

Course, she always bossed him around. And most of the time he let her. Though she was four years younger, they'd been friends forever, through high school and college. They'd remained close friends through the death of her parents, through his long engagement.

They'd even stayed friends after her brother had run off with *his* fiancée, leaving him literally stranded at the altar nineteen months ago.

Naked, Ethan stepped beneath a stinging spray of hot water and clenched his teeth against the surge of discomfort that radiated to his limbs. He braced his hands on the tiled wall, dropped his head forward and closed his eyes.

God, if he'd had sex with her, he didn't know if they could remain friends. Rosie was a marrying kind of woman, not a one-night stand. And he would never consider marriage again.

What the hell had he done?

"HOW MANY EGGS do you guys want?"

"Two."

"Three."

"Rosie," Riley said with a long, exaggerated sigh, "what's going on?"

Rosie Carrington glanced over her shoulder at Riley. He was a big man, so she cracked three eggs for him, same as Harris. "I'm just making breakfast, Riley. No big deal."

"Yeah, right. Just making breakfast—at Ethan's, dressed in his shirt, probably on the proverbial morning after."

"You're too smart to make assumptions, Riley."

Harris and Buck looked at each other, then snorted. Oh, they'd made plenty of assumptions, all right. Not that she blamed them. It was a rather damning situation.

Riley paid them no mind. "Okay, so what are you doing here? Last I saw Ethan at the party, he was flirting with that sexy redhead and you were fuming mad at him for, as you put it, acting like an ass again."

Rosie concentrated on not overcooking the eggs. Last night…well, she had been fuming mad. Come to that, she was still a little peeved. Most of the time Ethan was the best man around, easy to respect, easier to love. He was hardworking, levelheaded, conscientious. A firefighter with a moral code bone-deep. True, he'd become something of a hound dog, but a good-natured one nonetheless.

Yet whenever people brought up his ex-fiancée, he went from being a great guy to a shallow, chauvinistic jerk who grabbed the first available woman. Rosie assumed he did that to prove to everyone that he was over his fiancée, that he'd recovered. The opposite was true. It showed that he was still hurting—and that hurt her.

It had been over a year and a half, for crying out loud. She'd had enough. It was time to take matters into her own hands.

Rosie knew the men were uncomfortable to have found her here. If all went as she planned, they'd just have to get used to it. Besides, she was now decently covered—sort of—in a ratty old housecoat that she'd located in Ethan's closet.

"You're being evasive, Rosie."

"Gee, Riley, I'm twenty-six years old. I thought that meant I didn't have to answer to anyone for my personal life."

Harris scratched his head, making his black hair more disheveled than ever. "You and Ethan have a personal life?"

She ignored him as she poked a fork at the pound of sizzling bacon in the cast-iron skillet. Four men, all of them big bruisers, needed a lot of food to maintain their energy levels. "You know, I'm amazed you guys planned to go fishing all day without breakfast. It's the most important meal of the day. You shouldn't skip it."

The men smirked at that ludicrous comment. As firefighters, Ethan and Harris kept in the peak of health. Their jobs allowed nothing less. Buck owned a lumberyard and physical labor was part of his daily work week. He had muscles on his muscles.

And Riley—Rosie peered at him again. Riley was an evidence technician for the police department. A former member of the SWAT team, he now owned a self-defense studio where he taught sparring, grappling, Jeet Kune Do and Silat knife fighting.

Next to Ethan, Riley was the most intriguing, appealing man she knew. He could break a person in two without effort. But more often than not, he was as gentle as a lamb—especially where women were concerned.

There wasn't much call for a SWAT team in the small city of Chester, Ohio, thank God, but Riley had only lived here about five years. Before that, he'd evidently suffered some bad times, not that he ever spoke of it much. He tended to be a very quiet man.

Except for now, when he chose to badger Rosie.

"I think we'll all survive fishing on an empty stomach." Riley's voice was dry, teasing. "Now you won't have to."

Harris leaned forward, sniffing the eggs. "This'll be better than the pork rinds Buck packed."

Buck shoved him in the shoulder. "I'll just eat them all myself then."

"Hey." Harris acted wounded by Buck's selfishness. "You know I was just placating Rosie."

After wrinkling her nose at the lot of them, Rosie began toasting bread. She had half a loaf out and hoped that'd be enough. Ethan wasn't much on domesticity and therefore didn't have an abundance of groceries. His apartment was a pigsty, his kitchen a disaster and his cabinets all but empty.

She glanced at the clock. She'd give the big coward two more minutes tops, then she'd drag him out of the shower whether he wanted to face them all or not. If he was still naked and wet— well, she wouldn't cavil. In fact, the idea appealed to her.

Dragging him out proved unnecessary when not five seconds later Ethan appeared in the doorway. His mellow brown eyes were bloodshot, his blond hair still wet and only finger-combed, his feet bare. He'd pulled on clean jeans and a gray T-shirt, and to Rosie, he looked better than breakfast.

Her heart felt full to bursting. "You okay?"

He sent her a cautious sneer, hooked a chair, yanked it out from the table and dropped heavily into it. "I'll live, if that's what you mean." His mean, red-eyed look moved around the room to encompass each of his friends. "I'm not going fishing today."

"Of course not."

"We understand."

"You're an ass, Ethan."

That last was from Riley, of course. He seemed to love provoking Ethan. Rosie shook her head. They'd all known each other forever—with the exception of Riley who was late to the group, but had quickly become a good friend. They lived to give each other a hard time, so presumably, they were letting Ethan off the hook this time because of her. Since she and Ethan needed to talk, she didn't object.

Without a word, she set a cup of strong black coffee in front of Ethan. He drank half of it, cursed when he burned his tongue, then glared at her. "You're not my housekeeper or my cook."

"With the way you live, you couldn't pay me enough to be either."

Harris snickered. Buck held his breath.

Riley said, "You are a damn slob. When was the last time you cleaned?"

"What's it to you, Mom?" He drank the rest of the coffee and Rosie silently refilled his cup. He muttered his grudging thanks.

Riley lounged back in his seat. Because his censure was so obvious, his silence was more annoying than chatter would have been.

Rosie served the men. When she started to take

her own seat, Riley stood to pull out her chair. Ethan growled at him, and Riley growled back.

Men. They could be so unaccountably strange. "Dig in, fellas."

The next few minutes were filled with sounds of appreciation as the men practically inhaled the enormous amount of food she'd set on the table.

In all the time she'd known Ethan, she'd seen him drunk twice—this being the second time.

It amazed her that Ethan could eat such a hardy meal after a hangover. Other than his bloodshot eyes and listlessness, you wouldn't know he'd been so miserable just half an hour before.

Harris finished first. "Damn, that was good, Rosie." He patted his flat stomach. "If I come back tonight, will you cook dinner, too?"

Ethan pierced her with a direct stare. Rosie smiled. "Sure, Harris. Come on by my house around six. I planned on making stew today."

His brows shot up. "Really? I mean, I was kidding, but hell, I'm always up for your stew."

Buck pushed back his empty plate. "If that sorry sack is invited, then naturally I'm coming, too."

"I'll make plenty." Rosie loved to hang out with the guys. Because she'd had a tendency to tail her older brother wherever he went, she'd grown very close to the lot of them. She had very few female friends, thus the guys had become the sum total of her social circle.

Riley shook his head. "You're both mooches. But what would one more matter? Count me in."

Ethan's chair scraped back across the floor. He snatched up his empty plate, caused an awful clatter as he roughly stacked the rest of the empty dishes, then moved to the sink. He kept his back to them all as he scraped the plates before nearly throwing them in the dishwasher.

The men looked at each other, shrugged, then prepared to leave. One by one they gave Rosie a hug and a hardy thank-you, with Riley choosing to go last.

He tipped up her chin. "I'll be back by three. You want to come by the gym? Maybe work off some tension?" He gave a meaningful nod of his head toward Ethan's rigid back.

"I suppose that'd be better than killing anyone, huh?"

Riley laughed. "You're getting good, sugar, but not that good. Not yet."

Ethan jerked around. "Just what the hell does that mean?"

Harris and Buck hunkered out, muttering to Riley that they'd meet him in the truck.

Riley crossed his arms over his chest and faced Ethan. "She's taking lessons."

With an expression of incredulous disbelief, Ethan looked from Rosie to Riley and back again. "What kind of lessons would those be?"

His tone was so suspicious that Rosie laughed. "Self-defense, mixed with some knife fighting." She took a stance and chopped the air with a fist. "I'm going to be lethal."

Rather than appeased, Ethan appeared more livid. "What the hell are you doing that for? Has someone been bothering you?"

She resisted the urge to say *you* and shook her head. "I just like staying in shape and knowing I can take care of myself. I'm single, remember?"

Ethan's face turned red and he strangled on his reply.

Pulling the tiger's tail, Riley said, "Don't worry, Ethan. I'm real gentle with her."

Rosie thought Ethan's eyes might cross. Instead he fumed in silence for nearly a full thirty seconds before stalking out of the room.

"Oh, boy," Riley rumbled under his breath. He gestured for Rosie to precede him as he headed to the front door. Ethan waited for them there, holding it open, his impatience to be alone with Rosie plain.

Riley walked out into the hallway. "Be good, kids."

"You know I'm always good. But I can't make any promises for Ethan."

He winked at her. "You'll keep him in line."

Ethan snapped the door shut, then turned both locks with a dreadful sense of finality. When he faced Rosie, she decided a strategic retreat was in order; he did not look like a happy man.

In fact, he looked very unhappy. Or maybe "riled" was the word. Yeah, he looked downright riled. She supposed Riley's teasing flirtation hadn't helped matters.

Ethan was used to Harris and Buck razzing her. After all, they'd all grown up in the same neighborhood. The three of them had been best buds with her brother—until her brother had slipped off with Ethan's fiancée.

Riley was new to the mix, and while they all liked him a lot, Ethan apparently didn't take Riley's teasing the same at all.

She'd made it all the way to the bathroom when Ethan caught her arm. "Rosie."

There was so much warning in the way he said her name, she kept her back to him. "Hmm?"

His sigh parted the back of her hair. "Don't play games." He caught both arms and turned her around. "What were you doing here this morning in my bed?"

"Sleeping?"

His jaw worked, his eyes narrowed. Reaching inside the neckline of the housecoat, Ethan fingered the collar of his shirt. His gaze settled on her mouth. "Why aren't you wearing your own clothes?"

Very slowly, realization dawned on Rosie. "Oh, my God. You don't remember, do you?"

An arrested expression crossed his features. His pupils expanded until only a thin ring of light brown remained. His straight, dark brows pulled together. "Just what am I supposed to remember?"

Indignation reared up, followed by humiliation. "Ethan Winters. You have no idea what happened last night, do you?"

He blustered with his own dose of exasperation. "I know damn good and well we didn't have sex."

Rosie gasped, not because he was wrong, but because he was so sure that he hadn't touched her. What was she? Chopped liver? She felt just contrary enough not to reassure him. "Yeah, and how do you know that if you don't remember?"

Muscles tensed, Ethan let his smoldering gaze take a leisurely trip over her—but he only got as far as her breasts. "You were wearing a shirt. And panties. When I have sex with a woman—" his gaze rose and locked on hers "—she's buck naked. Not half-dressed."

Rosie dropped back against the wall with a thud. Her heart had started bouncing around with his first hot look, and his words had nearly brought her to her knees. Oh, she could only imagine what Ethan did when he had sex, but she believed him: the woman wouldn't be wearing clothes.

She cleared her throat, then had to clear it again when he flattened both hands to the wall on either side of her head. At five-nine she was a tall woman, but Ethan stood six-two and towered over her. He leaned in the smallest bit, probably trying to intimidate her—and doing a good job of it, but not for the reasons that he might assume. She wasn't afraid of Ethan and she never would be.

But she was extremely aware of him as a man. She stared at his sternum and gave an irrefutable reminder. "You were drunk. You couldn't have gotten your own clothes off, much less mine."

Ethan considered that, then smiled. "True. And being that drunk, I doubt I could have gotten a boner no matter what you did."

With another gasp, Rosie shoved him hard—with no visible effect. "I didn't do anything."

"You must have taken off your clothes, because as you just said, I was too damn drunk to accomplish it on my own."

Her eyes narrowed. "Not too drunk to flirt with that redhead."

He stared past her shoulder. After a second, his eyes lightened and the right side of his mouth kicked up. "Yeah, I remember her now. Where'd she go?"

Oh, that was one nasty little shot too many. Rosie stomped on his toes. Given that she was as barefoot as he was, it wasn't an overly painful move. But he did jerk back, giving her a chance to duck under his arm. She stormed into the bathroom and slammed the door. Hard. She took a lot of satisfaction in clicking the lock into place.

Ethan didn't beat on the door. He just said, "You have to come out sooner or later."

She felt like beating on the door. Or on his

head. Instead she took two deep breaths to gather her calm. "My clothes are in your laundry room. Your precious redhead dumped her drink on me, so until you run them through the wash, I can't wear them again. I'd smell like a lush."

Silence stretched until Ethan finally said, "Oh."

"Yes, oh." Inside the bathroom, Rosie stripped off the housecoat and his shirt. "Why don't you throw them in the washer while I shower?"

"Sure thing."

She could hear him whistling as he walked away, secure in the knowledge that nothing of a sexual nature had occurred between them.

But he didn't know that for sure, and no way would she tell him. Let him stew. Let him wonder.

And maybe, just maybe, he'd think about it enough that he'd start to like the idea.

Rosie grinned as she stepped into the shower. She had a plan, and oh, boy, it was going to be fun.

CHAPTER TWO

SHE WALKED INTO the kitchen with his toothbrush sticking out of her mouth.

In the process of shaking out a large plastic garbage bag, Ethan froze. Rosie's hair was still wet, pushed straight back from her forehead and hanging in long twisted ropes down her back. Over *his* housecoat.

Which was now the only thing she wore.

Ethan knew that because she leaned into the laundry room and pitched his shirt onto the pile of dirty clothes, then turned and stuck her folded panties into her purse, which was on the counter. With foamy toothpaste dripping down her chin, she headed back for the bathroom.

It took Ethan a moment to get his eyelids to work so he could blink. When he did, he couldn't help but notice that her behind, without benefit of underwear, jiggled just a little more beneath the terry-cloth robe. He jerked around, grumbling and too warm and feeling somewhat hunted.

"Damn irritant." He shoved an old pizza box into the garbage bag.

Five minutes later Rosie emerged again. She gave him a big toothy smile and said, "I used your toothbrush."

"Yeah, I noticed." He would not keep staring at her.

"You don't mind, do you?"

He started to say, *Of course not*; after all, they'd been friends a long time, shared drinks, once even an ice-cream cone. He wasn't worried about her germs.

But she didn't give him a chance. "I figured after last night, it wouldn't be any big deal."

Ethan went rigid. "Nothing happened last night."

"Did you put my stuff in the wash?" Apparently unconcerned with his emotional turmoil, Rosie pushed in a kitchen chair, closed a cabinet.

Shaking his head to clear it, Ethan said, "Yeah, they should be ready for the dryer in about ten more minutes." He continued to stuff empty food containers and soup cans, plastic cups, newspapers and junk mail into the bag. He shouldn't have felt so awkward with Rosie. He never had before—but then, he'd never slept with her before, either.

He glared when he realized that she intended to help him clean. Not only that, but she'd accomplished more in two minutes than he had in ten. Women, he decided, just had a knack for being efficient with housework.

"Leave that stuff. I'll get it." He glanced around at the remaining mess and for some stupid reason, felt compelled to explain. "I've been on a night shift all week. Had two nasty calls, one right before the banquet. Had to use the Jaws of Life on a guy who got caught in his car. Damn thing was on fire..." At her look of horror, his voice trailed off. He shook his head. "I got behind on stuff, but I planned to clean today anyway, since I have the next four days off."

"You're okay?"

Damn it, she didn't have to sound so anxious. She was a friend, not his keeper, not his sibling, not his wife. "I'm fine."

For a long moment she didn't look convinced, then she shrugged. "I don't mind helping." She wrung out a dishrag and wiped off the stove. "I've got nothing else to do until my clothes are done, then I have to head into the office. I have a house to show today."

As a real estate agent, her hours varied.

"I don't want you to help."

She blinked up at him with fresh-faced provocation. "Why?"

Damn, she looked cute straight from the shower. Rosie had never, in his opinion, needed much makeup. Her skin was fair, framed by silky brown hair that didn't contain a single hint of red. Her brows were dark, finely arched, her lashes long. Though her eyes were blue, they weren't an ordinary blue. They looked softer than ordinary blue, sort of smoky and smoldering, and when she got annoyed or excited, they turned stormy gray.

Would they turn gray when she was sexually aroused?

Ethan's scowl intensified. "Women always think they have certain rights after cleaning a guy's place."

"Wow, no kidding?" Her brows rose higher. "That's like…really profound. Your grasp on womankind is nothing short of astounding."

She was baiting him, maybe even poking fun at him. "My grasp is astute enough to know you can't be trusted, that you wait for a reason to screw a guy over or to confuse him so that he screws himself over or—"

Rosie stuck her fingers in her ears and said, "La, la, la, lalalal—"

"Stop that!"

She struck an arrogant, annoyed pose, her hands on her hips. "Then stop spouting nonsense."

Ethan shook his head at the gesture, until he realized that her stance made the robe gap just a little above and below the belt. It showed a length of her legs—which he'd seen a gazillion times, for crying out loud—and her cleavage, which he knew she had but he *hadn't* seen much before now.

Everything male within him went on alert, and he mumbled, "It is not nonsense."

"Are you talking to me or my boobs?"

Flabbergasted, Ethan jerked his gaze up to her face, saw her smile and wanted to shout with frustration. Ruthlessly he beat his male instincts into submission. "You."

"Huh. And here I was certain my ears were on my head, not my chest."

In a ridiculous show of temper, he threw the garbage bag down on the floor. "Damn it, Rosie, what is wrong with you? What are you up to?"

She shrugged, then groaned dramatically. "I need some aspirin."

Dismissing him, she turned to the cabinet and began riffling around until Ethan said, "Here, I keep them over the stove.'' He shook out two white pills and handed them to her. A new thought occurred to him. "You hungover, too?"

She lifted the aspirin off his palm, tossed them into her mouth and bent her head into the sink to grab a drink of water straight from the tap. When she'd finished, she shook her head. "No, of course not.''

He hadn't thought so. Rosie was never much of a drinker. Come to that, he wasn't, either, and he was thoroughly disgusted with himself for overindulging last night. "If you're not suffering from too much drink, then what's your problem?"

"I just have a headache from lack of sleep, actually." She sent him a calculated look. "We didn't get to bed till late."

His chest constricted. Why hadn't she gotten enough sleep? She'd been dead-out when he'd awakened.

The washer buzzed and Rosie stepped into the small laundry room off the kitchen to put her clothes in the dryer, giving Ethan a moment to think.

There had to be any number of reasons why she'd been in his bed, other than the most distressing one. Why she didn't want to tell him, he couldn't say. Sometimes Rosie could be difficult for no apparent reason.

But he'd get the truth out of her, one way or another.

"Hey, Ethan?"

He stayed in the kitchen, unwilling to test his resolve by getting near her again. "Yeah?"

"Did you mean that I couldn't be trusted, or women in general?"

Oh, hell, he didn't want to have this discussion with her. He jammed a carton of sour milk into the bag with more force than was necessary. Just getting the garbage off the countertops and off the floor made his place look much cleaner. Normally it didn't get so bad, but on top of the lousy week, he'd really been dreading the party last night. For days, cleaning had been the last thing on his mind.

"Is this a tough question, Ethan?"

Knowing she wouldn't let it go, he gave her the truth. "I meant all women."

"Really?" The silence was telling. "Including me?" She strolled back in, her eyes a flat gray— not a good sign.

"Rosie, let's drop this, okay?" Ethan could already tell she was up for an argument. He wasn't. He needed to know that he hadn't... touched her. And then he needed more sleep.

"No, it's not okay." She crossed her arms under her breasts. "You've insulted me."

He stared at the ceiling so he wouldn't be tempted to look at her breasts again. "How about if I just apologize?"

"Not if you aren't sincere." She sighed, sounding a little defeated. "You know, I fully intended to tell you everything."

Everything? He gave up his study of the ceiling and met her gaze. "What the hell does that mean?"

"You know." She flapped a hand. "Why I'm here, what I want, stuff like that."

What she wanted? Ethan tied the bag shut and set it aside. If she kept this up, his head would explode. "Okay, let's get this over with. What do you want?"

Her mischievous smile came slowly, accompanied by a twinkle in her eyes. "Oh, you'd like to rush me through this, wouldn't you? But why? You weren't in a rush last night."

He reached for her and she ducked away, laughing. "I still can't believe you forgot everything from last night."

Two deep breaths didn't help Ethan to contain

his temper. "There wasn't much to forget, now was there?"

"There was enough."

His jaw ached from clenching his teeth. "If that's true, then you took advantage of my drunken state—which proves what I said. Women can't be trusted."

"Some women, maybe."

"Like a woman who sleeps with a guy she knows is drunk?"

She winced, pretending to be wounded, but her grin told the real story. "Okay, let's back up. When you spout all that baloney about women not being trustworthy, you make yourself look really pathetic."

"Is that right?"

"Yep. It shows that Michelle really did a number on you and that you let her."

Oh, no, no way. He didn't want to talk about Michelle. He didn't even want to hear Michelle's name. Not now, not ever. "Be smart, Rosie, and keep her out of this."

Of course she didn't listen to him. She wouldn't be Rosie if she did. "Why? That's what this is really all about, isn't it? You got jilted and you've been playing the wounded swain ever since."

"It's none of your business. You're a friend, not my mother, not my confessor."

"Damn right I'm your friend."

She put her hands on her hips again, but this time Ethan was too annoyed to admire her cleavage. Rosie's anger struck him in waves and left him a little awed. He'd only witnessed her fierce temper a handful of times.

"I've had enough of you dragging around with your tail between your legs."

"I don't."

"Don't growl at me, Ethan Winters. What would you call it? You date every single girl within a three-hundred-mile radius—but only once. You make cracks about women all the time—and in case you've failed to notice, I'm a woman."

"I noticed."

That shut her up, even left her bemused, but only for a moment. Her chin lifted. "Yeah, well, when you belittle half of humanity—"

"The female half. And I don't belittle them, I just look at them realistically. I see them for how they are."

She rolled her eyes. "You make yourself look defensive." Her expression softened. "You make yourself look...well, lovesick."

The humiliation of being jilted in front of half the town and all his friends and family would be burned on his brain for the rest of his life. It wasn't the sort of thing that a man just got over.

It wasn't the sort of thing that Ethan would ever forget.

Rosie took a step closer to him. "Getting drunk and picking up strange women is certainly not the behavior of a hero, a role model for the community."

Because he didn't like the way she looked at him, and he especially didn't like the topic, Ethan backed up. "Screw that. I never asked to be called a hero."

In fact, part of the reason he'd started drinking last night was the ceremony honoring him. It had been every bit as bad as he'd imagined. He'd felt ridiculous, the center of attention for the first time since the wedding. And he'd felt undeserving.

"Ethan." Rosie's tone chastised as she continued to advance, nearly backing him into the pantry. "You're a firefighter and that's heroic enough. But you risked your life to save those people."

He sidestepped away from the pantry and found himself in a corner, next to the stove. "I did what any guy would have done, especially a firefighter. I did my job. That's all there is to it."

"In near-zero visibility? Knowing that the house could have collapsed at any moment?"

Ethan dropped his head back against the wall and stared at the ceiling. Three weeks ago when he'd entered the flaming residence, he hadn't had heroism on his mind. Through the crackle of burning wood and shattering glass, he'd heard people calling, pleading for help. Their voices had been raw from the thick smoke, desperate. Weak. Ethan had simply reacted.

He'd done what he was trained to do.

It hadn't been easy to carry the man out while dragging the teenage son. Everything was ablaze, the smoke so dense he couldn't see his hand in front of his face. He'd made his way through, inch by inch, but he'd managed, and they'd all lived. He was grateful for that—and embarrassed that so much hoopla had been made about it. He didn't ever again want to find himself as the focus of a crowd; it always reminded him of that awful wedding day when he'd been left standing alone at the altar.

Yet there he'd been last night, at the damn ceremony, being applauded by the very people who'd looked at him with pity the night his bride had failed to show. He'd been dressed up then, too, and he'd felt just as numb.

The memories assailed him, churning through his blood, ringing in his ears. He breathed hard, nearly panting, but it didn't help.

God, he was going to puke again.

Rosie touched his chest, gently stroking his right pectoral muscle. Her fingertips grazed his nipple.

It so startled him, the awful memories faded beneath a new emotion. He felt his body stir with sexual awareness.

"I was so proud of you, Ethan, when they gave you the Fire Commission's Valor Award. But then I'm always proud of you. You risk your life all the time without a second thought. You do what most men won't do—to help others. You're always so tall and commanding and direct. And last night you looked so incredibly handsome in your dress uniform."

Trying to ignore his unwanted arousal, Ethan focused on her soothing voice and eventually on the familiar features of her face. Rosie smiled at him and rested her palm over his heart.

"You know, you owe it to yourself for the person you are, and to the community for the person they see you as, to stop being a self-pitying jerk.''

He lurched at the shock of her words, such a contrast to the mood she'd created. Rosie poked him in the chest. Her voice was no longer quite so soothing. ''I understand how you feel, Ethan—''

''You can't have a clue.''

That seemed to make her angrier. ''You're obviously, *rightfully,* embarrassed that Michelle jilted you.''

''In front of two hundred people.'' He hadn't meant to shout, not that it fazed Rosie at all. No, if anything, she stepped closer until he felt her legs against his.

She tilted her head way back so she could stare him in the eyes. ''When you carry on the way you do, it looks like you're still pining over her.''

Ethan snorted. Personally, he thought just the opposite to be true. People saw him with different women, saw him enjoying his bachelor life, and it proved that he was over Michelle, that he didn't care.

That she hadn't ripped his heart out.

Leaning closer still, until her nose nearly touched his chin, Rosie said, ''But I know you're not lovesick, Ethan. I know, because you *didn't* love her.''

Ethan grabbed her shoulders to keep her from getting any closer. He would have moved away from her, but she had him boxed in. That thought almost made him smile. He weighed a smidgen off two hundred pounds, and Rosie couldn't possibly go over one-thirty, yet she did her best to intimidate him with her body.

Her best was pretty damn tantalizing, he admitted, when he felt her soft belly against his crotch.

All humor vanished.

She stared up at him, her eyes the color of an approaching storm. ''You want people to know you're over Michelle, that she didn't really affect you? Well, I have a better suggestion than what you've been doing.''

Ethan could barely breathe. Her mouth was right there, so close he could smell the toothpaste she'd just used and damn, it looked good. He wanted her, whether he denied it or not, whether he wanted to or not. Unable to move, he growled, ''What suggestion?''

''Get involved with a nice girl.'' Her gaze dropped to his mouth and her voice lowered, went husky in a way he'd never heard from Rosie before. "Quit playing the sexist Neanderthal and get serious again. Stop running scared."

"I'm not—"

She touched his bottom lip, stealing his thoughts, making him tense. She whispered, "Let me love you."

ETHAN KEPT TO THE SHADOWS of the large elms that lined the street, skirting buildings while trying not to look too furtive. He wanted to see her without being seen himself.

He couldn't believe he was doing this.

Actually, everything he'd done in the past twenty-four hours fell into the realm of the "not to be believed," starting with getting rip-roaring drunk, and ending with Rosie in his bed. So what did one more idiotic thing matter?

It didn't. Besides, his curiosity was too keen to keep him away. Luckily, Riley's studio had an enormous front window, so he'd be able to see what kind of lessons Rosie was taking without her knowing he spied.

He could only imagine what she'd think if she knew. The silly goose already thought herself in love with him. If she thought, even for a second, that he returned that overly valued emotion...

Ethan grunted, but deep inside himself something warm had started stirring the moment she'd said those four little taunting words. *Let me love you.*

He knew it was only lust. And no wonder with the way she'd been coming on to him. An ordinary woman he could have withstood, but Rosie…he hadn't wanted to chance it.

Nearly panicked, he'd sent her on her way with the explanation that he loved her, too—as a friend, and only a friend.

He'd looked her right in her beautiful blue eyes and lied through his teeth, telling her he didn't want her sexually, that he saw her as asexual, like a pal. Totally sexless. No sex thoughts involved at all. Sex, no. Friends, yes.

Rosie was not stupid.

She'd sighed, patted his chest in a curiously tender way and told him she'd give him a little time to get used to the idea.

He had a week.

Then she'd dressed and left and he *still* didn't know what the hell had happened last night in his bed. He'd be deranged with curiosity in a week. He had to find out something soon.

The sun was bright, baking down on his head and back. July had started on a heat wave that showed no signs of relenting. Shimmering hot waves rose from the blacktop parking lot. Ethan wore his aviator-style mirrored sunglasses, but still he had to hold a hand up to shield his eyes when he reached Riley's.

There were few people out on this sweltering afternoon, so he stood alone on the sidewalk with only the occasional passerby. Still, he maintained a casual air of indifference so he wouldn't look suspicious. The second he peeked inside, he spotted Riley rolling around in the middle of the mat with someone. It took Ethan less than three seconds to realize the person in the baggy T-shirt, snug shorts, sneakers and headgear was Rosie.

Calm control took a flying leap.

In three long strides Ethan had the door open and had advanced halfway across the gym. He ripped off his sunglasses to better see their shameful behavior. "What in the hell are you doing?" The rafters trembled with his bellow.

Riley, his head stuck between Rosie's thighs, looked up in surprise. His voice was a bit strangled, due to the way she had her legs clenched tight around his neck, when he said, "It's called the North South Position."

He grunted, did a quick flip and ended up on top with Rosie peering at Ethan, her face red with exertion, her head now between Riley's thighs.

Ethan gawked and fought the urge to bodily separate them. "That's...that's *obscene*."

Rosie tried to buck Riley off—and that only made matters worse from Ethan's perspective. His vision started to blur.

"I'm learning...leg...chokes," Rosie managed to gasp around her panting breaths. To Ethan, it appeared her eyes were starting to water.

He was more than ready to intervene when they rolled again and Ethan had to jump to keep from getting caught in the fast-churning tangle of arms and legs. When they stopped, Rosie was on top and she had Riley's arm caught in an awkward position, using her whole body to keep a steady pressure on it. Riley, around his strained laughter, cried uncle.

Rosie jumped up, punched a fist in the air like a world conqueror, and gave a ferocious battle cry. "Ha! Gotcha with a chicken wing."

Riley stood, too, grinning from ear to ear, but he shook his head at her. "You hadn't sunk it good enough. I could have gotten loose if Ethan hadn't been standing here breathing fire."

Rosie gasped in high indignation. "That's just like a man to claim he lost to a woman only because of *another* man."

Riley slipped his arm around her. "We'll keep working on it." He winked at Ethan.

At that particular moment Rosie wasn't the least attractive. Her hair stuck out in crazy clumps around the headgear, some long tangled tendrils loose, some looped in and around the straps. Her face was flushed and there was sweat on her forehead and upper lip. The wrinkled, sweat-dampened clothes she wore couldn't have been less appealing.

And Ethan wanted to throw her over his shoulder, smack her behind soundly, and remind her in no uncertain terms that she'd not only professed her love, but she'd given him a week to get used to it.

Instead, trying to hide his disgruntlement, he said to both of them, "If anyone taped your *lessons,* they could sell them for porn videos."

Cocking one shapely hip and giving him a siren's come-and-get-it smile, Rosie quipped, "Gee, honey, ya really think so?"

The pose should have been ludicrous given her present appearance. Instead, Ethan choked on a surge of lust.

Laughing, Rosie turned and sashayed her way out of the gym, heading for the showers. "Be right back."

The second she disappeared from sight, Riley dropped against the wall and grabbed his shoulder with a loud groan. "Man, she about tore my rotator cuff. She's good."

Ethan stared at him. His eyes narrowed the tiniest bit.

Doing a double take, Riley asked, "What?"

Ethan stared some more, no civil words coming to his mind or mouth.

"Oh, come on, Ethan." Riley pushed his sweaty hair back and grunted. "I'm teaching her to defend herself with legitimate defensive and offensive moves. As a real estate agent, you know she finds herself with male clients in empty houses a lot."

"Well, I hope if a guy attacks her, she doesn't stick her face in his crotch. I seriously doubt that'll deter him."

Riley tried and failed to stifle his laugh. "She's learning different ways to utilize the chicken wing—and as I said, she's getting good at that. She's also learning some good leg chokes. Usually, a woman who is attacked finds herself on her back with the assailant on top. I'm teaching her how to get out of that hold."

It made sense. God knew, Ethan wanted her safe, but still...

"I'm also teaching her the Guard, the High Crotch Series and some Silat knife moves."

"What's the…never mind. I don't want to know." By silent agreement they moved off the mats and to a bench lining one wall. Ethan plopped down, stretched out his legs, dropped his head back against the cool wall and sighed. "Damn, I'm beat."

Totally deadpan, Riley asked, "Long night?"

But Ethan was actually glad that he'd brought up the subject. Slowly, he swiveled his head toward Riley and opened his eyes. "Did Rosie tell you anything?"

"She's not one to kiss and tell."

"I didn't kiss her."

"No? Well, whatever you did, she wouldn't be talking about it. I've never once heard her mention a date or what she might have done on a date, have you?" Rather than wait for a reply, Riley continued. "And you know, now that I'm thinking about it, that's strange, huh?"

Ethan knew he'd rather walk into another burning building than think about Rosie with other men. It never failed to set him on edge. "We didn't have a damn date, and I didn't kiss her."

Rosie reappeared, and Ethan thought she had

to have taken the fastest shower in history. Then he realized she hadn't changed, had only removed the headgear and combed her hair.

She was still sweaty.

"You," she said, pointing at Ethan, "don't know what you did."

He snared her gaze with his own and wouldn't let her look away. "So tell me, Rosie. Did I kiss you?"

Her cheeks turned pink and she shrugged. "Maybe I don't remember, either."

Ethan slowly stood to approach her. "Oh, if I'd kissed you, Rosie, believe me, you'd remember."

She squared off, facing him like a prizefighter with her hands on her hips, legs braced. "Yeah? And why's that?"

He jutted his chin forward to match her stance. "Because I'm a damn good kisser."

"Maybe."

"It's true." He reached back to nudge Riley with a fist. "Ask Riley, he knows."

Riley almost fell off the bench. "What are you talking about?" His voice rose to a shout when Riley almost never shouted. "I sure as hell haven't kissed you!"

"Excuse me?"

They all turned toward the front door, and there stood the redhead from the night before. Her glorious hair—Ethan did love the color—was piled on top of her head in loose, very feminine disarray. She wore a pale green, knee-length skirt with a crisp white blouse and very high heels. An enormous satchel was hooked over her arm.

Great, Ethan thought, just great. He needed this like he needed a four-alarm fire.

Much provoked, Riley stood and immediately shouted, "I have never kissed Ethan, swear to God."

Rosie moved with the speed of light to position herself in front of Ethan.

Ethan started to laugh. He couldn't help himself. He was still a little hungover, still very confused by Rosie's recent offer, and horny as hell to boot. Could his life get more muddled?

"It's true," he confirmed. "Riley is as macho as they come. Hell, he's so macho he has hair on the soles of his feet."

"I do not." Riley turned to glare at him. "And don't help me, all right?"

Biting back his smile, Ethan said, "By the way, Riley, I was talking about those twins who wanted to double date, remember? The one told you I was a great kisser and she wanted to test you out to see who was better?''

Riley's frown lifted, a smile started and he said, ''Oh, yeah.''

The redhead looked beyond confused, on the verge of bolting. Her apparent nervousness kept her shifting her feet and twisting her hands. ''Are you open?''

Obviously dismissing Ethan and his memories of the twins, Riley looked her over, crossed his arms and said, ''I could be.''

Clutching her satchel, Red said, ''I need to learn some self-defense.''

Riley cocked a brow at that, Rosie scowled and Ethan felt mired in guilt. ''Good God, I didn't assault you, did I?'' He never should have gotten drunk. He never should have...

''No, of course not.'' Her green-eyed gaze darted to Rosie, to Ethan and back to Riley. Her slim brows puckered in a suspicious frown. ''Am I interrupting?''

''We were just about to leave.'' Rosie took Ethan's arm and tried to drag him behind her.

He planted his feet and refused to budge. ''If I bothered you last night, I am sorry. I don't usually drink like that.''

Red's smile was distracted when she forced

herself to look away from Riley. "You were fine," she assured him. "Mostly you just talked about a woman."

Ethan groaned. He felt moronic enough already, but, God, if he'd been waxing poetic about Michelle, he'd have to leave town.

Rosie elbowed him hard to show her displeasure. He grunted, caught her lethal pointy little elbow so she couldn't inflict more damage to his ribs and said to Red, "Again, I'm very sorry. You should have shoved me under a table or something."

"I didn't mind." Red's expression softened. A small smile teased her mouth. "Actually, I thought it was rather sweet that you're so obviously in love with her."

Ethan stiffened, embarrassed and outraged. "I am *not* in love with Michelle."

"Michelle?" Red frowned and again looked around at each person in the room before settling back on Ethan. "But...I thought her name was Rosie?"

CHAPTER THREE

ROSIE DID HER BEST to hide her grin as she turned off the Crock-Pot and dished up heaping bowls of thick stew. She'd gotten home half an hour ago, quickly showered, then changed into cutoffs and a T-shirt. She'd barely finished before they'd arrived.

All of them.

She sneaked a peek at Ethan and felt her heart patter in excitement. He sat at her small round dinner table, behaving like a surly badger, but at least he'd shown up.

He hadn't wanted to. He'd even refused—until Riley suggested to Rosie that they could do a little more practice after they'd eaten. Ethan had immediately changed his mind about dinner, and Rosie was starting to hope that jealousy motivated him.

Just as she finished serving the stew, the bread machine dinged and she carefully removed the hot loaf to a cutting board. The men were all sniffing the air impatiently. Harris even smacked his lips together, making her laugh.

"Ethan, will you pour everyone something to drink? And get the butter out of the refrigerator."

He grumbled an incoherent reply, then fetched a tea pitcher and began filling glasses.

Riley took a long drink and said, "Did you know that Red is a reporter? She was there last night to do a story on Ethan."

Ethan froze with the pitcher poised over Buck's glass. "Oh, shit."

Rosie dropped the large carving knife, almost removing her big toe.

"Hey, be careful there." Riley frowned at her.

She snatched up the knife and rinsed it in the sink. "A reporter? You've got to be kidding."

"Nah, but she's different from a lot of them. She's real sweet. She said she realized Ethan was drunk, so she's going to contact him for another interview."

Buck nudged Ethan to get him to pour the tea, then peered at Riley. "You like her?"

"Yeah, sure. She's a jumpy little thing, and her imagination is a bit much."

Rosie hated the idea of the woman being alone with Ethan. She wouldn't tolerate it, not since she already knew Ethan found her attractive. When she interviewed Ethan, it would have to be with Rosie present to protect his virtue. "What's wrong with her imagination?"

"She has some goofy notion that people are out to get her. She's a little paranoid, if you ask me."

Harris began buttering a thick slab of bread. "What's her real name?"

Grinning, Riley said, "Get this. It's Regina Foxworth." He laughed. "And she is foxy, but 'Red' suits her better than Regina."

Harris and Buck stared at Riley in complete and total bafflement. It was the very first time they'd ever heard him make such a comment concerning a woman.

Rosie couldn't help but grin. Well, well, well. It would gratify her immensely if Riley staked a claim. More than anything else, that would ensure that Ethan stayed free of the woman's clutches.

Ethan reseated himself at the table. "Hell, I don't want to be interviewed. Not by her, not by anyone. I had enough of that crap back when the fire first happened."

"It's good for the department." Harris pointed a spoon at him. "Captain is hoping you'll get us new funding."

"The captain can damn well—"

"If you don't willingly meet with her," Riley interjected, "she said she'd be forced to use what information she got at the ceremony last night."

Rosie made a disgusted face. "And that would be what? That Ethan can't hold his liquor?"

"Probably something like that."

Ethan ignored them to dig into his stew. "Mmm. Terrific, Rosie. Thanks."

The others followed suit, showering her with compliments. She thanked them, took a breath, then forged on manfully. "You know, you could all eat home-cooked meals more often if you'd just settle down."

Harris had his mouth full but he still managed to sputter. "I'm plenty settled."

Buck had the good grace to first swallow. Loudly. "No time. The lumberyard is a demanding mistress."

Harris laughed and thwacked him on the back for that quip.

Riley shrugged. "Maybe someday. But not yet."

Ethan remained conspicuously silent.

"You could all start with a nice house. I see terrific deals all the time." She tried not to stare at Ethan. "There's a nice tight ranch not far from where you already live, Riley. One hundred per-cent financing. New windows, new furnace.''

Ethan stood. ''Mind if I get some more stew?''

Deflated, Rosie waved at him. ''Go ahead. Help yourself.''

For fear of not getting seconds, the other guys jumped up and got in line for the Crock-Pot. Rosie tapped her fingertips on the tabletop. They were all so stubborn.

''I'd waive my fee, you know.''

Riley patted her head on his way back to his seat, his bowl almost overflowing. ''Course you would, hon. It's not that. I just don't think any of us are anxious to get into the home-and-hearth routine.''

Squaring her shoulders, Rosie twisted in her seat and faced Ethan. ''You used to be. Don't you remember when you were wanting kids and a dog and a house with a picket fence?''

A heavy silence fell around them. Other than a quick look in her direction, Ethan paid her little mind. ''It'd be hard to forget, but that was a long time ago.''

''Nineteen months. Not all that long.''

He pierced her with a lethal look. ''Long enough.''

Riley cleared his throat and attempted to help

Rosie by changing the subject. "So, Ethan, you gonna meet up with Red? You know how reporters are. It's easier not to fight them."

"Yeah, what the hell. I'll talk with her."

"She's probably left a message on your machine by now. Let us know how it goes."

"You know," Ethan said, gesturing with a piece of bread, "a good reporter would be covering something more important, like the damn fireworks. The Fourth is next weekend and I don't know about the rest of you, but I'm dreading it already."

Harris lifted his glass of tea in a toast. "Count me in on that. Every year someone sets a fire or gets burned. Why is it the majority of people who want to play with the damn things are idiots?"

"Are you expecting trouble?" Rosie asked.

"Every year." Arms folded on the table, Ethan glared down at his half-empty bowl. "And with the new bill just passed, a lot of the pyrotechnics we hate most are now legal for adults to use. Only adults aren't the only ones getting their hands on them."

"Firecrackers, Roman candles, bottle rockets." Harris leaned back in his seat. "Did you know about twelve thousand people get sent to emergency rooms every Fourth of July? Over fifty percent of them are kids, and ten percent are permanently injured. It sickens me.''

''And,'' Ethan added, ''we have a fireworks dealer in town who's known to be a little less than reputable. I'd love to shut him down, but for now, all we can do is keep an eye on him.''

Since Rosie had never heard Harris speak so…passionately on a topic, she was enthralled— and unaccountably worried. By the nature of their work as firefighters, Ethan and Harris faced various levels of danger daily. She'd tried to get used to that, especially since Ethan always seemed determined to be the first man in, the last man out, and the quickest to volunteer. He might not want to admit it, but he had hero tendencies that were as plain as his hair and eye color, there for all the world to see.

But this sounded more lethal than the usual day-to-day stuff, and she couldn't quite keep the worry from her tone. ''Will it be dangerous for you two?''

Ethan scowled over her concern, even as he shook his head. ''No, but seeing a kid burned is about the most awful thing in the world.''

''I know it's something I'll never get used to,'' Harris conceded.

Looking thoughtful, Riley said, ''Maybe Red

can help. She could at least get some of the facts in the paper, right?''

Buck slanted him a look. ''Just how well did you get to know her this afternoon?''

Riley shrugged. ''We talked about an hour. I told her what the lessons would cost, how often she should come in—stuff like that. She wanted a starter lesson today so we spent another hour on that.'' He stretched. ''I worked up quite an appetite, I can tell you.''

''Hell,'' Ethan muttered, ''if you showed her the same stuff you were doing with Rosie, the two of you might be having kids soon.''

Riley laughed out loud at that, and Rosie blushed.

''We've seen.'' Harris grinned at her, and his blue eyes were glittering with mischief. ''Wanna wrestle, Rosie?''

''No.'' She stood and collected bowls, hoping no one noticed her heightened color. ''Anyone want ice cream for dessert?''

Buck and Harris both cackled at the way she tried to change the subject.

Ethan wouldn't let it go. ''What do you mean, you've seen? You two have been down there watching?''

Buck nodded. "Hell of a show." He and Harris clicked glasses.

Flustered, Rosie smacked them both in the back of the head. "Now you two just quit it. And you, Ethan. You're making a big deal out of nothing. Why, Riley's the one teaching me the moves and he doesn't laugh about it."

She glanced up in time to see Riley wipe the grin off his face. "All right, that's it. Forget dessert. You can all go home now."

Immediate apologies followed, along with a lot of schmoozing hugs and entreaties. Rosie could barely catch her breath, they were all talking so fast and squeezing her so much.

"Enough already! All right, you can stay." Her eyes narrowed. "But no more razzing on my lessons. Understood?"

After they'd all dutifully nodded, Ethan stood. "I'll get the ice cream. One of you lazy slugs get the bowls."

Together, the men managed to serve themselves since Rosie was still peeved and it showed in the way she crossed her arms tight and kept her mouth flat.

The bowls were no sooner filled than the phone rang. Glad for something to do, Rosie answered it on her kitchen wall phone, but then excused herself from the guys to take the call in private. No one seemed to mind that except Ethan, who scowled and asked, "Who is it?"

"A client, nosy." She started to tell them not to wait for her, then saw that Buck already had his mouth full and Harris was soon to follow. "You're all social misfits, do you know that?"

They shrugged. Rosie shook her head and walked out.

The interruption was timely, in her opinion. She needed a few minutes to form her next plan of attack. Bringing up home and hearth hadn't worked, so she'd have to hit Ethan on a more basic level.

Damn it all, she was going to have to seduce him.

THE SECOND Rosie was out of hearing, Ethan said, "Finish up and get out of here. I want to talk to Rosie alone."

Riley bit his upper lip, but refrained from saying anything. Buck wasn't so subtle. "You two hooked up now?"

"No, we're not 'hooked up.' What the hell's wrong with you? Rosie is a friend and you know it."

Harris rolled his eyes. "A *female* friend, and

that's all the distinction she needs far as I'm concerned.''

"That's about it," Buck agreed.

Riley set his spoon aside. "Have any of you ever thought of Rosie in a...you know, sexual way?" He saluted the air with two fingers, giving the first admission, and Harris and Buck quickly lifted their hands, too.

Ethan gawked at them. "You can damn well stop thinking of her that way right now!"

"Impossible."

"No way."

"Sorry."

Ethan shoved his chair back. "You're all..."

"Normal? Healthy?" Riley laughed. "Gifted with perfect eyesight?"

Buck added, "Male."

And Harris tacked on, "Single."

"I don't believe this."

Unconcerned with Ethan's escalating temper, Riley took another bite of ice cream. "You know, Ethan, you're thumping your chest over nothing. Rosie has always treated us as just pals." He pointed his spoon at him. "'Cept for you."

"Lucky bastard," Harris mumbled with feigned but good-natured envy.

Stone-faced, Ethan paced away. Damn it, he was losing his mind. Ever since he'd awakened with Rosie draped over him, he'd been unable to stop thinking about her. But for the most part he'd forcefully kept those thoughts chaste, not carnal. *For the most part.*

But now, with his best friends putting thoughts in his head, well, how the hell was he supposed to *not* think about it? The woman was plain hot and that was all there was to it.

Rosie didn't help any, prancing around in those Daisy Duke cutoffs with her rounded ass and long legs on display. Oh, yeah, he'd noticed the other guys stealing a peek every few minutes. Course, they did that to all females. But still— This wasn't just any female. This was Rosie.

His Rosie, damn it.

Riley dropped his spoon into his empty bowl with a resounding clink, catching Ethan's notice. "She seems a little different since this morning, huh?"

Emotions roiling, Ethan asked through his teeth, "What do you mean?"

"It's like she's on the make or something. The way she's watching you—her body language."

His throat constricting, his eyes burning, Ethan repeated, "Body language?"

"Yeah." Riley turned to his cohorts. "You two've seen it, haven't you?"

"Yep." Buck gave a decisive nod. "She wants him."

"Bad."

"Stop it!" Ethan paced again, more furiously this time. But he couldn't outrun his own thoughts. It was too late. Their words were already bouncing around in his brain, making him sweat, causing his muscles to cramp. Last night he'd done…something with her. This morning she'd been so warm and soft and his bed still smelled like her, sexy and female and utterly Rosie.

He breathed hard, walking faster 'round her kitchen, the three stooges looking on. He couldn't banish the images of Rosie seducing him, touching him, kissing him…

"That's it." Ethan grabbed up their bowls and put them in the sink. "Go home. Go away. Just go."

Harris made no effort to hide his laughter. Buck had to quickly grab for a napkin as Ethan shoved him toward the doorway.

Riley hung back, grinning like a fool. "One thing, Ethan."

"What?" Ethan could barely breathe and seriously doubted he could manage a chat with Riley.

Somber now, Riley crossed his arms over his chest and stared at Ethan. "Don't do anything to hurt her. Remember that she is my friend and I care about her."

Ethan struggled for control. More than anything he wanted to knock Riley on his ass. How dare he act territorial now when seconds before he'd been all but throwing Rosie at him? He looked at Harris and Buck and they nodded, too, equally protective, equally serious about it.

Riley wasn't done. "She's a real nice woman, Ethan, with a huge heart. Don't use what her brother did against her. She had no part in that."

"Goddamn it," Ethan exploded, infuriated that Riley thought such a warning was necessary. He would never hurt Rosie and Riley should have damn well known it. "How dare you bring that up?"

Rosie stepped around the corner, the disconnected phone held loosely in her hand. She frowned in worry, her gaze darting back and forth between the men. "Bring what up? What's going on?"

Refusing to back down, Riley continued to

watch Ethan. Harris and Buck moved to flank Rosie—as if she needed protection.

From him.

"Leave," Ethan said to all three of them. "Or I will."

Rosie bit her bottom lip. "Ethan? What's going on?"

Riley stepped away from Ethan. His expression changed when he tugged Rosie up against his chest for a long hug. "Just guy stuff. Nothing important."

"Don't give me that." She shoved back, her eyes filled with annoyance. "You guys are—"

"Drop it, Rosie." Ethan waited, his temper growing more fractured by the second as each of them took a turn embracing Rosie. Harris even sighed. Buck touched her cheek with poignant regret.

You'd think she was a virgin they'd decided to sacrifice to some evil spirit! Hell, he cared about Rosie, too, always had. Even during his engagement, she'd remained one of his closest friends. The night his fiancée had jilted him, it was Rosie he'd gone to because he'd been too shamed to face anyone else. He could talk with her, just *be* with her, easier than he could anyone.

Looking back on it now, he realized there was

significance in their complete and total trust of one another. There'd always been a special bond between him and Rosie. She liked all of them, hung with all of them, but only he shared that extra closeness with her.

He was the only one she wanted in the sack.

Oh, hell.

Ethan strode to the door and jerked it open. "Enough, all ready. Violins are going to start playing if you guys don't stop being so melodramatic."

As they filed past Ethan, they all grinned and winked and bobbed their eyebrows suggestively. Riley clutched his heart and pretended to swoon. Now these were the guys he knew and loved. He even laughed a little at their antics. "Idiots."

He closed the door behind them, leaned back on it and surveyed Rosie with new eyes—and undiluted male interest.

She looked worried. "Uh…what's going on?"

Ethan pushed away from the door. Just thinking about getting her into bed now, about doing everything he hadn't done last night, made him hot. Holding her gaze, his hunger growing, he murmured, "God, I've been dense."

She took a step back, her eyes wide, locked on his. "Yeah, so what's new?"

Her sarcasm couldn't quite hide her nervousness. Ethan felt like a superior male, ready to gentle the little woman, ready to give her what she evidently wanted, what he now knew he wanted.

"No more games, Rosie."

Her chest rose and fell with deep breaths and she planted her feet, done with backing up. "Okay."

"Do you want me?"

She blinked hard, twice. "You mean... sexually?"

Just hearing her say it nearly tipped him over the edge. His voice turned husky. His chest constricted. "Yeah."

Silky brown hair shimmered around her shoulders with her nod. "I have for a long time now."

"Is that right?" Ethan didn't want to know how long—it might kill him. He stopped two inches from her. "Nothing happened last night, did it?"

"No."

"Not even a kiss?" He wanted it confirmed that if he'd kissed her, she'd damn well know it.

"No." She stared down at her feet. "Your redhead accidentally dumped her drink on me, so I had to leave. You were too drunk to drive and so you asked me to call you a cab.'' She looked up, determination darkening her gaze. ''I decided to take you home myself to be sure you made it safely, and well…I didn't want to leave.''

''I see.''

She rushed to add, ''I did refrain from taking your pants off you.'' She made it sound like a huge concession on her part.

Ethan smiled. ''I appreciate that.''

''You do?'' She started wringing her hands and frowning at him in confusion.

''Oh, yeah.'' Her uncertainty in the face of the bizarre circumstance was rather endearing, Ethan decided. It was rare indeed to see Rosie suffer such a human emotion as self-consciousness. ''I damn well want to be sober when I lie down with you, so I can remember every little detail.''

Her eyes widened like saucers. ''I was going to seduce you,'' she blurted.

''What?''

She nodded hard. ''I was. But it's your fault.''

''My fault you were going to seduce me?'' Following Rosie's train of thought proved impossible, especially when he was already so horny.

''Yes. You were being so stubborn about it, refusing to see me as a female and—''

"I've always known you were a female, Rosie." He wouldn't lie to either of them. "Not once did I ever confuse you with Riley or Harris or, God forbid, Buck."

Her mouth fell open, then snapped shut. "Really?"

She sounded so hopeful, Ethan's heart turned over in his chest. He'd always considered Rosie a very special friend. Now he realized she was very special—in all ways. Especially as a woman. "Hell, yeah." Then he scowled. "So have the other guys."

"What other guys?"

The way she asked that made his worries disappear. She wasn't aware of their interest. And she'd made it clear she wanted him. It was enough. "Never mind."

"But..."

"Shh." He took hold of her shoulders and gently caressed her, hoping to calm her and himself. She felt so soft, so warm. He'd touched her shoulders before, for crying out loud, but this was the first time he'd done so with sexual intent. It was different. How he felt was different.

Rosie deserved the best he could bring to her, and that meant not jumping her bones and dragging her down to the carpet, even when that was what he most wanted to do. He needed to be gentle and considerate. And slow.

Ethan closed his eyes. It was going to be a close call, but he thought, all things considered, he'd manage. "Being that we're both here, alone, and finally in agreement about what we want to do, maybe we should—"

She didn't give him a chance to finish. With an exclamation of delight, Rosie launched herself at him.

Taken off guard, Ethan staggered under her weight, but quickly righted himself. He was already half hard with expectation and now, feeling Rosie hugged up tight to him, her breasts against his chest, her belly against his groin, he lost what little control he'd been hanging on to. "Damn."

"Ethan." She caught his face and kissed him, awkwardly at first but with so much enthusiasm, he groaned. "Ethan," she said again, his name almost a wail.

"Easy," he tried to tell her even as he stroked his hands down her back to that perfect heart-shaped bottom. Her shorts were very short and it was nothing for him to slip his fingers under the frayed edges to tease her firm, rounded cheeks. Her skin was so silky, he felt sure his blood would boil.

Rosie bit his bottom lip. She wasn't overly gentle, either. He jerked, but she knotted her hands in his hair and brought his mouth back to hers so she could suck his lip into her mouth, tease it with her tongue.

"Jesus, Rosie, slow down."

"No." She sealed their mouths together and Ethan tilted his head so he could take over, thrusting his tongue into her mouth, swallowing her moan. It was the first deep kiss they'd ever shared, and boy, it was good.

"Wait." She shoved him back and reached for the hem of her shirt. "I want you to touch me. I've been thinking about you touching me for days."

Oh, no. Hell, no. In very Rosie-like fashion, she was running the show. Ethan couldn't let her do that. She probably had no idea that she drove him wild, that he might lose control at any moment. She'd never driven him wild before, so how could she know?

He caught her wrists and held her still, even when she struggled against him. "Damn it, Rosie. Give me a second." He panted, trembled, while she continued to fight him. He should have expected as much; Rosie wouldn't accept any man's control easily, not even a man she wanted.

Above the lust, that struck Ethan as funny, and he laughed roughly.

Rosie glared at him. "What?" she demanded, still pulling against his hold.

"Let's go into your bedroom." Maybe if he could get her pinned beneath him on the mattress, he could slow her down a little.

"The bedroom? Oh, okay." She tried to turn and hurry in that direction.

Ethan pulled her up short, a little desperate. "Honey, this isn't a race."

She turned around and yelled right into his face, "You'll change your mind!"

She looked so vulnerable, so unsure of herself. He'd been a pig, not seeing what was right in front of his face. "No," he told her very softly, smiling to reassure her. "Not a chance."

"Then why—?"

"Ever since I woke up with you this morning, my imagination has been in overdrive." He touched her slightly parted mouth with trembling fingertips. "Hell, Rosie, thinking about you, wanting you all day, has been like indulging in foreplay for hours and the result is that I'm working with a hair trigger here."

Her eyes darkened to a deep gray. "You've been thinking about me?"

"About getting you naked and under me, yeah." Saying it made him see it, and his stomach cramped with need. But she deserved to hear everything. "I've also been jealous as hell."

"Jealous? Of who?"

Ethan released her and rubbed his face. The need to laugh struck him again, lightening the urgency—at least for him—just a little. Rosie could be so single-minded in her determination she noticed nothing beyond her objective. Of course, he'd been the same, blind to the fact of his friends' interest.

But no more.

Ethan caught her hand and led her toward the bedroom. "Everyone. Any guy who looks at you."

"Really?"

"Especially that damned Riley." They entered her bedroom and Ethan pushed the door shut. "He knew it, too, and kept egging me on."

Disbelief had her wrinkling her nose. "Riley?"

Ethan stared down at her, so overwhelmed with tenderness—with newfound love—he could have choked on it. "And Harris and Buck."

"You've got to be kidding."

"No." His smile came naturally. So did the

love he felt for her, until it filled him up, making him feel whole for the first time in ages. Loosely looping his arms around her, Ethan kissed her temple. "I knew all along that I thought you were hot, but they think it, too."

She snorted. "They do not."

"They do." He smoothed her cheek, her silky-soft brown hair. *Rosie.* He couldn't get over the shock, or the rightness of it. "But you only want me, right?"

She stared at him a long minute before squeezing him tight. "I'm not her, Ethan. Of course, I only want you. Michelle was the biggest fool alive to walk out on you. And as much as I hurt for you when it happened, I was so glad you didn't marry her."

Ethan closed his eyes, cut by her words. He hadn't meant to bring that up, hadn't even been thinking in that direction. Hell, the humiliation Michelle had inflicted couldn't possibly invade his thoughts, not now, not with Rosie in front of him, ready to take him to her bed. He took one breath, then another, but it didn't help.

Leaning back, Rosie saw his pained expression and flattened one hand on his chest. "You didn't love her, Ethan. I know you didn't."

"Rosie…"

Her small hand smoothed over his chest then down his abdomen, and lower. He caught his breath.

Still staring up at him, she touched his fly, gently, curiously. He was fully erect, straining his jeans, and Rosie traced her fingertips up and down his length. "I'm not a fool," she said. "How could I want any other man but you?"

"Yeah," Ethan murmured, barely able to think much less discuss the past. "Right now."

Her smile affected him as much as her touch. "I'm ready."

She stepped back and this time when she reached for the hem of her shirt, Ethan didn't stop her. He stood there, every muscle in his body tense, as Rosie disrobed as naturally as if she'd been baring herself to him for a lifetime. She threw the shirt aside, unhooked her bra, and still he stood there, just watching—and catching on fire.

With slow precision, playing the tease naturally, she unsnapped her shorts, slid down the zipper, and bent to push them off, taking her panties with her. When she straightened, she was beautifully naked.

A slight blush colored her cheeks when she lifted her face and looked at him. Shaking, Ethan closed his hands on her waist and brought her up against him.

''Rosie,'' he whispered, and he took her mouth as he lowered her down to lie flat on the mattress. He'd waited long enough.

He couldn't wait a second more.

CHAPTER FOUR

ROSIE FELT HIS MOUTH on her throat, open, damp, hot. One big hand rested on her ribs, just beneath her right breast. He laid half-atop her, heat pouring off him, *and he wanted her.*

She closed her eyes and luxuriated in the moment. She loved him so much she hurt with it, and now finally she could tell him.

His long rough fingers slid gently over and around her breast, teasing, making her skin prickle, before he cupped her fully. She could feel his hot breath against her shoulder, near her ear, disturbing the fine hairs at her nape. His breathing was rough, uneven, sounding so sexy, so male. He continued to place openmouthed kisses here and there, until Rosie couldn't catch and hold a thought.

She was already squirming, unable to stay still, when his thumb brushed over her stiffened nipple once then returned again and again. The effect was startling, wonderful. Her heart raced and everything she felt intensified to an acute ache.

Rosie looked at him, and all she could think was that this was Ethan, finally. He was hers. "Ethan…"

He groaned, lowered his head and took her nipple into the wet heat of his mouth.

An overwhelming wave of sensation made her thighs stiffen, her toes curl. "Oh, Ethan…"

She arched hard, but Ethan held her steady. "Look at you," he murmured, and his breath drifted over her wet nipple. "So pink and soft. So sweet."

He switched to the other breast and Rosie thought it was almost too much. She'd wanted this, wanted him, for as long as she could remember.

"Take your shirt off, too, Ethan. Please." She barely recognized her own voice, but Ethan understood. He came up to his knees, straddling her hips, and yanked his shirt up and over his head. He started to return to her breasts but she flattened her hands on his shoulders and held him back.

"Let me touch you," she whispered with wonder. She'd seen Ethan without his shirt before. They'd played softball, gone swimming, and he'd helped her move in. Each time he'd pulled off his shirt, as most of the guys had. It had been so hard not to stare, not to let her love for him show through. All of them were impressive, but they all weren't Ethan.

Now he was here, with her, and she intended to get her fill.

Slowly, savoring the moment, she smoothed her palms over him. He felt perfect to her, hard and sleek and hot, with soft, crisp hair lightly scattered from pectoral to pectoral. His body hair was shades darker than his blond head, a rich brown, matching his brows and lashes. A very sexy line of silky hair teased down the middle of his abdomen and disappeared into his low-riding jeans. Awed, Rosie shoved him onto his back.

He smiled up at her, eyes twinkling with amusement. "You are so pushy, Rosie."

This time she straddled his hips—and he shut up as she settled atop his erection. "I can feel you beneath me." Her eyes closed, her breath caught. "I can't wait until you're inside me, Ethan. Until I can feel all of you."

Heat flared in his eyes and he growled, "Come here."

She evaded his hands and moved to the side

of him. "You need to take off your jeans." She flipped the snap loose and grabbed for his zipper.

"Rosie, wait." His long fingers curled around her wrist. She looked at his face and saw that his pupils were dilated, his nostrils flared. Arousal colored his high cheekbones.

He wanted her, and she loved him. It was more than enough.

She bent and kissed his navel.

Ethan stiffened, but Rosie continued to kiss him, each rib, across to a hipbone—the hard ridge of his erection through his jeans. His stomach tautened until each muscle was defined. "Rosie, honey…" He gasped and his hands fell to his sides.

Satisfied, she licked the hot, taut flesh of his abdomen as she carefully lowered his zipper. "Raise your hips," she murmured, so anxious to have all of him that she couldn't stop trembling.

He did as she asked and she worked his jeans down his muscled legs, then his underwear. It took her a moment to work off his shoes and socks, and then finally he was completely, wonderfully naked. Like a feast laid out in front of her, Ethan was irresistible and she couldn't stop devouring him with her gaze. She heard a rough, rumbling purr and realized the carnal sound was her own.

Relishing each broken breath he took, the way his strong fingers fisted in the sheets, Rosie reached out her hand and touched him. The feel of his penis amazed her, warm velvet over flexing steel, alive, pulsing. Ethan made small desperate sounds as she explored him, but she barely paid him any mind, too intent on what she wanted.

She bent toward him again and his rough fingers tangled gently in her hair.

"You smell so good." Nuzzling into him, she breathed deeply, filling herself with the wonderful musky male scent.

With the smallest nudge, Ethan guided her mouth to his straining erection, and she obliged, anxious to taste him as she'd so often dreamed of doing.

She wasn't disappointed with his reaction. The first touch of her tongue on him and he froze, his powerful body shaking. "Oh, damn."

Rosie stroked her tongue over him, licking along his length then up and over the broad head. With a rough growl, he tried to pull away. "I'm going to lose it, honey," he warned.

"Okay," she purred, and opened her mouth,

taking him in. His taste was delicious, turning her on even more. She heard him moan again—and she sucked.

A great shudder went through Ethan; his fingers clenched in her hair to hold her closer and his hips lifted with a small, unintentional jerk. She took more of him, sucking gently, moving her wet tongue over and around and...

"Enough." His strength took her by surprise as he pulled her away and up to his chest. "Rosie, baby, that's enough." Before she could protest, he turned and caught her beneath him. His mouth covered hers and he kissed her with rough determination, his tongue wild, his hands stroking everywhere.

Wanting him now, Rosie opened her thighs for him, but instead of accepting her invitation he slid down a little and again kissed her breasts. He wasn't so gentle this time, sucking strongly at her nipples, nipping with his teeth. She cried out, stunned by his urgency, which made her own need escalate, but still he didn't stop. He slid lower and one hand moved between her thighs.

The shock of it had her stiffening, but he didn't seem to notice. They both paused and she heard Ethan groan as he carefully began exploring her, his fingertips gliding through her curls, pressing in, parting her. It seemed the oddest caress, so intimate, so hot and stimulating and, judging by the hungry sounds he made, Ethan enjoyed touching her as much as she enjoyed his touch. She didn't know what she had expected, but the gentle, insistent way he continued to stroke her made her wild.

His five o'clock shadow rasped against her belly as he turned his face inward to kiss her, leaving small, tingling love bites. By slow degrees, he went lower and lower until taking a single breath was too difficult to accomplish.

Rosie struggled to assimilate all the new feelings—and then he pushed one finger into her and she jerked, her eyes rounding, her body rioting with sensation. "Ethan."

"You're tight." His voice was nearly soundless with arousal. "And wet."

She bit her lip to keep her groans to herself, but she couldn't stop the automatic rise and fall of her hips. Ethan had large, hard, wonderful hands.

"Yeah, that's it. That's what I want." He worked another finger in, stretching her, just as his breath touched her most sensitive flesh.

"Ethan?" This was all very new to her, though he couldn't know that. "I…"

With his fingers buried deep inside her, he covered her with his mouth. The scalding heat struck her first, then the gentle damp rasp of his velvet tongue. The sensation was so intense she couldn't bear it, but she couldn't stop him, either. No matter how she twisted, how she moaned, Ethan didn't stop.

If anything, he pressed closer, holding her motionless with the weight of his broad shoulders, and then his mouth closed around her clitoris, suckling at her while his fingers pushed, withdrew and sank in again.

Her climax hit her without warning. Rosie had thought about this moment so many times, about how she'd act feminine and sexy and she'd lure Ethan so that he wanted to have sex with her again and again.

Instead she shouted like a crazy person, her body arching hard, uncontrollably. His hold tightened and he drove her until every nerve was alive, tingling.

As the spiraling explosion faded, she heard Ethan moan, felt his hands settle on her hips, tenderly squeezing. When she lay flat again, stunned and more or less quiet, he pulled away.

Rosie couldn't move. Her legs were sprawled around him, her thoughts scattered. She simply hadn't expected such a thing, such a wild bombardment on her senses.

Ethan rested his cheek on her belly and hugged her. She still gasped for breath, astounded by what had just happened, when he whispered, "I love you, Rosie."

Her heart slammed to a halt. It took her two tries to catch her breath, to believe he'd actually said those special words, and then she started to sob. She didn't mean to, but once the tears started, she couldn't stop them. And damn it, she wasn't a pretty crier. She wasn't very quiet, either.

Ethan lifted his head to look at her, and his smile was lopsided, a little silly. "I've never seen you cry, Rosie."

"Shut up." She sniffled, wiped at her eyes and stretched her arm to the nightstand for a handful of tissues.

Watching her with that endearing grin in place, Ethan said, "So surly."

"I'm embarrassed, all right?"

"Why?"

"I'm not very dainty about crying." Her brother used to tease her that she sounded like a drunken walrus when she wept.

"You're not very dainty about coming, either,

but hey, I'm not complaining." He stood beside the bed. Rosie froze in the middle of blowing her nose.

Dear heaven, he was gorgeous.

He lifted his jeans from the floor, pulled his wallet from the back pocket, located a condom and, casual as you please, opened the package and put it on. Rosie bolted upright in fascination. She'd never seen an erection in a raincoat.

Then she remembered she'd never seen an erection—not up close and personal anyway.

She started to comment on the process, but then Ethan was there, pushing her back down on the bed, crowding over her.

He kissed her cheek, up to her damp eyelashes, to her temple. Very softly he said, "I love the way you cry, and I love the way you come." He cupped her face. "I love *you*."

The tears came again, this time in a torrent. *"Ethan."* She wrapped her arms tight around him and bawled. She felt stupid for her loss of control, but she couldn't count the nights she'd lain awake and prayed that someday he'd say those three special words to her. Now that he finally had, her heart wanted to burst.

In a butterfly caress, he kissed her shoulder— and nudged her thighs wider apart so he could settle between them. "Shh," he rumbled lowly, sounding indulgent. "You'll make yourself sick."

"I don't—"

He pushed into her.

"—*care!*" Rosie clenched down hard as his cock slid deep inside her. It burned a little as he filled her, and felt so good she lost her breath again. "Oh, my—Ethan. *Ethan.*"

He actually laughed. But the laugh trailed off into a groan. He kept his hips flexed, straining against her, maintaining the pressure, pushing deeper and deeper. "Relax for me, honey." He kissed the corner of her mouth. "I want you to take all of me."

All of him? Rosie bit his shoulder, trying to silence her roar of pleasure as he rocked against her, slowly giving her more, then more still. Without thinking about it, she lifted her legs and locked them around his waist—and he sank in another inch.

Just when she thought it would be too much, he stopped and rested against her. "Rosie?"

She swallowed, shivered and finally choked an indistinct, "Mmm?"

"You were a virgin?"

There was only one answer she could give. "I've never wanted anyone but you."

Ethan didn't tease her, didn't crow about his conquest, he simply gathered her closer against him, kissed her mouth in a long, slow, deep kiss—and began moving.

The friction proved beyond incredible. Ethan kept kissing her. Long, lazy, consuming kisses. Hot, frantic kisses. He started to move faster and his breathing deepened, his muscles tightened.

Suddenly he levered himself up on stiffened arms. His thrusts were hard, slow, deep. Rosie stared at him, enthralled by the sight of his corded neck, the bunched muscles in his shoulders and biceps. His narrowed eyes were golden brown, bright, fevered. His jaw clenched.

And then she knew he was coming. She watched him through a haze. Their labored breaths mingled and she moaned with him, so excited to see him like this.

Moments later Ethan dropped sluggishly onto her, his face in her neck. Her legs went slack and slipped to the mattress. He was still inside her. It wasn't easy, but Rosie managed to lift one hand to stroke the nape of his neck down to his sweaty shoulder. "I love you, too, Ethan."

He gave an incoherent reply and tightened his arms.

Smiling, happier than she ever thought possible, Rosie asked, "When can we get married?"

He stopped breathing.

One second he was sucking air, sounding like a marathon runner, the next he was perfectly still. She barely felt his heartbeat—until it started drumming madly against her breast.

He raised his head, eyes agog. *"Married?"*

He appeared so horrified by the idea that Rosie considered slugging him. "Don't say it like a dirty word, Ethan."

"Well, no, but...*marriage?"*

Oh, she didn't feel like crying now. She was spitting mad and very determined. "I'm marrying you, Ethan Winters, so you might as well get used to it right now. And, by God, we'll live in my house and plant flowers in the summer and get a damn dog and eventually have some kids and—"

The shock cleared from his face and he started to laugh. Rosie shoved at him, but he didn't seem inclined to stop. "You think me being a mother is funny?" she demanded.

"No," he gasped around his chuckles. "No, I swear."

"Buffoon! Get off of me."

Instead he dropped his whole weight on her and got his chuckles under control. He wore a tender smile and his eyes were twinkling when he said, "Rosie."

"Don't you 'Rosie' me!"

He kissed her, but it was a funny kiss because she was fighting him and he was snickering again.

"I love you," he reminded her when she tried to twist his arm behind his back. "Ow, ouch. Rosie, I love you! Now stop that."

Mulish, a little hurt, she let him go but glared at him.

He still looked entirely too close to hilarity. "Honey, I *love* you." He touched her mouth, teasing. "You just took me by surprise, that's all."

He sounded sincere, she had to admit. "I've always known I loved you, Ethan."

"Yeah, well, I've only had it figured out for a few hours, so how about just giving me some time?" He cupped her face, kissed her again, a tickling teasing kiss.

"And time will make you realize that we need to be married?"

He tried to sound somber when he said, "I'd consider myself a shallow ass if it didn't."

Relief washed over her and she found her own smile. "All right."

With one last kiss, Ethan moved away from her. "Stay put. I'll be right back." Naked, gorgeous and far too sexy, he went out into the hall and then she heard water running in the bathroom.

Ethan loved her. The rest would come. It had to.

ETHAN TOOK HIS TIME removing the condom, finding a washcloth, soaking it with warm water. *Marriage.* Damn, but Rosie only knew one speed—Mach.

She'd left him in the dust that time for sure. He'd been doing his best to reconcile the fact that he loved her, that she'd been a virgin, that she was a regular wildcat in bed—and bam! She'd planned out their whole lives, complete with a dog and kids.

But now that she'd brought it up, the idea appealed to him. He did love her, no doubt about that one. Once he'd admitted it to himself, the feeling had expanded and grown and all but consumed him. He couldn't believe it had taken him so long to realize what was firmly rooted in his heart. The strength of what he felt for her was even a little scary.

Ethan knew he couldn't bear the idea of any other man touching her. So far, no other man had. If he played his cards right, no other man would. She was his in every sense of the word—and by God, he'd keep her. If that meant marriage, then so what? It wouldn't make him care more for her, but if she needed that, then he'd give it to her.

A quiet little ceremony, with only two witnesses…yeah, he could do that. He wouldn't like it, and he assumed some pretty ugly memories would plague him. But Rosie was worth any emotional discomfort.

He took a steadying breath, wrung out the washcloth, and headed back to the bedroom.

She hadn't bothered to cover herself.

Ethan almost tripped over his own feet. He'd always known Rosie was pretty, and that she was built nice. But naked, stretched out on a bed, she was about the sexiest thing he'd ever seen.

Her head turned toward him when he stopped in the open doorway. Her hair was tumbled around her face, her body still flushed in selective places—such as her breasts, her belly, her silky thighs.

Damn, he was getting hard again.

Ethan cleared his throat and sat beside her on the mattress. "I'm going to clean you up."

Now she moved, darting under the covers so fast she was a blur. "You most definitely are *not.*"

Ethan grinned. "Wanna bet?"

"Don't even think—"

He had the covers completely off the bed in a flash, which left Rosie squawking and ready to tussle. He obliged. Wrestling with Rosie wasn't at all like wrestling with other women. For one thing, she refused to understand that she was the weaker sex. Instead, she fought hard, determined to get the upper hand. By the time Ethan had her hands pinned above her head and his hips settled firmly between her spread thighs so she couldn't kick him, they were both panting from exertion.

And he was fully aroused again.

He grinned down at her, but she didn't smile back. No, her eyes had turned all molten and she was staring at his mouth. The way he held her left her breasts on display and Ethan had a hard time keeping his gaze off her tight pink nipples and on her face.

He lowered his forehead to hers. "You're distracting me, Rosie."

"Good." She lifted her hips in an undulating roll, stroking him with her body. "Let's do it again."

Hell of an idea. "You're not too sore?"

She shook her head. "No. Well, maybe just a little, but…no." She lifted her long lashes to stare up at him. "I want to watch you come again. You are so sexy."

Feeling a little self-conscious with her bold statement, Ethan laughed. "You don't act like a virgin, you know that?"

Her thighs closed around his waist. "If you stay the night with me, I'll try to act more virginal." Since she made that promise while leaning up to nip his chin, Ethan could only nod his agreement. It felt damn good to be wanted so much, especially by Rosie.

"You have more condoms?" she asked.

"Just one," he told her.

"Then let's make it last." She pulled her hands free, pushed him to his back, and Ethan groaned as she climbed atop him.

Loving Rosie was going to be a lot of fun.

As the night wore on, so did Ethan's determination to legally bind her to him. The rest of his life wouldn't be long enough to love her. He'd discuss it with her in the morning, and then they could make plans. With any luck, they could get the marriage business over with on his next day off.

WHEN ETHAN AWOKE, he found Rosie at her dresser, putting in earrings. He smiled, thinking how delightful she looked standing there in her slip and nylons, her beautiful hair twisted atop her head.

He scooted up in the bed and stretched. Rosie turned to face him, smiled, and came to him for a good morning kiss.

"I've got coffee in the kitchen if you want some."

He pulled her onto his lap. "I was hoping to find you naked in bed beside me, not half-dressed."

"Sorry." She pushed away and checked her hair to make sure he hadn't messed it up. "I have to see a client in about half an hour." Absently, she stroked his chest hair, and her gaze warmed. "You look good in my bed, Ethan."

"Is that a hint?"

"That I'd like to see you here more? Absolutely." She stood and went to the closet to pull out a tailored dress, which she stepped into and buttoned up. Next she slipped her feet into medium-heeled shoes and she was done.

It felt right to watch Rosie dress, to be privy to her little morning rituals. He should have awakened in time to shower with her. Tomorrow he would.

Ethan swung his legs over the side of the bed, stood and scratched his chest. When he reached for his jeans, he realized that Rosie was just standing there, staring at him, and he grinned.

"You know," he said as he pulled on the jeans, "I was thinking about this marriage stuff."

Her breath caught. "And?"

"I think it's a hell of an idea."

She stood still for almost fifteen seconds before she let out a squeal and bounded around the bed to reach him. Ethan caught her, whirled her around once, then laughed out loud as she choked him with a tight hug. "I knew you'd be reasonable!"

Still laughing, Ethan said, "It has nothing to do with reason and everything to do with loving you." He cupped his hands over her bottom and kissed her. "Do you think we could get it done next week on my day off?"

"Next week?" Her face went blank. "Of course not. I have to order a dress and rent a hall and find a preacher and invite everyone... weddings take time, Ethan.''

His heart sank like a stone into his stomach. ''Rosie.'' Gently he set her away from him. ''I want no part of a big, fancy wedding. I thought we could just go to a justice of the peace and be done with it.''

''But...I don't want to just 'be done with it.''' She looked stricken, a little pale. ''I want a big wedding.'' She tried a smile that went flat, and teased, ''I'm only getting married once, you know.''

Ethan couldn't bear to see her hope. He turned away, stalking to the window to look out. Her small backyard was immaculate, perfect for the dog and kids that she wanted. He gave a muffled curse.

The silence behind him was suffocating, but damned if he could think of anything to say to her. The idea of a fancy wedding with guests staring at him...no. He couldn't do that.

''Ethan?'' She touched his bare shoulder. ''I *love* you.''

''I know.''

Her arms came around him from behind. ''I would never do anything to hurt you.''

''I know that, too, Rosie. But I swore I'd never

again put myself in that position.'' He turned to face her. ''If we had a big wedding, you know what everyone would be thinking? They'd be remembering the last time, how I was left standing there looking like a goddamned fool when your brother ran off with my bride.''

Rosie backed up a step. Her chin lifted. ''You weren't the only one humiliated that day, Ethan Winters. Every person at that wedding wanted to ask me about it, too, to see if I'd known what my brother was planning.''

''Did you?''

Her eyes narrowed, her mouth trembled. ''I'll pretend you didn't ask me that.''

He rubbed his face. ''Shit. I'm sorry.''

''You weren't the only one to lose someone you loved, either.'' Her voice got shaky, her eyes a little liquid. But she didn't look away, didn't lower that stubborn chin. ''I haven't seen my brother since. With Mom and Dad gone, he's the only family I have left, but until you forgive him, until you let everyone know that you're over Michelle, I have no one.''

Ethan hadn't thought of it that way, and now he felt sick. ''You have me.''

She didn't smile. ''Yes I do, and I love you. But...maybe that's not enough.''

She waited, and he knew what she wanted. Rosie never bothered with subtlety. But Ethan couldn't relent.

With a resigned sigh, Rosie glanced at her watch. "Wow, look at the time."

"Rosie..."

"Darn it, I have to go or I'll be late." She tried to look chipper—and failed.

"I'm off today," Ethan told her. "I'm going to see if I can get the interview with Red out of the way early this afternoon, then I'll come back here. We can talk more tonight." He hated to give her false hope about a big wedding, when just the thought of it made him break out in a cold sweat and sent cramps to his stomach. But he also hated to send her out the door when she was upset.

"All right." She turned thoughtful, and Ethan had the faint suspicion she was plotting something. "I'll be back around five. Make yourself at home, okay?"

"Coffee first, then your shower." He touched her cheek. "Could I have a key?"

This time her smile was natural. "On top of the fridge in the basket. I had it made for you months ago."

Ethan slipped his arm around her and started

her toward the front door so she wouldn't be late. "I appreciate your confidence in my intelligence. You knew I'd wise up, didn't you?"

Rosie laughed. "I couldn't bear to think otherwise."

CHAPTER FIVE

AT ONE O'CLOCK, Rosie parked in front of the entrance to the park where she'd set up a meeting with Regina Foxworth. The reporter said she'd be in the area to talk with a fireworks dealer located nearby, then at two, she would be interviewing Ethan over lunch at the diner across the street. She agreed to give Rosie half an hour first, plenty of time to set the record straight.

Rosie had rearranged her schedule, but still it had been difficult to get to the park by the designated time. Luckily, when she shaded her eyes and looked around, she found Regina just seating herself on a park bench in front of a decorative fountain.

Rosie strode forward, a woman on a mission. Ethan might be resistant to the idea of a big marriage now, but she'd get him around that somehow. In her heart, she knew he was over Michelle. She just needed him to know it, too.

Regina was another matter entirely. She believed Ethan when he said he loved her, but he'd also made his admiration of the reporter plain. Rosie had waited too long to have Ethan to take chances now. She wanted Regina to understand that Ethan was already involved in a relationship. "Hello, Regina."

The pretty redhead smiled up at Rosie and extended her hand. She was dressed in a chic summer-weight suit and a camera hung from a wide strap around her neck. "Nice to see you again, Rosie."

"I appreciate you making the time for me." After a friendly handshake, Rosie sat beside her on the bench. Though the day was hot, the park buzzed with life. Children were playing everywhere and she could hear the occasional happy bark of a dog chasing a Frisbee. Someday in the near future she and Ethan would bring their children here and watch them on the swings. She sighed.

"No problem." Regina crossed her legs and smiled. "You've got me curious, so I wanted to meet with you first. When I interview Firefighter Winters, I don't want to be distracted."

Rosie clenched her teeth. Jealousy was new to her and she didn't like it at all. "Please, call him Ethan—I know he'll insist."

"All right."

A man and a woman jogged by. Regina
waited, not saying anything more, leaving it up
to Rosie to explain herself.

She got right to the point. "Why do you want
to interview Ethan?"

Regina's brows rose. "Just the obvious reasons. Ethan has a history of heroic deeds and he
was rewarded for it. The ceremony was a big deal
and I got some great photos, but obviously Ethan
wasn't up to an interview then."

Remembering how foolishly Ethan had be-
haved chasing the woman beside her, Rosie
scowled. He'd thrown himself at her and the only
surprise was that Regina hadn't jumped on the
chance to be with him. Rosie would have.

"The paper has already done a couple of articles on him," Rosie pointed out.

"True. But in a town this size, a man like
Ethan quickly becomes a role model. Pride for
one of their own is top-notch news. Everyone
wants to hear about him, about the ceremony the
other night, his past good deeds and what's happening with him now."

"What do you intend to ask him?"

If Regina thought her questions intrusive, she
didn't say so. "You're protective of him, aren't
you? I can understand that. His behavior at the
ceremony was..." She searched for a word and

finally shrugged. "Well, as big and strong and capable as he is, he seemed vulnerable to me."

That startled Rosie. "He was drunk."

Grinning, Regina said, "That he was." She tipped her head. "Does he drink often?"

"No. Almost never, actually."

"But he drank too much that night." She nodded. "I think that's because he was so ill at ease. Being uncomfortable in that situation is a startling contrast for a man who enters burning buildings without a qualm."

Regina sounded far too admiring to Rosie. "Ethan doesn't like all the fuss made over him."

"Maybe." She watched a butterfly flit by, turned her face up to a warm breeze. The seconds ticked by and finally she shrugged. "I'm sure you know Ethan better than I do, but I don't think that's it." She turned toward Rosie. "I think it's the ceremony itself he didn't like."

Regina sounded so sure of herself, Rosie grew uneasy. "Why do you say that?"

"I skimmed some of the other articles done on him the last few weeks, just to get a bare-bones history on him, and in every case he spoke freely about his duties as a firefighter, posed for the occasional picture, even ribbed his chief a little. He was totally at ease, comfortable. He didn't mind the one-on-one attention at all, or the publicity in the papers. No, it was the crowd, every-one looking at him and making him the center of attention at a formal affair that got to him.''

Rosie dropped back against the bench, stunned by how blind she'd been. And she'd accused Ethan of being dense. Realization pounded through her, causing her heart to ache. Knowing she might have hurt Ethan with the awful way she'd pressed him for a big, elaborate wedding was a weight on her chest. She'd been so insensitive.

Regina reached over and patted her hand. ''Forgive me for sticking my nose in where it doesn't belong, but...well, I *am* a reporter.'' She grinned at that. ''I couldn't interview Ethan the night of the ceremony, not because he was so drunk, but because all he wanted to talk about was you.''

She'd said that at the gym. At the time Ethan hadn't given her a chance to ask Regina any questions. He'd rushed Rosie out of there so fast her feet had barely touched the floor. ''What did he say?''

Ticking off comments on her fingers, Regina said, ''You're funnier, sweeter, pushier than any other woman he knows. You drive him nuts with your smart mouth, smother him with your moth-ering tendency—he grinned when he said that, by the way. You're honest, loyal, a great cook with a big heart and..."

Rosie covered her face and groaned. "Oh, God."

Sympathetic, Regina patted her again. "He hadn't mentioned this Michelle person until I saw you both at Riley's gym. And seeing you both side by side...well, it didn't take a genius to figure out you're in love."

Rosie had few female friends and she wasn't close with any of them, not like she was with the guys. But she found she liked being able to confide in Regina. The woman wasn't at all as she'd first assumed. "He was engaged to Michelle. I thought...I thought he was still upset because of what had happened between them."

"I found articles on that, too. She jilted him— in front of the whole town." Regina shuddered delicately. "I can only imagine how that would affect someone like Ethan. It'd be tough on any man, but firefighters are naturally arrogant and more proud than most and to be humiliated that way...I'm sure it wasn't easy for him."

Rosie found herself wringing her hands. She needed to see Ethan, to make it up to him, to assure him that having him for her husband was all she ever really wanted. "You're not going to ask Ethan about that at the interview, are you?"

"Heavens, no. For one thing, I try very hard to be fair and up front in my reporting. That means sticking to pertinent facts." Then she wrinkled her lightly freckled nose. "Besides, I imagine Ethan would walk out on me if I invaded his privacy that way."

When Rosie just sat there, pondering her own guilt and how she'd tried to coerce Ethan into a big wedding just to prove he was over Michelle, Regina cleared her throat. "Was there anything else you wanted to talk to me about?"

Rosie considered it for only a moment. "Yes. Would you like to come over tomorrow night? I was going to invite Riley and a few of our other friends, as well. Ethan will be there, too." At least she hoped he would. She had to get home to him and apologize first. "I know you're new to town and I think we can be friends."

A little surprised, Regina smiled. "I'd like that. Thank you."

Just then a young man came barreling up behind the bench, his attention on the ball he meant to catch. He collided with the bench and nearly toppled over into Regina's lap. Rosie steadied him with both hands, but Regina gave a short scream, whirling around in what could only be described as near panic.

With the ball safely captured, the man turned

fiery red and apologized all over himself. When Regina seemed incapable of replying, Rosie told him not to worry about it, and he ran off, glad to escape.

"You okay?"

Nodding jerkily, Regina pressed a hand to her heart and closed her eyes.

Watching her, Rosie remembered Riley claiming that Regina was "a little paranoid." Seeing her now, Rosie understood. She was white as a sheet. "What's going on?"

"Nothing. I'm sorry." She opened her eyes, looked around again and, somewhat distracted, checked her watch. "I should be going if I hope to make it back here in time to meet Ethan at the diner. The address I have for the fireworks dealer is supposed to be in this area but I'm not sure where exactly and I don't know how long it will take me to find him."

Considering all the insight she'd just gained into Ethan, Rosie felt she owed the other woman. This would be a good way to repay her in part. "If you don't mind the company, I'd be glad to walk with you to the address. I'm a real estate agent and can pretty much find any building."

"You're sure?"

"I've got an hour free."

Regina looked vastly relieved. "Thank you. It

shouldn't take me long. I've already found some background information on the guy, so mostly I just need to ask a few questions and take some pictures.''

''He agreed to be interviewed?''

Regina winced. ''Not exactly. At least not until I told him I'd run the story with or without his input. He, uh, well, he wasn't happy with my persistence. But with the Fourth almost here, and this guy's reputation not quite aboveboard…''

Rosie fought a smile. ''It's okay. I can be persistent, too, when I want something.''

''This job is important to me. Riley told me how Ethan and the others feel about all the illegal fireworks that show up every Fourth of July. He suggested the public could do with a little more knowledge on the subject, and I agreed. So…'' She made a face. ''I'm going to do something of an exposé.''

''He does know you're coming, right?''

''He knows. But under the circumstances, I'll understand if you don't want to join me.''

''No, I'll go.'' Now Rosie felt honor-bound to help protect Regina from the surly man. Besides, it felt like an adventure. As they started on their way, Rosie said, ''Do you hope to uncover some illegal activities on his part?''

Regina laughed. ''I wish, but it's doubtful. It's

just that I found out from Riley that Ethan is concerned over this guy. It seems he's had several violations over the years. No fire alarm, narrow aisles. He didn't have a guard posted at the door last Fourth of July and someone lit an exposed fuse. There was a small fire that could have been really bad. He waits to get cited, *then* he fixes the problems.''

''Why does he need a guard?''

''To make sure no one carries a lighter or matches into the store, so that there won't be any fires. State safety regulations have been strengthened over the years. But from all accounts, this guy's something of a shady character and he walks a fine line on keeping his shop legit. And since he's a nasty-tempered fellow, too, he'll make a good counterpoint to Ethan's natural heroism. When I interview Ethan, he can add to the discussion on fireworks safety. I think my editor will run the articles side by side as a special feature.''

To Rosie, it did sound interesting.

They had no trouble finding the building, but once they did, Rosie stared in dismay. Though it was only two blocks away, she felt as though they'd crossed over into another city. The atmosphere of the industrial area was very different; darker, more desolate from that near the park.

There were no children around, no joggers, only a few ominous, shadowed silhouettes hanging in deep, open doorways.

This was not an area of town for two women alone.

The buildings were spaced close together and included an abandoned factory and two warehouses. Large trucks were parked on the street and in alleys. A wolf whistle came from somewhere. Rosie admitted to feeling a little apprehensive.

The fireworks store sat between two other two-story brick buildings, one selling risqué novelties, the other a pawnshop.

Rosie stared at the front door of the fireworks store with its crooked Closed sign and frowned. "It's awfully rundown for a business, isn't it?"

Regina shrugged. "I'm told he sells mostly to companies that put on displays for large groups. I guess he considers this a warehouse of sorts."

"It's closed."

Regina gave her a telling look. "Doesn't that seem strange to you? It's the middle of the afternoon, surely part of his business hours."

A pane of glass was missing from one of the upstairs windows, but darkened curtains blocked any view to the inside. A profusion of weeds grew in a narrow patch of dirt between the street and the building. The front stoop was littered with debris.

"It's an eyesore, but that'll only make it a better contrast." Regina took several photos of the front of the shop, all the while glancing around nervously. "Let's try around back."

The narrow alleyway was overgrown with some type of scraggly vine that spread up the brick walls, into the gutters, and across every surface. They had to step around broken pieces of glass, empty boxes and garbage overflowing from a Dumpster. The gate to a rusted chain-link fence hung from one hinge and squeaked loudly when Regina pushed it open.

They rounded the corner and saw that the tiny backyard was nearly filled with a gigantic oak tree planted too close to the structure. The tree had likely never been trimmed; branches spread out over the roof and kept everything so shaded that not a speck of grass grew on the small square of spongy ground. The back door stood open. Rosie could hear men caught in a heated debate.

Regina took a breath and approached the door, cautiously stepping over twisted, exposed roots from the tree. "Hello?"

No one answered. The voices were farther away, down a hall. There was no door blocking the interior doorway, only a thin curtain tacked up and pushed partly open. The women looked at each other, but when Regina went inside, Rosie followed.

They were apparently in a back storage room and despite Rosie's untrained eye she saw a catastrophe waiting to happen. Open crates overflowing with firecrackers were stacked to the ceiling against one wall. Opposite that was a narrow flight of stairs lined with boxes of sparklers and snakes and other gimmicky fireworks. To Rosie, it appeared someone had been riffling through the boxes, given how some of the packages had been opened and products cluttered the floor.

Regina lifted her camera and snapped off several quick shots, getting a close-up of the exposed fuses. Rosie stepped around some boxes and moved to the stairs. There was a small bathroom built beneath the stairs and Rosie stared at it in disgust. Beyond being filthy, it also held several bottles of cleaner and a rag mop and bucket. Regina caught Rosie's wave and took more pictures.

At the very top of the stairs, Rosie could see more boxes. She couldn't tell what they were, but they looked different from the ones downstairs. She was ready to investigate when a large man came bursting into the room. He stopped in the curtained doorway and glared darkly at Regina.

"Here now! Just who the hell are you? You ain't allowed in here to take pictures."

Frowning at his tone, Rosie took two steps forward. Regina quickly attempted to introduce herself. "I called earlier. I'm a reporter with the—"

Suddenly a loud crack sounded like the blast of a gun, and the man whirled around. "What the hell!" His eyes rounded at something Rosie couldn't see and he shouted, "What are you doing? No!"

A whoosh of fire shot through the doorway, caught the curtains and flared up into his face. Cursing, he staggered backward and jammed into Regina. They both went down.

"Regina!" Rosie tripped over a box and almost fell, too. She fetched up against the wall, bruising her arm. Before she could straighten herself, the burning curtains fell to the floor and the fire spread to lick around the crates of firecrackers. Seconds later, they began to explode, the sound almost deafening.

Horrified, Rosie saw that Regina had hit her head and was badly dazed. The man, who had started to run out without her, apparently thought better of it and quickly threw Regina over his shoulder. He raced out the back door, leaving Rosie inside, alone. She tried to call out, tried to scream, but the roar of the fire and the noise of the fireworks swallowed up any sound she made. The man hadn't seen her, so he hadn't even known she was inside.

The fire spread too quickly, and Rosie's alarm was almost as choking as the smoke filling the room. Hot flames blocked the back door, leaving her only one other way to go. Up.

Praying, Rosie quickly scaled the stairs. She had only a second to see that the upper floor was congested with bottle rockets, flares and Roman candles—then she saw the window and lurched toward it. She struggled to get it open, but her fingers felt numb in her fear; the window refused to budge. Behind her, the roar of the fire grew, angry and menacing. Tears ran down her face from the blinding smoke, but she brushed them away, forcing herself to think. Finally she pulled off a shoe and smashed it against the window-pane until all the sharp shards of glass were gone.

Leaning out to gulp in fresh air, she looked for Regina, but she couldn't see her or the man. However, about four feet in front of her, a thick sturdy branch from the oak tree reached out like a lifeline.

Several explosions sounded below, making her jump in terror. Rosie covered her ears before new determination gripped her. She'd just gotten Ethan, damn it, and no way was she going to let some stupid fire keep her from him now. Thanks to all the lessons she'd taken with Riley, she was strong, agile. She would save herself.

She kicked off her other shoe, crawled onto the window ledge and stretched out her hand. She couldn't quite get hold of the branch, no matter how she tried. There was only one thing left to do. She's have to jump to the tree—and pray she didn't miss.

HIS THOUGHTS had centered on Rosie all day. He had to be the biggest fool alive not to have realized earlier how much he cared for her. She was his best friend, his better half and his perfect match sexually. When he considered all the time he'd wasted, he wanted to kick himself.

When he remembered how sexy she was in bed, how soft she felt and the way she held him when she came...he could barely breathe. Rosie did everything with an abundance of energy and involvement. Lovemaking had been no different. Damn, he was lucky because out of all the men in the world, she wanted him.

She also wanted a big, formal, fancy wedding. Ethan closed his eyes and groaned.

He needed a distraction in the worst way and his appointment with Regina Foxworth would serve as well as any other. He was just starting into the diner when he heard the explosion and saw the smoke in the sky. It wasn't far away, and he knew fire engines were probably already on their way. Still, before he even knew it, he was halfway there, his long legs eating up the distance. The closer he got, the thicker the smoke grew.

He reached the industrial area and pushed his way through a wall of people lining the street, watching the flames consume the old building. He recognized it, of course. This was the shady fireworks dealer he'd mentioned to Rosie. He wasn't surprised by the fire, all things considered, but he prayed no one was hurt.

"You people should back up," Ethan told them as his training naturally came to the fore. "At least go to the other side of the street." He got people moving even as he heard the sirens start off in the distance. Reluctantly, the crowd parted and shifted—and then he saw Red.

But...she was supposed to be at the Diamond Diner, waiting for him.

She sat on the curb, a thin trickle of blood running down her temple, her clothes dirty and torn. "Hey?" Ethan crouched in front of her. "Are you all right? What the hell happened? What are you doing here?" As he spoke he pulled out a hanky and dabbed at the blood on her head.

She opened vague eyes and blinked at him. "Ethan?"

"Yeah, it's me." Ethan wondered if she had a concussion or if she was in shock. Either way, he needed to move her a safer distance away from the fire. "Can you walk, Regina?"

Appearing desperate, she clutched his hand. *"Rosie…"*

"What?" Frowning, sure she was delirious, Ethan took her shoulders. "What about Rosie?"

She shook her head as if to clear it, then tried again. "Oh, God, I think…I think she's still inside."

Ethan stiffened, the bottom fell out of his stomach. *Still* inside? He looked at the flames dancing out every window, coloring the sky crimson. He took in the billowing black smoke that clung to everything, stinking up the air. "She's at work."

"No." Big tears clouded Red's eyes. "She was with me."

Numb incredulity gave way to rage. Ethan wasn't aware of roaring, wasn't aware of charging the building, but suddenly men were holding him back and no matter how he fought, he couldn't get loose. No, no, he wouldn't accept it. He hit someone, kicked someone else.

Riley appeared, though that didn't make any sense. "Ethan, damn it, no."

"Let me go," he snarled, fighting for his life.

Riley wrapped his arms around him and they fell to the ground ten feet from the building. Intense heat washed over them, and there was another loud boom. Half of the roof caved in. With Riley holding him flat on his back, Ethan twisted his head to stare at the destruction. He couldn't breathe, couldn't even really see. The smoke was so goddamned thick...

Then he heard her calling his name. At first he thought he imagined it even as hope sprang alive inside him. None of it seemed real. Why would Rosie even be here? And Riley?

He pushed Riley aside as if he were no more than a gnat. Before he'd taken two steps toward the building, Riley grabbed his arm and swung him around. "Ethan, there! There she is."

With his fist cocked back, Ethan hesitated. He heard her call him again and then he followed the direction Riley pointed. Two buildings down, Ethan saw her. She'd lost her shoes, her hair was singed, but she was running toward him and, damn it, he couldn't manage a single step. He started desperately sucking air two seconds before his knees gave out.

"Ethan." She stumbled to a halt in front of him, grabbed his arm and tried to haul him to his feet. "We have to move," she panted. "The place is full of stuff—bottle rockets and Roman candles and...I don't know. All kinds of explosive things."

Slowly his vision cleared until he could see again. Belatedly, his instincts kicked in and he struggled to his feet. "We have to move."

Rosie blinked at him. "That's what I was saying."

"Come on." He wrapped her protectively in his arms and together they jogged to the opposite side of the street, away from harm. Riley walked up to stand beside them, holding Red in his arms. Ethan hadn't even noticed him picking up the other woman, yet there she was, cuddled against Riley's chest. They all sat on the curb.

The men shared a look. "This is going to be one hell of an interesting story." Riley glanced down at Red and shook his head.

Beyond confused, still rattled with lingering fear and embarrassed over his reaction, Ethan scowled. "Just what the hell is going on? Why are you here?"

"I was just..." Riley glanced at Red, frowned

and shrugged. "I was just checking up on her. She was so damn jumpy yesterday and…"

Red, still holding Ethan's hanky to her temple, lifted her head. "You were worried about me?"

Riley looked disgusted. "Yeah."

"But I thought you didn't believe me."

He glanced at Ethan. "I believe you now." Suddenly he looked furious. "Damn it, Red, when I suggested you do a story on fireworks and safety, I didn't mean for you to go skulking around this part of town."

"I'm a reporter," she insisted, but with her face white and streaked with blood, her indignation was ludicrous.

Riley took the hanky from her and dabbed at her cut. "You're a fool." She started to protest and he pushed her head back to his shoulder. "I know why I'm here, but, Rosie, what are you doing here?"

Ethan's grip on Rosie was bruising, but he wouldn't, couldn't, let her go. She patted his chest in a bid to soothe him. "I was with Regina."

Ethan stared down at her. "Why?"

"I didn't want her to try to steal you away."

He looked thunderstruck, then outraged. "Of all the idiotic…"

Red lifted her head. "But I don't want him."

Rosie looked at Riley. "Yeah, I know that *now.*"

The fire engines arrived with a lot of flashing lights, noise and fanfare, drowning out any further possibilities for conversation. Men ran to the surrounding buildings, evacuating people, moving others to safety.

Without being told, Ethan and Riley strode farther away. Ethan kept Rosie tight to his side, and Riley still carried Red. Other members of the crowd weren't so easy to sway, and Ethan had to wonder at the idiocy of spectators. If the building should explode again, anyone close by could be hit with debris.

The firefighters went to work, pulling out hoses, surrounding the building and fighting the fire from the outside in an exterior assault. One look told Ethan that it wasn't safe to do anything else.

A concerned firefighter approached Rosie. "Was there anyone else inside?"

Her voice raspy from the smoke, she said, "We—Regina and I—heard two men arguing. Only one came out to talk to her, though. I don't know about the other man."

Riley gave her a sharp look. "What do you mean, he talked to her? What about you?"

"He didn't see me. I was by the stairs."

She leaned on Ethan and he pressed his face against her smoke-scented hair. All his training, everything he knew, had disappeared with his panic. But then, no woman had ever loved him the way Rosie did. She was his, and if he lost her…

When she continued, her voice was softer, a little frightened. "I had to go upstairs because the fire just…spread. Like a whoosh."

Ethan held her back. "Do you think it was deliberate?"

Rosie looked at Regina. Both women looked upset. "Maybe."

Regina nodded. "I saw a flash of fire, then I fell and hit my head. I'm sorry I can't be more help."

Riley patted her back. "Shush. Just rest."

Bemused by Riley's behavior, Rosie had to force her gaze back to the man questioning her. "The fire blocked the door where we'd entered and it was all around these boxes of firecrackers, and they were all spilled everywhere and half-opened so that the fuses were sticking out almost like someone had set it up on purpose. Regina took a lot of pictures but…" Her babbling came to a halt. "Regina, where's your camera?"

Regina looked down at where the camera had hung around her neck, then stared for several moments in disbelief before saying, "Well, damn." She glared at Riley as if it might be his fault. "It's gone!"

Rosie scowled. "I bet the man who carried Regina out took it. He did seem mad that she was using the camera. I don't know where he went but I did see him leave with her."

"You said you went upstairs?" Riley didn't seem in any hurry to put Red down.

Rosie nodded, sending her frazzled hair to bounce around her face. "I climbed out a window, into that big tree behind the building. The fire blocked the alley so I had to go two buildings over to cut back to the street."

The firefighter touched her arm. "Thanks. I'll want to talk to both you ladies later. In the meantime, if you see that man, let me know right away, okay?" He waited for her nod, then headed off to once again force on-lookers back.

Rosie lifted her face and touched Ethan's mouth. Her fingers were trembling, her eyes a little red. "I'm so sorry if I scared you."

"Scared me? I was more than scared, Rosie." He kissed her gently. "I love you, damn it."

"I don't want a big wedding."

Not sure he'd heard her right, Ethan frowned. "What?"

She fisted her hands in his shirt and tried to

shake him. "We're getting married at a justice of the peace as soon as possible, and that's that. Do you understand me?"

Ethan looked at Riley, who raised both brows and shrugged. Against his throat, Red murmured, "They're in love. They're getting married."

"I see." Riley kissed her ear. "Let's let the paramedics take a look at you, okay?"

"But I'm fine."

"We'll do it anyway."

Disgruntled, she said, "All right, but at least let me walk."

"No." Riley headed for the ambulance that had just pulled up.

Ethan watched him carry her off, a little surprised though he didn't know why. Riley was...well, he was more dangerous than any modern man should be. He'd joined their group after they all met on a fishing trip. Since then, they'd been good friends, but Ethan was always aware of Riley's sharper edge and thinly veiled civility. He hid it well, but there were times, such as now, when his primitive instincts shone loud and clear.

Ethan had seen hints of it with the way Riley fought, how he remained alert at all times, the precise gentleness he utilized in his everyday life, as if he had to concentrate on that because it didn't come naturally.

This was the first time he'd seen his armor crack around a woman. Interesting.

Shrugging away those thoughts, he gave his attention back to Rosie. "Honey, we can get married any way you want. It was stupid of me to—"

"You heard me, Ethan Winters." The rest of the roof caved in with a thunderous crash. Rosie jumped, gripped him tighter and raised her voice accordingly. "It'll be a small wedding, damn it, just us and the guys and well…maybe Regina." She looked worried, and watched him with a frown. "You won't mind that, will you? I like her and I kind of think Riley does, too."

"You kind of think, huh?" Ethan glanced over at the ambulance where a paramedic tried to convince Riley to set Red down. Ethan grinned, knowing Riley had just claimed a woman in the most elemental way known to man. No way would he relinquish his hold on her. "I'd kind of say you're right."

"I do love you, Ethan."

He sat—or rather his knees gave out—but he caught Rosie on his lap. "As long as I get you and the house and the dog and the kids, nothing else matters to me."

She beamed at him. Ethan pushed her singed hair away from her face and kissed her. "You're making me old before my time."

She sighed. "Well, as long as I'm the only one making you, I can live with that."

EPILOGUE

ROSIE LAUGHED as she got out of the limousine Ethan had insisted on hiring. They'd ridden to the small church with Harris, Buck, Riley and Regina. Her white dress was knee-length, simply cut, but it was lovely, the bodice overlaid with lace and pearls. The look on Ethan's face when he'd seen her in it had made her feel more beautiful than any traditional wedding gown could have.

The church was another thing he'd insisted on. And Rosie loved him too much to argue. Only two weeks had passed since the fire, which was still under investigation. They'd found the man who had carried Regina out, but no one else. He denied taking her camera, denied any wrongdoing, and claimed the other man Rosie had heard was just a customer.

He did agree that someone had deliberately set his place on fire. Unfortunately, he wanted to blame Regina.

So far, the fire was a mystery, but Riley was now convinced that Regina had reason to worry—and he'd taken it upon himself to keep an eye on her.

Rosie started for the front door of the church, but Ethan sidetracked her. "We need to go in from the back."

"We do? Why?" Everyone kept watching her, making her very suspicious. "What's going on, Ethan?"

His smile made her heart do flips.

"You're so difficult, sweetheart. Come on." He caught her hand and she had to trot in her high heels to keep up with him. Regina carried her bouquet for her—a beautiful creation of roses and baby's breath and lilies. There was a strange hush to the air as they traversed the cobblestone path to the rear. Rosie hesitated when she saw the flower-covered trellis, but Ethan didn't give her a chance to balk.

They stepped through the trellis—and into an elaborate setting of orange blossoms, crepe paper and hundreds of chairs filled with guests. A multitude of trees had been decorated with ribbons and a white outdoor platform, complete with a smiling minister, had been erected on the immaculate lawn.

Thunderstruck, her mouth hanging open, Rosie scanned the crowd of grinning faces. She recognized her neighbors, all the people she worked with, Ethan's relatives and co-workers and friends and…almost the whole town.

And there, right in the front row where her family belonged, was her brother with Michelle at his side. He looked at her for a long moment, his expression poignant, tender, then he grinned like a rascal and winked. Michelle gave a small, happy wave. Emotion choked Rosie and she started gasping, unable to catch her breath.

"Hey." Ethan slipped his arm around her. "Don't faint on me now."

She stared at him through a haze of tears. "Oh, Ethan…"

He caught her chin and tipped her face up to his. "I love you, Rosie."

She covered her mouth with a shaking hand, gulped, but it didn't help. Darn it, she never cried.

Ethan turned them both so that he blocked her from view with his body. Smiling, he used one fingertip to wipe the tears away. "You're going to ruin your makeup, sweetheart."

"But I thought you didn't want this." She sniffled, tried to pull herself together without much success. "Ethan, it's wonderful, it really is. But you're all that's important. Nothing else matters to me..."

"It matters to me, Rosie. I used to think if I did this, everyone would see me and remember how I'd been jilted." His mouth curled in a crooked smile. "Now I know what they're really thinking."

"What?"

His thumb rubbed under her chin, teasing her, keeping her face turned up to his. "That you're beautiful, and that I'm the luckiest man alive." He bent and kissed her to the roar of their guests. When he lifted his head, he grinned. "And I want the whole town to know that you're mine."

Rosie heard soft music begin, saw the guests all smiling and the flash of a camera capturing the moment.

Regina rushed up and handed her the bouquet.

Rosie stopped crying. She had everything—because she had the perfect man. Forever.

She caught Ethan's hand and dragged him to the platform. To the surprise of the other guests, Harris and Buck and Riley all whooped, cheering her name and swinging their fists in the air. But then, they were used to Rosie and her pushiness.

Once they were standing in front of the minister, Ethan pulled her close. "Love me forever, Rosie."

She laughed and threw her arms around him. "I already have."

*   *   *   *   *

Be sure to catch Riley Moore's story,
part of the
AMERICAN HEROES
miniseries in Temptation. Don't miss
RILEY,
Temptation #930, available in June 2003!

BURIED!
Donna Kauffman

CHAPTER ONE

HALEY BRUBAKER was somewhere over Texas when disaster struck. The pilot announced that an earthquake had just rocked Northern California. More important, the epicenter was being reported as just south of San Francisco. Which was exactly where Haley called home.

The extent of the damage was unknown, but they were being rerouted to a different airport well south of the area.

Her first thoughts weren't of family and friends, as she didn't communicate with the former and hadn't been in the Bay Area long enough to develop the latter. Okay, so it had been two years. Maybe she needed to come out of her home studio more often. But this new life, the new business she'd started, meant everything. Slavish devotion was to be expected.

But, at the moment, her jewelry-making business was the furthest thing from her mind. All of her lovely, painstakingly handmade pieces, which she'd just signed a very nice series of contracts to sell in small, exclusive shops from L.A. to Dallas, were tucked away in velvet-lined cases, back at home, awaiting shipment. Her whole future was in those little boxes, and yet she didn't give them even a passing moment of thought. She was only worried about one thing.

Digger. Her four-year-old Jack Russell terrier. The one and only living, breathing creature in the whole world who had never let her down, never turned his back in a time of need, never sneered at her big plans, never embezzled her hard-earned money, nor stomped on her too trusting heart. Digger. Her little four-legged fountain of unconditional love and affection. Possibly trapped... possibly worse.

She refused to think that, to allow herself to think that. The rest could be gone, she'd rebuild. She'd done it before. "Just let Digger be okay," she murmured as she stumbled from the plane, almost numb from worry, and headed directly to the nearest phone. Lines were jammed and she finally had to borrow a fellow passenger's cell phone to place the call to her pet sitter. Service was disrupted, so she tried the cell phone number. Finally, after a dozen tries, there was an answer.

"Mrs. Fletcher? Thank God! It's me, Haley. Please tell me you—" She paused, barely able to hear the older woman over the pounding of her heart. A heart that fell rapidly as what the woman was saying sank in.

"I knew you were coming home today and thought you'd enjoy having him there waiting for you," she was saying. "So I took him up to the house this morning." Pauline Fletcher, who ran a little pet-sitting service in the oceanside town of Blue Moon, down below Haley's house, was beside herself with despair. "I—I'm so sorry." She broke down in tears.

It took a moment for Haley to get the lump past her throat enough to speak. "The town—the damage—"

She'd already heard enough, seen enough on the airport television monitors, to know several small towns along the coast, just south of the city, had been particularly hard hit. Blue Moon was one of them. But she hadn't been able to gather any more specific detail than that. She knew she had to get to a rental car counter as soon as possible or there would be nothing left to rent, as many other flights had been diverted here, as well, and everyone was scrambling to find a way home. But she needed to know everything Pauline could tell her first.

"Have you seen the town? Are you okay?"

Pauline sniffled, cried, then finally sucked in a steadying breath. "I was up in the city when it hit. I haven't been able to get back. The road looks like someone took it and shook it, like a ribbon. It's all buckled. You can't get close. I'm stuck up here. I don't know." She started to cry again. "I just don't know."

Haley tried to reassure her, but she was just as bewildered, just as lost. They finally broke connection and Haley numbly pushed herself to a car rental counter. Then another, then another. It took almost two hours, but she finally got a car—a small sports car far beyond her budget, but literally the last car on the lot—and got on the road.

She'd shut her mind down, focusing on driving took every bit of her will. Mercifully left behind was the incessant reporting on the television monitors. She left the radio off. She'd fall apart completely if she had to listen to it anymore.

She knew enough to understand that getting close via the coast road was her best chance. The highways were jammed, huge parts of them sunken into the ground as if a giant had danced upon them. She couldn't let herself picture it, couldn't let herself think about it. She had to get home. Had to find out if Digger was okay.

The closer she got, the calmer she got. It was a surreal calm, but she clung to it, ticking off one mile, then another. Fighting the occasional log jam as she passed through each small town. It felt as if it took forever to reach the outskirts of her county, then her town. Her house was up a semiprivate road just south of town, which wound up into the hills to three houses built literally into the side of the mountain. There were originally more planned, but heavy rains and two serious mudslides had ruined the developer's plans and he'd bailed out. Leaving the three model homes at bargain-basement prices.

Haley had been at the right place at the right time, or so she'd thought. Unafraid of Mother Nature after mankind had already done a tap dance on her soul, she'd snapped up one of the houses. "I should have known Mother Nature would have as mean a streak as everyone else I've come across in my life," she muttered as the traffic once again began to clog up.

She was less than a mile south of town when her trip came to an abrupt end. It was late afternoon, a little more than eight hours since she'd been in that plane, hearing the news for the first time. It felt like a lifetime ago. A roadblock had been set up and as she pulled over and parked along the side of the road, with the media and television crews and other travelers, she got her first glimpse of what Mother Nature could do when she was really good and pissed off.

Haley sat there, in shock. No television monitor could prepare a person for the reality of it, the enormity. The road beyond the block looked just as Pauline had described: like a crumpled ribbon. Only it was a ribbon of concrete and blacktop. She looked up into the hills above the road, toward her house, but she was too far away and the trees hid her home from view anyway. Unless, of course, the trees were no longer there, sent tumbling like so many Pick Up sticks, her house along with it—

Again she shut that mental path down. Ruthlessly.

"Breathe. Stay focused," she schooled herself, then went about finding someone who could tell her what was going on. Men in yellow rescue-worker jackets and helmets swarmed like bees around the roadblock and the makeshift headquarters that had been set up in a gas station parking lot. In addition to the amazing numbers of media trucks with dishes mounted on top and cables running everywhere, there was rescue and emergency equipment, fire trucks and heavy machinery lined up, with more rolling in as she fought her way through the small throngs of onlookers and worried homeowners such as herself, looking for someone who might know something. Anything.

She stopped several men, but they all told her the same thing. A makeshift shelter had been set up at the high school gym a mile down the road. She needed to go back there and they would tell her what they knew, when they knew it. He said insurance adjusters were there, claims people, and there were forms she should start filling out. Just in case.

She couldn't even think about that now. "You don't understand. My dog—"

"They'll have lists," the man said shortly, if not unkindly. "Go to the shelter."

Lists. Haley felt a little dizzy. She knew what kind of list he meant. *No. No, wait.* She raced after him, wanting to know about the other lists. The people who were rescued, sent to hospitals maybe, or makeshift first-aid centers. Surely pets and animals were being rescued, too.

He'd already been swallowed up in the rapidly growing sea of people and workers. It was then she saw the dog. A black Labrador, trotting at the side of a man wearing the dark blue pants and T-shirt of a firefighter, but without the helmet and heavy coat. He had a dog. *He'd understand,* was all she could think.

Pushing through the crowd, ignoring the few who stopped and tried to direct her the other way, toward the shelter, she finally moved in behind him. The dog turned first, ears perked slightly, tail up, an animated look on its face. Tears suddenly surged forward and her throat grew tight. Haley fought them down as she put her hand on the man's arm and tore her gaze from the dog's friendly welcome. Would she ever see Digger's bright eyes, hear his friendly yip of hello? *Stop it. Don't think like that.*

The man stopped, turned. And for the first time in what felt like a lifetime of hours, minutes and seconds, she forgot about Digger, the quake, all of it. "Brett? My God, Brett Gannon?"

She'd been running from her past for several years; had escaped it entirely, in fact, when she'd settled in Northern California. But this was a blast from a different past, a happier past. Her college years. A time and place out of her regular life. If you could call anything about her life up to that point regular. She'd reveled in those years, her anonymity, her ability to be, for once, blessedly normal. Just another coed. Not Haley Brubaker, of the Litchfield County Brubakers. It had been a time for learning, for discovering who she was and for falling in love. Not with the younger man who stood in front of her. With his older brother, Sean.

Eight years had done a lot for the gangly sixteen-year-old, she noted. Couldn't help but note. Because Brett was far from a teenager now. He was all man, every six-foot-plus, perfectly muscled inch of him. He'd always been cute. The bright blue eyes that all the Gannon men had, the thick, dusty-blond hair like his mother's, the blinding bright smile. But whereas Sean's smile had been confident and a bit edgy, at least to her nineteen-year-old mind, Brett's had been more mischievous and fun-loving.

He smiled now and she noted the slight crinkles at the corners of his eyes, probably a result of the deep tan that gave him a somewhat weathered, surfer boy look. The eyes were just as bright, the hair bleached a great deal blonder. Total beach boy, very sexy. Except the last time she'd seen him, he'd been back home in Baton Rouge, at the Gannon spread on the Mississippi River.

"Haley? Haley Brubaker? My God, it is you!"
He grinned and pulled her into his arms for a
tight hug. Unlike her family—the polar opposite
in fact—the Gannons had always been an exu-
berantly affectionate bunch. Except for Sean.
Leave it to her to fall for the one Gannon who
wasn't in touch with his emotions, she'd always
thought. Of course, that was likely what had
drawn them to each other in the first place.

The brief hug was a shock to her battered
nerves; the hard length of his body an even
greater one. She wished he'd held her longer. Not
for any sexual reason, but for the sudden wave
of affection that managed to neatly destroy the
shaky wall of confidence that had brought her
this far. Tears firmly sprang to her eyes and her
throat completely closed over. There was no
wishing them away.

She felt a wet nose press into her hand and
looked down to find Brett's dog looking up at
her, tail wagging, eyes filled with concern. At
least, it looked that way to her. Which only made
the tears fall faster.

"Whoa, whoa," Brett said, turning her to face
him, pulling her, mercifully, back into those
strong arms.

Refuge, was all she could think. She wanted to

lose herself inside his embrace, burrow against him, close her eyes, drink in the smell of warm skin, laundered shirt and—well, man. *Just make it all go away.*

But that lasted all of ten seconds. She hadn't gotten to where she was by hiding when things got tough, much less letting someone else call the shots. The last time she'd done that she'd ended up bankrupt. Both financially and morally.

She fought to pull herself together. And to do that, she had to extract herself from his arms. But when his hands lingered on her elbows, his concerned face hovering above hers, she had to admit a momentary waver. "My dog," she finally managed to say. "Digger. He's up there."

She lifted a shaky hand and pointed to the long ridge that paralleled the ocean. "I don't know—" She stopped, took a breath, fought the gasp of a sob and definitely didn't look at the dog still wagging its tail by her thigh. Instead she looked up at Brett. And found strength in a sea of blue. "I don't know if he's okay."

"Come here," Brett said, his tone calm despite the worry clear on his face. "You need to sit down. Let me get you some water."

She yanked her arm free, suddenly ferociously angry. She knew it was the stress that she'd been

bottling up since the moment the pilot had announced the disaster, but she couldn't seem to
stop it. "I don't want to sit down, damn it! I
don't want water. And I don't want to go to the
shelter. I want to find my goddamn dog!"

Brett lifted his hands, palms out, at her sudden
outburst, but surprised her by smiling. "You
know, I don't recall you having a temper. Or
swearing, for that matter."

"A lot has happened since I last saw you,"
she said evenly, but was shocked to find her
mouth wanting to twitch, ever so slightly. That
had always been Brett's role in his rowdy, sometimes tempestuous family. The one who made
everyone laugh, broke the tensions that only a
large family could produce, with a quick joke, a
cocky grin. She should resent him for doing it
now, and so smoothly, so easily. But she needed
to regain her footing, needed to stay calm and
centered. He'd never listen to her if she was an
irrational, screaming mess. And getting him to
listen was critical.

Because she'd already decided he was her
ticket in. Her ticket up there. To whatever lay
beyond the flashing lights and grinding gears of
rescue equipment, the endless cables and collec-
tive drone of television reporters.

To her home. Her livelihood. Her life.

Because Brett and his dog, which she now realized had some kind of rescue designation strapped to its sleek, muscular body, was her ticket to finding Digger.

Once again she placed her hand on his arm, once again found her center in the steady, calm depths of his eyes. And found it amazingly easy to do the one thing she swore she'd never do again. Turn to someone else and ask for help.

"I need to know he's okay," she begged quietly. "He's everything I've got. Please help me."

CHAPTER TWO

BRETT WAS STILL in a bit of a daze. And not because this had been his third rescue mission in the past five weeks. It really was Haley Brubaker, the source of many a fevered teenage dream, standing right in front of him. And even all these years later, knowing he had no clue what kind of person she'd become, he found himself thinking his brother had been the biggest idiot on the planet to let her get away.

Of course, considering the path Sean had taken in life—dedicating every waking minute to the U.S. Marshal's service—breaking up with Haley right after college graduation was probably the kindest thing he could have done for her. Brett had given a fleeting thought then about looking her up himself. After all, he was a college man at that point, although just barely. But arrogant enough to believe she wouldn't let the scant few years in age between them mean anything, wouldn't let Sean's cool dismissal of what they'd shared keep her from looking to another Gannon brother for solace. As long as that Gannon brother was him.

But she'd left Stanford behind and gone back east, back home near her family in Connecticut. And Brett had followed Sean's path instead, to Stanford. Only the second Gannon to go to such a prestigious school. Hell, for that matter, one of only a handful of Gannons who'd made it to any form of higher education. Scholarship in hand, and nubile coeds galore, he'd eventually forgotten all about Haley Brubaker.

Until now.

She stood in front of him, all beseeching brown eyes, firmed-up chin and squared-off shoulders. The top of her head didn't even reach his nose. He didn't remember her being so short. Of course, he was a bit taller himself these days. Not that it would have mattered. In his teenage mind, she'd been a towering goddess, the epitome of style, grace, polish. The kind you could only be born with. So sleek he thought she surely slid through life with the ease that only the independently wealthy could.

He had no idea what had brought her back to California, or what had ever happened to her family, her wealth. He seemed to recall there was some strain there, which was why she'd spent every holiday with the Gannons, instead of with the Brubakers of South Kent, Connecticut. Still, to look at her then, you'd have never guessed she'd fretted about anything more pressing than where to buy the latest designer outfit or where to have her nails done. Not prissy, exactly, but…precise. Put together, as they say.

But there was nothing of that effortlessly-put-together girl in front of him now. No hint of the easy life he assumed she'd led, Brubaker fortune and college degree in hand. None of that easy style and grace. In fact, she looked…uncivilized. Her brown hair was a windblown mass of tangles, her face pale and pinched at the corners of her eyes and mouth, her eyes too big with unshed tears, her lips pressed firmly together. Struggling so hard to put on a brave, steady front, that he doubted she even realized she was shaking.

Haley Brubaker, the stuff of almost every one of his teenage fantasies, was a wreck.

And, despite the years that had passed, Brett Gannon discovered he still wanted to be the Gannon brother she turned to in her time of need.

Gently he took her hand from his arm and folded it in his own. It was cold, despite the late summer heat. He knew from the look in her eyes that any hint he was placating her was going to be met with resistance. Perhaps even hysterics. Given her recent outburst, she was a lot closer to falling apart than she thought she was.

But there was no way she was getting past the line of rescue trucks to head up that hill. Dog or no dog. And he, more than most anyone, understood the deep connection man could feel for those four-legged beasts.

"I need to ask you some questions," he said. "Get some information from you," he went on, gently but firmly steering her away from the front lines, toward his truck. Recon, his Search and Rescue dog and steady companion for the past eighteen months, trotted along beside them without having to be told to. "I promise I'll find out what you need to know."

She let him get her across the lot to his SUV, but she balked at sitting on the rear tailgate. Pushing her hair from her face, pulling from his grasp, she paced. "Fine, fine. I'm at 24143 Columbarra. There's only three houses up there." She pointed to the hills just above them. "About a mile down that ridge. The road winds down and comes out just about a quarter mile down the road past those trucks." She turned, faced him again. "Do you know if they—" Her lower lip

trembled hard, but she fought for control and
found it. "Do you know if any of the houses up
there were affected?"

"I just got here, but I can find out for you.
You need to sit here." He reached for the bottles
of water he kept stocked in the back. In fact, as
part of his commitment to being a SAR team, he
and Recon were packed and ready to go at a moment's notice, with gear that would last up to two
weeks. This time it was local. But less than three
days ago he'd been in Florida. Helping clean up
after Hurricane Evelyn. Before that they'd been
at a building collapse in Boston. Recon had been
brilliant in both scenarios. She was a disaster
dog, one of a growing number of advanced, specialty rescue dogs. Brett and the two-year-old
Lab had worked long and hard, for months on
end, to be certified. Worked long and hard still.
And would, for as long as they remained an ac-
tive team. And it had paid off this summer. This
long, brutal summer.

He looked back at Haley and the fatigue of
weeks spent on the road, pacing in airports, living
in makeshift tents and workstations was forgotten. Adrenaline coursed through him again. But
the new rush wasn't entirely work-related. He ignored that part. Okay, he tried. He shoved a water

bottle at her. "Stay here," he commanded, startling her a little. And himself. But they both
needed to get a grip. "I'll go find out what I can.
Okay?"

He stared her down, until she finally nodded.
Her shoulders slumped a little and she looked so
damn lost he wanted to pull her into his arms
again. Which would be a bad idea all the way
around. Nothing could distract him from what
he'd been called here to do. Not even her.

He thought about leaving Recon with her, both
for companionship and insurance that she'd stay
put, but where he went, his dog went. Period.

He signaled Recon and the black Lab fell into
place beside him as he wound his way back into
the fray. Huge, all terrain vehicles were being
loaded with gear and personnel, and several of
them had trundled past the front line, making
their way to the right, along a narrow path of
undisturbed roadside, between the buckled pave-
ment and the rising mountainside. To the left
there was a sheer drop to the rocks and ocean
below. They didn't get very far before they had
to abandon that idea and set out on foot.

Brett knew that he and Recon would be called
in shortly, along with the other SAR teams
headed this way, once the damage had been fully

assessed and a strategy for approaching the affected areas developed. Their job would be to search for survivors. He looked down the mountain ridge, to where Haley's home was still hopefully perched, and sent a private plea skyward that her dog was okay. That anyone left up there was okay.

The thumping sound of helicopter blades echoed incessantly overhead. Thankfully the media had been banned from the airspace above. It was bad enough having them in a tangle on the ground. The reports from the military choppers would be invaluable, giving them a bird's-eye view of the extent of the damage up above in the hills, along with the best way to approach.

He pushed his way over to one of the command chiefs he knew from his SAR training. ''What have we got up there?'' he asked without preamble.

Butch Gregory turned toward him, his face deeply grooved, his expression grave. ''One home gone, halfway down the hill. Trees down everywhere. We're trying to get confirmation, but word is the owners were away. Two more apparently unaffected, but the road up there is a mess. Ravines, splits, cracked wide open like someone took a sledgehammer to 'em. Hell of a thing,'' he murmured, looking beyond the line, up the hills, where crews were presently beginning to set up a relay line. ''Hell of a thing.''

Brett hadn't been in SAR all that long, not the decades-long career of the man in front of him, anyway. But he didn't suppose a person ever got used to the kind of destruction nature could so blithely wreak, and with so little warning. ''How many in the other houses?''

''We don't know yet. If we can't find an easy access route, they'll need to be lifted out of there. But with the tree coverage, the steep incline, that won't be easy.''

''When do we go up?''

For the first time Butch looked at him, then down at Recon. His face smoothed then, as Brett's often did when looking into the soulful eyes of the animals whose hearts were worn so obviously on their sleeves. He patted the Lab's head, then looked back to Brett. ''A couple of hours. Teams are just now trying to establish a route in. We'll know more soon.''

''Good. You happen to know the address of the house that went down? Name of the owner?''

Butch frowned. ''You got connections here? You know someone up there? Because—''

Brett knew that they didn't like sending in anyone directly affected by whatever disaster they were working. Most of the time, teams were so scarce, they didn't have much choice. But with the damage from this quake spreading up the coast for several miles at least, he could be re-routed, and he knew it. "Just trying to get some information for some people that stopped me. Might help us track the owner down. One less vic to search for."

Butch studied him a moment longer, but finally shook his head. "I don't have it. But I'll see about getting that information to you."

Brett nodded. "Thanks. Much appreciated." He tapped his thigh and Recon fell into a trot beside him as he headed back toward his truck. He was a dozen yards away when he noticed there was no longer a petite brunette hovering near his tailgate. He stopped and quickly scanned the area, but her pale yellow shirt and tan khakis were hardly going to stand out in this crowd.

Then he noticed the bandanna lying on his tail-gate. It was his, but it had been in the back of his truck, unused, when he'd left. Now it was crumpled and lying next to the half-empty water bottle he'd given her. He quickly crossed the remaining distance and let Recon scent the bandanna. She was trained to air scent, to pick up the scent of people from the skin cells they shed that clung in the air currents for hours afterward. Ground tracking would be all but impossible with the crowds around them, but air scent, with Haley so recently gone, was a higher percentage chance. He'd just given Recon the command to track when he happened to look up and spot her.

And his heart stopped before resuming at twice the normal speed. It had only been a flash of her face before she turned away, but he knew it was her. And it was a good thing he'd seen her face. Because with that turnout coat and helmet she now had on, almost swallowing her whole, he'd have never recognized her otherwise.

She was clambering onto the back of a truck. A truck heading out to join the small cluster beyond the front line, at the base of the mountain.

"What the—?" But a moment later her mission became terrifyingly clear. "Oh, God. No."

He was already moving, Recon matching his strides as he covered the distance as fast as he was able. He hit a dead run, even as he watched her get back off the truck, lose herself in the growing crowd of workers…then slip out of that jacket before disappearing unnoticed beyond the tree line.

To head up the mountain. Alone.

CHAPTER THREE

HALEY READILY ADMITTED this was probably the stupidest thing she'd ever done. More foolhardy than falling in love with the emotionally closed-off Sean Gannon. More foolish than believing her family would ever understand her need to follow her own path. Dumber even than falling in love again, this time with Glenn Everest. Suave, sophisticated Glenn, who was quite open emotionally, to the point of being needy. And, oh, how her undernourished heart had loved that. Being so wanted, so desperately needed.

She snorted, even as she scraped another pine bough out of her face and continued her scrabbling effort to climb the side of the mountain. If only she'd realized it was her bank account, not her sponge-soft heart that Glenn had so desperately needed. And since her family money wasn't available to him, he'd helped himself to her own hard-earned cash, which she'd put away so carefully for the day she could start her own business.

Although she was certain Glenn would have gladly helped himself to the entire Brubaker fortune, as well. And run through it just as fast.

She supposed for that alone she should be thankful she'd severed all ties to her family, both emotional and financial. It had been the only way really. A clean cut, right to the bone. Deep wounds bled less that way.

Now if she could just find a way to forgive herself for literally handing her money over to Glenn. *Just let me get my consultant business up and off the ground. We're partners, a team, right? Then it will be your turn.* Oh, yeah, she'd been the perfect helpful partner, putting her lover's needs above her own. "Proof positive that there is indeed a sucker born every minute," she muttered. "And I was sucker enough for at least a whole year's worth of minutes."

She lost her footing, grunted as her calf muscle protested the sudden backward slide. She ignored the stab of pain, once again found her footing, and once again began her painful climb upward. She'd tried to be quiet at first, so the ground crew wouldn't notice her, but she'd given up on that after the first hundred yards. Between the helicopters and heavy equipment below, they'd never hear her anyway.

She'd hoped to angle her way over to the road that led up to the cluster of houses at the top, but she'd heard enough from the crew on her smuggled ride in to know the road was not in great shape. She tried hard not to think what that meant about her house.

One house down. That single overheard comment was all it had taken to spur her into action. She'd forced her way to the front, begged for more information, but no one was listening to her. Well, surviving bankruptcy and a broken heart should be good for something. So she did what she'd learned to do over the past two years. She took matters into her own hands.

Hands that were now hopelessly scratched and bleeding from literally clawing her way up the mountainside. But until she found Digger, she'd do more than sacrifice the fingers whose nimbleness had been the foundation of her new career. Her new life, new source of confidence and pride.

She couldn't let herself think about what she'd do if it was all gone. But that was later. Right now she only cared about rescuing one thing. "Come on, Digger, you're my buddy, you're my guy," she murmured over and over again as she continued her ascent.

And after what seemed like days, years, she

finally got to the edge of the backyard—if you could call it that—of the first house of the three on her road. The house was still standing, looking fine, in fact. As she stumbled into the small but steeply angled area just behind the house, her heart wanted to burst, but more from emotional gratitude than from physical exertion. The deck still jutted out, giving the Smithings a perfect view of the ocean through the trees. To look at the house and the trees, you'd never know that devastation was so close.

She made her way around the side of the house and banged on the garage door. No one answered, but both cars were gone, the garage empty. Hopefully that meant the older couple had been out at the time of the quake. She only knew them in passing. But Patsy Smithing was a chatty sort and just from the occasional comment while Haley had been out walking Digger, she'd learned they were retired and that her husband, Judd, could usually be found on a golf course somewhere, while Patsy devoted her time to charity work.

Haley could only hope they'd managed to find each other in the aftermath. And hard-won independence or not, she wasn't so closed off emotionally that she didn't acknowledge the solace and comfort to be found in the arms of a loved one. In fact, she'd have given a great deal in that moment to have someone to hold on to.

Brett's unwavering blue-eyed gaze popped into her mind, along with the memory of what it had been like to be folded into his arms, held tightly against that oh, so sturdy chest.

She pushed that thought away, along with the twinge of guilt for abandoning his offer to help her. But she simply couldn't sit and do nothing. Not if it meant the difference between life and— *No.* She couldn't think it. Wouldn't.

She loped down the front gravel drive, her legs rubbery and unsteady after the hard climb upward. She tried to take slow, even breaths, to calm herself, to keep her heart from racing as she looked up the road. There was another house before she got to hers, perched higher up the ridge. All three backed to the steep incline of the mountain, with a panoramic view of the ocean below, albeit through the trees. Her house was at the top, above the tree line and afforded the best view of all. The fronts of the houses faced the narrow road connecting them all to civilization, with the mountain continuing to rise up just on the other side, before leveling off and sloping gently down to the valley on the other side.

Only there was nothing civilized or gentle about what Haley discovered as she stumbled to a stop at the end of the Smithings's driveway. Not ten yards below their drive, the road had split in two, as if someone had driven a monstrously huge spike right into the center of it. She didn't dare go close enough to see how deep the chasm was, as there was no telling how unstable the ground around it might be.

She tried to turn away from it, to look up the road, to devise the safest route to her house, but she couldn't seem to stop standing there, staring, openmouthed, at the magnitude of what had been done to her neighborhood. Such as it was. And this was just the road. She finally spun on shaky legs, to stare once again at the Smithing home. But it still looked untouched. Merely yards away from massive destruction, and yet it looked just as it always had.

Could she be as lucky?

She swiveled back, once again caught up in the shock of the gaping slash that had so recently been the road to her house. The only road to her house. Which meant that, even if it was still there, she couldn't stay here. How long would it take to repair something like this? And could it even be done? Could you just fill up a giant chasm like that?

Then she noticed the trees on the other side of the road. They had fallen to their sides, as though a strong wind had knocked them down, as if they were nothing more than toothpicks. Roots jutted up in the air, ripping ragged holes in the earth. And it occurred to her that there was nothing clean or bloodless about this cut.

She felt suddenly chilled, started to shake, and couldn't seem to stop. Couldn't seem to make her feet move. To even do as much as turn and look up the road, much less close the final distance to her house.

And that was how Brett's dog found her.

He circled her and started barking, startling her from the numb void she'd sunken into. Tail wagging and looking quite proud of himself, he continued his sharp barks, even when she tried to shush him. The sudden drone of helicopter propellers thwap-thwapped overhead, muting the dog and making her look up. It circled several times. Looking for her? No, she realized a second later, looking at the damage.

Her heart sped up again as she realized the Labrador was in work mode. Search and Rescue. With her being the rescue.

Moments later Brett came jogging around the side of the Smithing house and signaled the dog to be quiet. The dog bounded to his side, then fell into a trot next to him as Brett closed the final distance between them.

At any other time Haley would have been disgusted by his appearance. He was hardly flushed from the climb, much less scratched up and bloody. But there was a part of her that was too glad to see him, too glad to have someone—anyone else—by her side when she made...whatever discoveries were to be made down the road at her house.

The other part of her tensed up, preparing for the lecture she was sure to get and the argument that would follow. Because she hadn't come this far to turn back now. Braced for a fight, she turned to face him squarely, then stepped back as he came right up to her, surprising her by invading her personal space. All of it.

He stopped a mere breath away. She opened her mouth to explain in no uncertain terms that she was not leaving, even if he tried to bodily carry her off the mountain, which considering the look in his eye and his close proximity, seemed to be his intent. But he dashed her arguments before she'd even made them, and he didn't even have to say anything.

He lifted a hand, a hand she was pleased to see was at least a bit scuffed and dirty, and pulled a piece of pine bow from the wild tangle her hair had become. His own expression looked so fierce, so unlike the happy-go-lucky Brett she knew. "I would have helped you."

Not "You shouldn't have come up here on your own, you stupid idiot." Not "What kind of crazy stunt do you think you're pulling? You could have gotten yourself killed." Both of which she rightly deserved. Just chiding her for leaving him behind. And, despite the ferocity of his gaze, he also wore an unmistakable look of understanding. Which shamed her more than any yelling match would have.

"I'm sorry. That I worried you," she clarified. "I had to find him."

Brett let his hand fall away and nodded. "I understand, but—"

"Right now I'm not all that worried about something happening to me. Everything I have is up the road in that house. And I'm not talking about my furniture, or even my livelihood."

"I know. But you have to think beyond yourself, your personal safety. With choppers flying overhead, they were going to see you crashing through the trees. Did you stop to think what they'd do? Did you think they wouldn't send a rescue team up here after you when they realized what you'd done?''

She wrapped her arms around herself again. "I—I—no, I wasn't thinking that far ahead." She hung her head. "I wasn't thinking at all. I'm really sorry." This time she was completely sincere. She looked back up at him, deserved the quiet censure now in his gaze. "I didn't mean to put anyone else in danger."

"I know we haven't seen each other in a long time, that we don't really know each other anymore... But I would have helped you, found a way up here, found your dog. You promised to wait."

Now, completely unreasonably, she felt a smile tug at the corners of her mouth. "No, I didn't promise. You merely commanded me to stay. Like I was one of your rescue dogs."

She thought she saw him fight the same battle. "At least Recon would have had the good sense to obey me," he said grudgingly.

Her urge to smile faded, as did his. Finally she nodded. "You're right. I should have waited. But when I heard someone mention one house was down up here, I—'' She shrugged.

''Okay, okay. No point in rehashing this to death. What's done is done.''

He placed his hand on her shoulder, let it slide down her arm to cup her elbow. The Gannons had always been a touchy-feely bunch, overly familiar with other people, never thinking that they might resent such a personal intrusion. Surely Brett didn't realize how startling it was to her to be touched, even casually. It was as natural to him as breathing. At any other time, she'd have carefully stepped away, easing from that kind of familiarity, the kind that could become addictive to a person not reared with the same easygoing sensibilities. The kind of person who'd place too much stake on such things, then end up sorely disappointed when they didn't mean as much to the giver as they did to the receiver. Any other time she'd have stepped back, preserved that space she'd so carefully erected around herself these past two years.

But she didn't. His touch was calming, steadying, and she was too shaken up to find the strength to turn away from that. She told herself at least she understood her reasons for needing it, taking it, indulging herself in her time of shock and fear. Surely she could handle this much without risking anything. Because just as surely he was only offering her solace in his capacity of a rescuer.

Except, as her walls were so shaky, her confidence eroding, she had to admit that his touch sparked all sorts of things inside her that had nothing to do with being rescued. Things that made her aware of him, not as a rescuer or the not-so-little brother of an old flame. She shivered. Only this time it wasn't in shock, which was what made her pull away. *Danger, danger, Haley Brubaker,* she thought silently. *And it's not the earthquake that's the threat.*

"I'm not going back. I've come too far," she said, knowing she sounded stiff and unnatural, but then dealing with her sudden physical reaction to him was one shock too many for her system to bear. She supposed this is why people did things well out of character during times of deep stress. She'd heard about those primal urges that take over when people think they are in mortal danger. She shivered again, then shook her head. As if that would clear the sudden images crowding her brain. Images of Brett taking her in those strong arms of his, soothing away all her fears, making her forget her terror and fear of the unknown by drowning her in a sensual tidal pool of—

"I've got to find Digger," she stated flatly, pushing—no, shoving—those thoughts, those highly inappropriate, obviously shock-induced thoughts, firmly from her mind.

He took her arm as she spun away from him. "Whoa, whoa."

She merely stared down at his hand on her, working furiously to think of Digger. Only of Digger. He was paramount in her mind. A mind she was surely losing because she couldn't stop looking at that wide span of hand, those long, lean fingers, so easily gripping her, holding her in place. *Maybe that's it,* she thought somewhat wildly. *I need someone with big, strong hands to hold me in place. Otherwise I'm going to shatter into a million pieces.* She found her gaze drifting up to his, and she hated herself for the helpless look she knew damn well filled her eyes.

But there was no pity to be found in his. No censure, either. "I'm here now, Haley. And I'm trained for this. We'll go find Digger. Recon and me." His grip tightened. "Not you."

She began to shake again, and tears threatened, which made no sense. He was going to help her. He was going to get Digger. "I can't—won't—

sit here and wait,'' she said, her voice trembling. ''I've come this far, I—''

And then she was in his arms, tight up against that glorious, secure expanse of chest, and she couldn't help it, she reveled in it. Even for just a moment, just long enough to get her bearings, to find her strength, her control. Digger needed her and she'd be damned if she'd let him down when she'd come this far, gotten this close. ''I can't let him down,'' she whispered.

Brett tipped her chin up, looked down into her eyes. And grinned. It was a shocking, blinding thing, seemingly so out of place amid all the terror and destruction. And yet it was the perfect thing, the perfect gift. The shining beacon of confidence she needed to latch her own shaky foundation to.

''Then let's go get him,'' Brett said. And with her hand tucked firmly in his, they turned to face what lay ahead.

CHAPTER FOUR

IT HAD BEEN EIGHT YEARS and he was a long way from that gangly sixteen-year-old who'd fantasized about having the right to touch Haley Brubaker. But as he held her hand while they made their way along the side of the road, well away from the edge of the snaking split that ran down the center of it, to the second house on the road, he realized he was still the same dumb goober.

Her house was likely halfway to the ocean, her four-legged companion possibly lost forever…and here he was, thinking about how touching her felt even better than he'd imagined.

They rounded the bend in the road and she halted with a gasp. "Oh, no. Oh, my God."

"Yours?" Brett felt his heart turn to lead. All that remained of the house that had once stood on the lot to their right were foundation shards and half a deck that was no longer attached to anything. It bobbed drunkenly, barely supported by the one piling left standing.

Haley shook her head. With her hand covering her mouth, she stumbled forward, as if she was going to go and look down the side of the mountain. "Oh, my God."

Brett pulled her back. "Don't. You don't know how stable the ground is." He didn't want to explain about the other dangers, such as aftershocks. She was operating on a thin enough wire as it was, whether she realized it or not. "No cars," he noted with relief. "Do they work outside the home?"

She nodded. "The Smithing house was fine, and they're just right down the road."

"Don't try to make sense out of it, Haley. Tornados, hurricanes, floods, there is no rhyme or reason to any of the devastation they cause."

Then she spun around to face him, clutched at his forearms, her eyes bright with hope. "One house down," she said. "They said one house down! Which means—" She broke free and took off running before Brett could do anything to stop her.

He sent Recon off with her and followed at a run. "Stop, Haley," he called, knowing it would do little good at this point. "Watch where you're stepping. The ground is unstable."

She was already off the road, cutting through

the shrubs and trees to the house he saw beyond.
It was up on a sort of promontory. No trees
around beyond it, as if the earth simply fell away.
It was nothing less than a miracle that the house
was still there. But he was trained to know just
how deceiving looks could be in a situation such
as this.

"No!" he shouted, hitting his stride at a dead
run, whacking limbs out of his way as he came
into the clearing. Recon was right on her heels
as she cut the last corner and raced up her drive.
His legs were easily half again as long as hers
and yet some sort of super, adrenaline-powered
rush kept her just out of his reach. "Haley,
stop!" he commanded, his heart pounding more
in fear than from exertion. "You could send the
whole thing down! Stop!"

She literally skidded to a stop not ten feet from
the double doors of her detached garage, stood
like a frozen statue as she pulled herself together
and studied the ground around her, then the
building in front of her, obviously looking for
signs of structural damage.

"You can't always see it," he said, coming to
a stop beside her. "This thing barely clings to
the side of this huge pile of rock we're on as it
is. It had to be shaken pretty good when the

quake hit. Just because it looks okay, because that other house looked okay, doesn't mean—''

''Digger is in there.''

''I know.'' He signaled Recon to his side. ''This time you have to promise me,'' he said, taking her chin in his hand. ''We'll go get him.''

To her credit, she nodded without argument.

''But what if—'' she began.

''We're trained for this.'' He tugged his pack off his back and zipped it open, pulling out a long tool that looked like a cross between a claw and some sort of tire iron.

''It's a Halligan tool,'' he explained, noting her expression.

Her mouth dropped open as she spied the gear strapped and pocketed throughout the pack's lining. ''You ran up the side of a mountain with all that stuff?'' She looked at him. ''And you hardly broke a sweat.''

He grinned and gave her a little salute with his Halligan. ''Like I said, I'm trained for this. It's just nice to know that all that hard work pays off when duty calls.''

''Yeah, I guess it would,'' she said faintly, then looked again at his pack. ''I guess you are trained for this.''

''I'm not a sixteen-year-old goober, drooling,

pestering his big brother's girlfriend anymore, Haley.''

''I—I can see that.''

And for a split second, he could have sworn there was a snick of sexual awareness arcing between them. Which was ludicrous given the situation. *He* was aware, but then he always had been. Time didn't change everything, apparently. His grin firmed, but didn't fade. ''What kind of dog is Digger?''

''Jack Russell terrier.''

''Crated?''

She nodded. ''While I'm gone. Otherwise he gets into everything. Pauline had him at her place. She has outdoor runs and—'' She broke off, as if realizing she was babbling. ''The crate is in the kitchen. It's straight through the living room and runs the length of the back of the house. His crate is to the left, near the sliding-glass door to the deck. So he can see the birds and squirrels.'' Her voice caught on that last part and she covered her mouth again.

He rubbed her shoulder with his free hand. ''I'll get him, Haley, okay? You're doing fine. But I need you to stay here. The house doesn't need any more weight in it than necessary. Do you understand?''

She nodded, all big brown eyes and wavering lips. He never remembered her as being particularly helpless. Quite the opposite, in fact. He didn't think that was teenage hero worship, either. Digger meant a great deal to her. Recon pressed her nose against his hand and Brett understood exactly how Haley felt. "Okay. Good. Stay right here. Right. Here."

She nodded. "Just make sure he's okay. And—and be careful. I couldn't bear it if I caused—"

"This is what I do." Recon was all but vibrating at his side. "What we do."

Haley looked down at his dog. "He looks... excited."

Brett had the feeling she was going to say, "Happy." Which Recon was. She didn't understand the stakes. Search and Rescue dogs were trained to think of their jobs as one big game. An overdeveloped desire to play, hunt, seek and find were precisely the traits handlers used to select the right puppy for training. It had taken Brett almost fifteen months to find the right dog. And he'd ended up finding her at the local humane shelter, of all places. He'd known almost instantly she was the one. Recon loved the game, and she was very, very good at playing it. "She is excited. She lives for this."

"She? With a name like that?"

"Trust me, she earned it. Now listen, we might take a while. It doesn't mean anything bad has happened, just that we need to move carefully. Don't panic. And don't follow." He waited for her nod, then moved up the drive and picked his way onto the narrow front porch. The only way to the back door was across the deck. Which hung out over a very steep, very rocky incline that tumbled down to the road below. He'd rather go through the house.

He glanced back at Haley, who was still riveted to the exact same spot, fingers twisting together as she watched him. "Does he have any toys close to the front door? A leash?" he called.

"His leash and collar are on a small table, right inside to the left."

Brett nodded. It would give him a scent to put Recon on, if they needed to go that far. It was quite possible that tables, chairs, shelves, had all come crashing down. He'd seen too many people reenter houses after disaster struck, houses that looked perfectly fine on the outside, only to stumble back out in total shock at the devastation inside. Digger might be trapped in his crate, or could have escaped it altogether and still be trapped. Very carefully he went to pry open the door.

Haley called out to him. "Key! Under the clay squirrel. Right by the front step in the garden. I'm sorry, I forgot. I—I left everything in the rental car and didn't have time to get it when I—"

"Decided to hitch a ride," Brett finished, flashing her a grin. "No problem." He calmly retrieved the key. Steadiness was key, patience even more so, in this kind of job. Most SAR teams were made up of one very laid-back human and one very excitable canine partner. His team was no exception.

He eased the door open. The less vibration or pressure he had to put on any part of the house, the better. It could be just as rock solid as ever, but there was no point in taking unnecessary risks. He was glad to see the door swung freely on its hinges. Nothing warped. Digger wasn't sitting there waiting for them, which wasn't a bad sign, but he heard no barking or other signs that the dog was aware of intruders. Not a terrier's nature, as far as he knew.

He signaled out to Haley with a wave. "We'll

be out shortly.'' The "Do not follow us'' part
was clearly understood.

She nodded.

He looped the leash over the Halligan, lifting
it from where it sat on the table by the door,
which still stood upright. But one look at the
room beyond told him that was about all that had
remained intact. His heart tightened for Haley's
sake.

He dipped the leash down to Recon, who immediately went to work. ''Find,'' he commanded. Of course, Digger's scent was all over
the place, but Recon was trained to air scent and
immediately tracked to the kitchen, where the
strongest scent emanated from. She picked her
way through the clutter and mess with nimble-
footed grace. The floor creaked as Brett took a
step after her, and he signaled her to stop. He
tested the floor in several areas, applying pressure
with the tool, then motioning her to continue as
he followed at a slower, more careful pace. He
continuously checked the walls for cracks, the
floor for any unseen gaps. Recon and he trained
routinely on huge piles of rubble set up just for
that purpose, and, more recently, had experienced
the real thing. It had been a bitch of a few months

and both were unfortunately well used to moving over shifting mounds of debris.

But this time it was different. Not because it was any more or less dangerous, but because the shifting mounds of debris belonged to the woman standing out in her own driveway, heart in hand as she waited for him to emerge with the only thing she cared about. It made him wonder why. Not that people didn't form tight bonds with their pets. He understood that better than most. But she'd said he was the only thing she had in the world. He guessed she still wasn't close with her family.

Which made him wonder what had brought her back to the west coast, how long she'd been here. To think they both lived in the Bay Area and it had taken a disaster to reunite them. "Just my luck," Brett mumbled. His normal work schedule with the San Mateo Fire Department was demanding enough. His SAR work had only increased that demand. He and Recon had worked hard toward becoming one of the elite specialty SAR teams, certified by FEMA, the Federal Emergency Management Agency. They'd achieved that goal in the early spring. And had spent the summer proving their worth. He hadn't regretted his decision for a second.

But it was hell on relationships.

"What relationships?" he muttered, stilling again as the floor creaked. He signaled Recon to stop, then carefully shifted a landslide of books out of his path before testing the floor again. Deciding on his route, he sent her on ahead and continued to pick his way closer to the kitchen. He absently glanced at the titles as he shifted them aside. *Lapidary Journal, Gemologists Today, Jewels and Jewelry.* Her business, perhaps? He shook his head. He'd always figured her as the CEO of some Fortune 500 company. Perhaps his attentions had been a bit more hero-worship-colored than he wanted to admit.

Though the trip across the room to the kitchen was less than twenty feet, he and Recon were forced to stop half a dozen times, their forward progress slow, but thankfully steady and as safe as possible. It was a nerve-racking pace, but he had to do his best to ensure they didn't all three end up needing rescuing.

Finally Recon made it into the kitchen and it was only moments later she sent up her alert. She was trained to stand and bark when she'd found whatever she'd been sent after. In her case, it was usually people. And not always in time. But her bark wasn't agitated, as it tended to get when her "prize" wasn't as lively as she'd hoped. It was bright, perky, excited. Brett had, unfortunately, had plenty of opportunity these past several months to learn the nuances of Recon's alerts.

He climbed carefully around the last bookcase, then gingerly slid her kitchen table, now on its side and almost completely blocking the door, to the side. Finally he made it into the kitchen. Digger stood in his crate, or vibrated would be more accurate, tail stub wagging furiously, mouth open in soundless yips. Brett realized why he hadn't heard the dog bark or signal for intruders. He'd long since lost his voice, poor guy.

"It's okay, Digger. We're here for you." He signaled Recon to cease her alert. She stopped barking, but there was no settling her down. An other buddy to play with! Brett smiled and righted several cane chairs before kneeling in front of the crate. "Yes, Recon, much more fun prize than usual, huh, girl?" He rubbed his dog's head and gave her a reward from his pocket. Her favorite—dried hot dog pieces.

"Okay, Dig, let's see about getting you out of here, buddy." Fortunately his crate was small, so Brett could pick up the whole thing. Despite the dog's obvious glee in being rescued, in his highly agitated and terrified state, there was no telling what he'd do if let go. Better to keep him confined. Digger's leash was tucked in his pack, so he hoisted the crate, and began the arduous climb back out. The house continued to creak ominously and given its precarious perch on the mountainside, he wasn't taking any chances. Though it was tempting to just head straight for the door, directly over the rubble of furniture, he followed the same careful path he'd charted on the way in, slowed by the dog-filled crate he was now hauling with him. Once outside, he'd get Haley to put her dog on lead, then they were all climbing their way off this mountain.

He sent Recon out of the house first, then hit the front porch the same instant Haley hit a dead run toward them.

Her expression was one of pure, unadulterated joy. "Digger! My little baby!"

Digger yipped soundlessly and banged around inside his crate.

"Whoa, whoa," Brett said, trying to hold the suddenly quaking cage. "Let's get back, away from the house." It was the safe thing to do, but he also didn't need her dealing with the destruction inside just yet. Let her enjoy her reunion with Digger.

"What's wrong with him?" She was reaching for the crate.

"He's barked himself hoarse. I imagine the quake shook him up quite a bit. Some animals are hypersensitive to seismic movement, sensing it even before we do." He kept talking as he eased them off the porch and away from the house. "Let me carry him until we're clear of the house. His leash is in my pack. You can take him out and hook him up as soon as we get clear."

Haley literally dogged his heels all the way down the drive to the road. It wasn't until she'd knelt and let an amazingly wiggled-up dog out of his crate, caught him to her chest and hugged him tightly, nose buried in his wiry fur, that she looked at him again. Eyes shining as brightly as Digger's, mouth stretched wide, teeth flashing, she was amazingly beautiful. Even with scratches on her face, hair sticking out at every angle and dog hair plastered all over her, she took his breath away.

"Thank you," she said, then impulsively reached up on tiptoes and kissed him right on the mouth. He wasn't sure who was more shocked.

Her lips were warm, sweet, and had she not been standing in front of her partially demolished house, rescued dog clutched to her chest, he'd have likely reached for her and found out just where this friendly thank-you kiss might lead. Damn, but he'd waited a long time to taste Haley Brubaker. And it had been well worth it. Quake and all.

When she pulled back, her eyes were bright with more than gratitude, her skin flushed with more than relief. She held his gaze for what seemed like an eternity. But just when he was going to lower his head again, to find out if the fireworks between them were as real as he suspected they were, Digger reached up and licked his cheek, making them both laugh.

"He thanks you, too," Haley said, hugging the dog again.

"Thank you for doing this, Brett. I know I had no right, compromising things, but I can't say I'm sorry. You don't know how much this means to me."

Seeing Digger's tongue lolling happily and the bright light shining from her eyes gave him a pretty clear idea. "Not a problem. I'm just glad he's okay. You'll probably want the medics down below to check him out. There will probably be at least one vet on scene. Either one could probably recommend something for his throat." He tugged out the leash and smiled. "As much as I know both of you would rather you carry him out of here, it would be better if he were on lead.''

The ''just in case'' was implied. The slightest frown creased her forehead and for the first time she looked back at her house. ''I hadn't even thought about what comes next. Is it—is everything really okay in there?'' The color that had come back to her cheeks when she'd been reunited with Digger had brightened to a flush with their kiss. Brett knew it wouldn't be long before true emotional and physical toll began to set in. And it would be best if she was down at the base, with help at the ready, when that happened.

''Do you have family, friends, in the area?'' He motioned back down the road. ''That road is impassable and will be for some time.''

''But my house? It's really okay?''

Brett sighed. He hated to say anything, but he refused to lie to her. ''Things got shaken up a bit. Some of your dishes are broken, your furniture got jumbled up pretty good. I'm not sure how serious the damage is. I'm sure a lot of it just needs to be put to rights. But they'll have to send inspectors up here, engineers and whatnot, to check everything out before they'll give you the okay to go back in.'' *If they do at all,* he added silently, but saw she understood that anyway.

She opened her mouth, then looked at her house and closed it, sighing. "I'm just happy you're okay," she murmured, pressing her face once again into Digger's now more settled body. "That's all that matters."

There had been fear on her face, worry, maybe a moment of yearning, before resignation had taken over. Brett thought of the books he'd seen on her bookcase. "You said something down at base, when we first hooked up, about your livelihood."

She nodded. "I make jewelry. I—I was just coming back from a business trip, setting up some new accounts in other cities."

"So most of your stock is already in stores?" He felt a little better then. She'd have insurance. Surely they'd replace her supplies, tools.

Then she shook her head. "No. Several boutiques around the Bay Area handle a few pieces, but I'd been stocking up, preparing for this trip. I have one case of some of my best pieces, packed with my luggage." Her mouth dropped open. "Oh, my God, I never got my luggage! I was so worried, I—"

"It will be there," he told her. "We can get it later."

"We?" She shook her head. "You've already gone way above and beyond—"

"Do you have someplace to stay? Where you can take Digger?"

She simply stared at him, then down at Digger, nonplussed for a moment, before finally marshaling her control once again. "We'll get a room. I'm sure they'll make exceptions, all things considered."

"I've got tons of room." He raised his hand. "My family would never forgive me if I didn't help out."

A small smile tugged at the corners of her mouth, but she only said, "How are they? Everyone still in Baton Rouge?"

"All but me and Sean." He dug his hands into his pockets. Mostly to keep from reaching for her again. It was the damnedest thing, but he had this feeling that all this had happened for a reason. Maybe not the quake, he didn't need anything so literally earthshaking as a sign. But...he couldn't ignore the feeling that this—meeting her again— was somehow, some way, meant to be. "Your work. It's in there?" He nodded to the house.

Surprisingly, she shook her head and motioned

instead to the small, detached garage. "I turned that into a workspace. I have a small safe in there to keep finished work I haven't sent on consignment. Four contracts' worth of work is in there." She said the latter more to herself than to him.

Brett had no idea what had happened between her and her wealthy family, but it was clear she wasn't living off any kind of trust fund. Her furniture had been nice, but basic and functional. There were no fancy gadgets, no high-end stereo system, no pricey appliances, much less any objets d'art, at least none that he had seen. As far as he could tell, her jewelry business was her sole source of income.

He studied the garage. "Is it a key safe, or a combination safe?"

Understanding dawned immediately on her face. "No, I can't let you do that. It's all in there and safe. I've seen that with my own eyes. I'll— It'll be all right. I'm sure my clients will be more than understanding, given the circumstances."

Brett had been in and around enough disaster situations to know that while insurance companies did the best they could to help their customers out, and the state did what it could to help, restitution took time. And, in some cases, insurance money simply wasn't enough. Acts of God, as quakes were termed, didn't always come under the heading of benefits. And he doubted, given her circumstances, she'd taken out any pricey earthquake coverage.

He shot her a grin, his cockiest. "Wouldn't hurt any to at least get the pieces out of there, where they could be earning you some commissions, right? You'll have enough on your hands, dealing with the rest of this. Knowing you at least fulfilled your initial obligation would go a long way toward—"

"Brett, thank you, but I can't ask you to do that." She looked at the garage then away again. Her future, everything she'd worked hard for, was right inside that little building.

Even if things did move swiftly, with the road the way it was, she wouldn't be let back up here on any kind of permanent basis for a long time. And he wasn't sure what kind of means the state would provide for the families up here to get their belongings down off the mountain in the meantime.

She was looking at the garage again and he pressed his advantage. "Just give me the combination."

"I wouldn't know where to begin. And it's not

something you can haul down the mountain in your backpack. None of it is wrapped and—''

''Just what kind of jewelry are we talking about?''

She smiled finally. ''Unique. Wire, beads, jewels. Most of it somewhat fragile. At least, in terms of hiking and backpacks.'' She finally knelt and put Digger down, snapping on his body harness and lead. She ruffed his ears, scratched his rear haunches, then finally stood. Recon and Digger set about getting to know one another and she smiled. ''I have everything I need.'' She looked at him again. ''But thank you.'' She nodded toward the garage. ''It will be okay, don't you think? I've got clothes and stuff in my luggage. Enough to handle things for a while, anyway. We'll be fine. Or as fine as we can be.''

It was ridiculous, really. Here he was, the trained professional, and he was the one wanting to take stupid risks—for the civilian who was being rational about the whole thing.

But she wasn't any civilian. And he knew she hadn't a clue what she had yet to face. ''Let me at least look inside and check on things. I don't know when you'll be let up here again.''

She smiled. ''Or your family will never forgive you?''

He smiled, too. "Not in this case. I take full responsibility for this act of idiocy."

She put her hand out as he turned. "Brett, really—"

He just grinned over his shoulder. "I'm a big boy. And I'm well trained."

Recon chose that moment to bark, as if in total agreement, making them both laugh.

"Okay," Haley said. "But only if I at least get to come to the door and tell you what to take." She held up her hand when he went to protest. "Those are my conditions. Take 'em or leave 'em."

He tried to stare her down. It didn't work. He sort of liked that. Not that he'd tell her. Let a woman know something like that and she'd be running roughshod over you in a heartbeat. Not that he thought he'd mind a whole lot, he found himself thinking. If the woman was Haley Brubaker.

"Just to the door," he said, wagging a finger. "And hold on to Digger." He put Recon in a sit/ stay as Haley slapped her chest and her little dog literally sprung off its haunches, all the way into her arms.

"Nice trick."

"You're not the only one who's well trained,"

she said smugly, then motioned for him to lead on.

Rather than lift up either of the roll-top doors, Brett opted for the small, windowed door around the side. The footing wasn't as good there, as the hill sloped down directly behind him. But the bay doors would shake the building too much. There was a small railing and stoop, both of which he made use of. He motioned her to stand back. "Let me take a look, then I'll go in and roll up the doors if I think it's okay. I don't want you this close to the edge."

She nodded.

He stepped inside, but even with the door open, it was too dark to really see anything. He felt around the door frame until he hit the switch. Nothing. No power. No real surprise there.

"I have a generator," she called. "We lose power up here all the time."

"I'll use my flashlight." He'd just pulled it out of his pack, stepped inside as he turned it on, when Recon began to bark. It was one he didn't recognize. He stepped back out, saw his dog still in her sit/stay, but barking in what, for her, was almost a high-pitched frenzy. "Recon," he called, then gave a signal for her to come. She bulleted toward him.

Digger started squirming in Haley's arms, too, and she was looking around, trying to discover the source.

Brett had a really bad feeling, but before he could do anything, the ground began to roll like water beneath his feet. "Move! Move!" he shouted, wanting Haley away from the structure. As he stepped back out onto the stoop, it gave way, sending him back into the building. The ground rocked more violently and Recon danced outside, barking.

Brett tried to make a leap past the stoop that was no longer there, to the ground just a few feet away, but he couldn't get a grip with his feet.

"Brett!"

Haley was screaming his name. He didn't know what to tell her, other than to get away from the buildings. But it didn't mean the earth wouldn't split wide open and swallow her whole anyway. Goddammit, what had he been thinking to waste time up here as he had! Flirting, for all intents and purposes. Not that it would have made much difference. They wouldn't have made it far anyway. For all he knew, they could have ended up in a landslide of trees.

He reached out for anything to hold on to, then the ground heaved him up in the air as though he weighed less than a Popsicle stick. He landed hard. On what, he had no idea. He could hear Recon barking, Haley screaming.

Then nothing.

CHAPTER FIVE

IT WAS LIKE WATCHING something out of a movie, only it was all horrifically real. The ground rolled like a giant wave beneath Haley's feet. She clutched Digger close to her body, struggling just to remain upright, but the ground literally was pulled out from under her, sending her sprawling to the road. Digger popped loose, but Haley managed to snag the leash and wound it around her arm, clinging to it like a lifeline. Only she was very much afraid there was no such thing anymore. For any of them.

She managed to get to her knees. Recon was beside her, barking wildly at the garage. Haley watched in an oddly detached way as the surreal happened right in front of her. Her garage actually began to tilt, then list to one side, as if drunk. Her mouth opened in soundless horror as it literally shuffled right off its foundation...and moved closer to the edge. Her little stoop was already gone.

"Brett!" she screamed. Recon suddenly leaped beside her and she turned enough to see that the road was beginning to split and buckle behind her, right where the dog had been standing. She looked wildly around her, wondering which way she should go. One step in the wrong direction could mean—

And then it all stopped, just as suddenly as it had begun. It seemed as if the ground had been shifting beneath her for hours, and yet the whole episode had likely lasted less than several seconds.

Recon was standing just a foot away, no longer barking, but so agitated she was almost vibrating. Digger had burrowed himself beneath Haley, who was still on her hands and knees. Unaware of the scrapes to her knees and bloody cuts on her hands, she finally managed to stand. "Get a grip. Be calm," she murmured, needing the sound of her own voice. "Think."

She took a breath, then another one, then did a slow and complete turn, steeling herself to whatever she might see. She'd made it this far, she wasn't about to lose it now.

The road behind her was split from side to side, with giant snaking cracks leading from either side. It wasn't passable. The only way down was over the edge behind her. And that wasn't climbable. "Don't think about that yet," she schooled herself. Digger jumped against her leg and she slapped her chest. She caught him tightly to her as she finished her turn.

The garage.

And then she remembered, and realized she wasn't as together as she thought. "Brett? Brett!" she screamed. He was inside the garage. What was left of it. "Oh, my God, oh, my God. Brett!" She carefully picked her way closer. There were no cracks between the ground where she stood and the garage. The back corner of which had collapsed and disappeared over the edge beyond. "Stay calm, stay calm." Digger must have sensed the gravity of the situation, because for once he remained still and compliant in her arms.

She got within five yards of the two rolling doors. The side door was no longer there. She blanked her mind against the image of Brett standing in that doorway only moments ago, refusing to think the worst. "Brett?"

She waited, straining to hear any sounds from inside the garage.

I take full responsibility for this act of idiocy. She tried to get Brett's words out of her mind, tried just as unsuccessfully to squelch the wave of guilt that threatened to drown her. There would be plenty of time for that later. Right now she had to figure out how to check the garage. Brett could be lying in there, trapped, hurt…or worse.

Then she felt Recon's nose press against her thigh and turned to find the dog staring up at her expectantly. She had no idea how to command the dog to search, and wasn't willing to send her inside that tottering building anyway. ''He needs help,'' she told the dog, rubbing her head, stroking her velvety ears.

Recon barked, tail wagging, eyes alert, focused, as if waiting for her orders.

Haley tried to stem the defeating sense of helplessness creeping in on her. Damn it, she wasn't helpless. She'd carved a whole new life for herself, hadn't she? A life free of the demands and controls of her family, a life free of lying, stealing lovers, a life free of any commitments save the ones she decided to commit to. Which, right now, was her dog and her business. They were the only partners she needed, the only ones she could handle. As for a warm body in bed at night, well, Digger fulfilled that role as best as he could.

He wasn't exactly a strong pair of arms, but at least he was dependable.

She thought about Brett's strong arms, his warm mouth on hers. Okay, so maybe she wanted more. And if she'd allowed herself to think about it, she'd have admitted she didn't want to live alone forever, that she would want to be with someone again. Someday. And Brett was definitely the first man to even make her think about that day. But this was hardly the time or place to consider—

Recon barked again, panting heavily as her gaze flipped from garage to Haley, back and forth, as she waited. Waited for Haley to *do* something. And Haley realized that the time of being only accountable for herself and her dog had ended the moment she'd made the mad dash up the side of this mountain.

She turned to Recon and commanded, "Sit. Stay." She didn't remember the hand signals Brett had used with the command, but apparently she didn't need them as Recon planted her butt obediently on the ground. Haley carefully avoided looking past her, to the snaking cracks and crevices that snaked through what had been her road. All she could do was pray there were no more aftershocks until she got them all off this godforsaken mountain. What the hell had she been thinking coming up here?

Just then Digger licked her chin, as if reminding her that at least one creature was thankful for her rash decision. She sighed, hugging him close, suddenly feeling very near to tears. Which would help no one at the moment.

She sniffled once, pasted a determined look on her face and told Digger in no uncertain terms, "Keep still."

The dog observed her solemnly, which for a Jack Russell was akin to a miracle. It was only a shame he wouldn't sit and stay like Recon. She wanted her arms free, her hands free, but there was nothing to tie him to. The trees were across the road, on the other side of the giant cracks.

"All right," she announced, hoping a confident bearing would instill trust in her ragged troops. And herself. "I'm going to try to get around the other side. There's a small, high window. I'm going to see if I can look inside, figure out if I can roll up the doors without sending the whole thing sliding."

Both dogs merely blinked at her. *So trusting,* she thought. She only hoped she didn't let them, or Brett, down. After all, they hadn't let her down when she needed them.

The left side of the garage was farthest away from the edge. She gingerly, carefully, walked around to that side, testing the ground with each step for stability. Not so much as a piece of gravel shifted. She clung to that hopeful bit of news.

"Brett?" she called again, now only several feet from the window. "Can you hear me? Are you okay?"

Slowly, she made her way to the window, almost tiptoeing the last few steps. The building actually leaned away from her now, listing toward the edge. The tiny window had been high on this side to begin with. Now it was just beyond her height, even on tiptoe. She'd have to jump up and look in. Any other time she wouldn't have hesitated, but she had no idea what even the impact of her body weight on the earth around the building would do. It was already shifting off its foundations. That couldn't be good news.

"Brett?" she shouted again, as loud as she could. Then the air was filled with the sudden thwap-thwap of helicopter blades. She looked up, but between the house and garage, and the tree line beyond the house, her view in the direction of the sound was limited. She debated leaving the garage, moving back out on the driveway, closer to the cracks and crevices, and waving to get their attention, but the sound grew more distant and the chopper was gone without ever coming directly overhead.

"They'll be back," she told Digger. And herself. "And we'll all be ready for them." She studied the ground just next to the foundation, then looked up at the window, then at Digger. "I'm going to have to put you down for a moment. Behave."

Digger shocked her by actually plopping down on his butt right next to her feet. Apparently he'd had a good enough scare being left in that house during the quake, he wasn't going anywhere without her. She smiled, her heart filling with the love she had for her little furry companion. "I'm not going anywhere without you either, don't worry."

He tilted his head to the side, as he often did when she spoke to him. It was adorable and endearing and gave her the moment she needed to gather her confidence. "Thanks," she told him, but firmly looped the leash on her arm nonetheless. Then turned to the window. "Okay, here goes nothing." She counted to three in her head, then jumped. If the situation had been any less threatening, she'd have laughed at herself for the wimpy, scaredy-cat little hop she took. That wasn't going to get the job done. And the fewer times she had to jump, the better. But just as she was gearing up for another leap, she heard a sound. From inside the garage. A groan.

"Brett! Do you hear me?" She jumped then, without having to think twice. She'd only had a split second, but she'd seen him easily. With the power out, she'd expected to have to strain her eyes to see. She hadn't counted on the fact that the entire other side of the garage was now gone, making lighting a moot issue.

Brett was sprawled dangerously close to the edge. It was hard to see all of him as one of her large workbenches had toppled over in front of him.

"Don't move," she shouted, unsure of how groggy he was. Apparently something had come flying at him, or he'd fallen and hit his head. Whatever, it looked as if he'd been knocked out. "Stay very still. Help will come soon." She hoped. She wanted to jump up and look in again, but didn't want to pound the ground any more than necessary. "Can you hear me? Are you hurt?"

There was a grumble, followed by a few

choice swearwords that had her smiling even as she worried about him. "I'm—I'm okay."

He didn't sound okay. She'd only been re-united with him for a matter of hours, but the Brett Gannon she knew hadn't changed that much. His voice was strained, tense, not the usual calm, smooth, full-of-confidence tone she easily associated with him. Of course, under the cir-cumstances, that was to be expected, but she still sensed something more was wrong. *What more wrong does he need? Trapped in a building half-gone, the rest ready to slide away at a moment's notice?*

She ignored her little voice and concentrated on his. "Can you move or are you trapped?"

A few seconds passed and she worried that maybe he'd blacked out again. Then she heard, "I'm not trapped." She breathed a sigh of relief, then he added, "But I can't move all that well. My ankle is—not right."

Not right. "Broken not right or sprained not right?"

There was a pause, then another string of swearwords. "Sprained," he called.

My ass, she thought, but hoped he was telling the truth, for his sake. "Do you think either of the roll doors would move up enough for you to slide yourself out?''

"Not worth the risk," he called back.

She bit back the hopelessness that rose in her again. He sounded steadier, which was a good thing. Better to stay focused on the positive things. Now she just had to figure out how to get him the hell out of there before another aftershock hit. She tried not to think about the fact that standing where she was at the moment was no great guarantee of safety, either.

"Are you okay?" he called. "Recon? Digger?"

"Yeah, we're all fine. Your dog is worried about you."

"Just don't let her in here after me."

"I won't. She's a good dog, well trained, like you said. Brett, listen, I'm so—"

"Don't. I chose to come in here. I knew an aftershock could happen. It's my fault for not getting us off this mountain the moment we had Digger in hand."

"We'd have only been a few yards down the road and it's split all to hell now," she said. "I'm sorry I got you into this."

"I've gotten into worse. It was my decision."

There was no point in arguing about it, she

decided. They both needed to focus on a solution. "What do you want me to do?" she called.

"Keep me company," he said. "That helicopter will be back here soon enough."

So, he'd heard the chopper. It was probably what had roused him. "What happened?" she called. "Did you get knocked out?"

"Yeah, I guess. I have a lump on my head that says I did. But I'll live."

She heard the grin in his voice and wondered how he could joke at a time like this. But, then again, maybe this was the best time to keep spirits up.

"My folks have always said I was hardheaded. I guess they were right."

She heard a rustling sound inside the garage. "Be careful," she called.

"Yep," he responded, then whistled. "Boy, now this is what I call living on the edge."

"Ha, ha, very funny. We should be figuring out how to get you out of there."

"There is no getting me out of here. The only way I'm going is by chopper. If I could just find my damn radio—"

"Do you want me to try to make some kind of signal?" She heard more rustling. "What are you doing?"

"Strapping my ankle. I have some stuff in my bag. I hope you don't mind if I help myself to some of your supplies in here to shore it up with. What do you do with rebar anyway?"

She couldn't help it. She found herself smiling. "Please. Take what you need. I use the rebar for support structures."

"I thought you made jewelry. What kind of jewelry requires support structures?" She heard several grunts, then a few more swearwords. Then, "Ah, there it is. Figures."

"What?"

"My radio. It must have flipped out of its holder when I got tossed around like a rag doll. It's…well, let's just say it's beyond reach."

Halcy could only hope he meant beyond reach inside the garage somewhere. She didn't want to think that he was dangling out over the edge, looking down the mountainside. Although she wouldn't put it past him.

"So, when did you start up your jewelry business?" he asked conversationally, as if they were out to dinner somewhere and not in the middle of a life-threatening disaster.

But then again, maybe he wasn't as calm as he sounded. He had to be in pain, and regardless of his training, dangling over a cliff was never going to be a casual thing to deal with. Maybe the distraction of conversation would help.

"Ah, about two years ago."

"Is that how long you've been back out here? I thought you went back east after college."

"I did." She really didn't want to go into her life story, certain he wasn't really interested. "Things didn't go as I'd hoped and I needed a fresh start. So I guess I came back to the place where the memories were the best."

"Good memories, huh? I guess Sean would be glad to hear that."

"How is he? Still with the Marshal's service?"

"Yep, they've been married for eight years now. No kids. I keep on him about getting a dog, but they like being alone, just the two of them. Him and his duty to God and country."

Haley had to laugh. It didn't surprise her to hear that Sean was still single. He would never be dedicated to anything as completely as he was to his job. "You're one to talk. Unless—" She hadn't even thought about that, and gave a little dry smile at her momentary fantasy of being held in his arms on a more permanent basis, kissed with that smart mouth of his. It had only been the shock and fear talking anyway. Still, the thought of him married, with a couple of tow-headed kids running around, sent a little pang to her heart.

"Nope," he responded, understanding the question before she asked. "I guess, in a way, I'm just as bad. My job takes a great deal of time. But at least I still know how to have a good time."

She thought again about his smile, his bright blue eyes, his easy laugh. Those big strong hands, his hard, fit body. *Yeah, I bet you do.* She sighed. "At least you got a dog."

She heard his laugh, felt a tiny bit better for giving him that, at least.

"True," he said. "I'll have to remind Sean of that the next time I see him."

"So, how do your parents handle having two of their kids in such dangerous occupations?" Both he and Sean had been to an Ivy League school, and yet he was in rescue and Sean worked for the government. Some parents would have a hard time with that. A fact she knew all too well. She was using her business degree, just on a very small scale, with a company consisting of one employee. Her. Definitely not the dominate-and-conquer method of doing business the rest of the Brubakers considered a mandate. And yet it didn't bother her that her degree was essentially gathering dust while she made jewelry for a living. Those four years had given her a whole lot more than a degree. That had been the least of what she'd gained. But there was no telling that to her family. She'd eventually given up trying and walked away.

"You know my folks," Brett said, "they're just happy we're well adjusted and earning an honest living."

Haley nodded, knowing he spoke the truth. She wondered if he had any idea how lucky he was. "What about your younger brother, your two sisters? Are they all done with school now?"

"Clay is just now out of college," he said. "Baby of the family with a degree. Who'd a thunk it, huh?"

"Did he go to Stanford, too?"

"Nah. He stuck close to home. Where Mom could still spoil him. Brat."

But he'd said it affectionately, and it made Haley remember her time spent with his boisterous family. Used to the cool reserve and carved-in-stone Brubaker rules of decorum and behavior, the Gannons had intimidated her with their easy familiarity and gregarious natures. But they had ignored her unease and sucked her right into the chaos. She'd been overwhelmed, but also fascinated. And thankful that they didn't give her a hard time for her less than natural ability to return even their casual affection. Although she'd done her best. And that had always been good enough for Gus and Marie Gannon.

"And your sisters?" she asked, enjoying the trip down memory lane. She had so few good ones, and it had been a long time since she'd recalled this particular part of her life. And it helped her ignore, for a few moments anyway, that Mother Nature had just tried to swallow her whole.

"One married, with a baby girl on the way."

"Isabel?" She was the oldest Gannon, older than Sean by a couple of years and the definite mini-matriarch of the family. Although Marie did a formidable job on her own.

"Nope, my younger sister Carly. Izzy is still single. I swear, she makes Sean look relaxed and laid-back. Talk about workaholic. I'm pretty sure it's her picture, not Sean's in the dictionary. Although maybe they have them both, side by side."

Haley laughed, then moved back from the side of the garage, around to the front, getting as close as she felt she could. She could hear him better that way. She sat on the ground, pulled Digger into her lap, then motioned Recon over. She loped over in her easy, graceful trot, and when Haley said "Down," she immediately dropped and lay by her side.

"Haley?"

"I'm here. Just repositioning the troops."

"You know, my family missed you. Your name still comes up occasionally."

She snorted. "It does not."

"Does, too. When we look through the photo albums. You remember the Gannon Christmas tradition. Mortify the children by rehashing their most embarrassing moments? Complete with film at eleven."

Haley smiled. She'd forgotten about that. Her family would have been mortified by having anyone mention their foibles in front of company. Besides, Brubakers didn't make mistakes. They merely had learning opportunities. The Gannons on the other hand, considered their faults as fodder for the family grist mill, and laughed over them as much as the triumphs. Seemed far healthier to her, in retrospect. "Well, I hope I'm not part of that embarrassing past," she joked. There was a long pause, and she actually tensed. "Brett?"

"He did you a favor, you know," he said finally.

"What?"

"Sean. Breaking up with you. He did you a favor."

"I know that. I mean, I didn't at the time, but I realized it pretty soon afterward. He was good enough to keep in touch, at least for a little while. And—well, you're right," she said, leaving it at that.

"But we did miss you. A lot."

"That's really sweet, but I was just—"

"I missed you."

There was something in his voice. And she couldn't help remembering how his mouth had felt on hers, his hands on her, his body, so— She stopped, had to stop. He needed her help, not her stupid needy fantasies. "Brett, I—"

"I had a major crush on you. Did you know that?"

She opened her mouth, then shut it again and merely shook her head, forgetting he could only hear her.

"I'm embarrassing you."

"No," she said quickly. Too quickly? "I mean, I—I didn't know." And just thinking about it was almost too tantalizing, too filled with possibilities.

"I'm surprised you didn't notice I was all but drooling every time you came home with Sean. I thought I was pretty suave in hiding it. But let's face it, I was all of sixteen at the time. How suave could I have been?"

"I always thought you were adorably cute and sweet. And funny."

"Ouch."

She smiled despite herself. "It's better than me remembering you as a drooling teenager with a crush, isn't it? And I didn't mean it in a bad way. I've—I've always had fond memories of you. Your whole family," she added quickly, though not sure why. He'd brought up this conversational path. He'd been the one making the revelations. And, while truth be told, she'd never thought of Brett in a romantic or sexual way back years before…it seemed she couldn't think of him in any other way now. And that was with the world literally falling apart around her. Imagine where her thoughts would go if they were actually to spend some normal time together. And, as simply as that, she realized she wanted to.

"I dreamed about you," he said.

She didn't know what to say to that, either. Tell him she imagined she'd dream about him now, too?

"I'm glad we met up again, Brett," she said, deciding that was a truth they could both handle. "Sorry for the reasons, but glad nonetheless."

"Me, too. Which is good. Because now you have to come home with me."

"Home? To Baton Rouge?"

"No, home to San Francisco. It's where I live now. In my undamaged home. Where I'll be, with my bum ankle. Laid up for some time."

She grinned. "Ah, playing the sympathy/guilt angle, are we?"

"Is it working?"

"It might be."

"Good. Because I was serious earlier. I have a spare room. Plenty of workspace in my garage. Recon will be more than glad to share her food and water. Although Mr. Squeaky is not up for grabs. Just a friendly warning."

"Mr. Squeaky?"

"The god of all dog toys."

"I'll make sure Digger knows."

"Then it's all set."

"But—" Her response was drowned out by

the thwap-thwap of helicopter blades. Only this time they didn't fly away.

Help had finally come. They were all going to be okay.

The helicopter maneuvered into place, the wind thrust from the blades making the treetops thrash, while bits of dust and rubble swirled up from the road. They lifted higher and for a moment Haley thought they were going to fly away, but she soon realized they were just adjusting their height to diminish the force of downward thrusting air. Shortly afterward, a man in yellow rescue gear was lowered on a cable and dangled there as they maneuvered him around so he could inspect what was left of her garage. Then they shifted slightly, but the motion was enough to swing him over to where she and the dogs huddled.

"You okay?" the man shouted, barely discernible over the sound of the chopper above.

Haley nodded vigorously. "Fine. Animals are fine," she shouted.

He gave her a thumbs-up, then spoke into the mouthpiece that was attached to his headgear. Moments later the chopper shifted again and they began the painstaking chore of determining how to lift Brett from the shorn-off remains of her garage. After what seemed like hours but was—amazingly—probably less than thirty minutes, they'd managed to get a harness to him and lift him from the rubble.

Haley's heart was in her throat the entire time he was winched up and finally, thankfully, hauled safely into the chopper. Then the cable dropped again, this time with a rescue worker attached. The helicopter shifted and they motioned her and the dogs back and shouted down through bull horns for her to turn away and close her eyes. She did so, keeping the dogs huddled until she felt a tap on her back. She jumped, but was quickly held in place by the strong hands of the rescue worker—who, as it happened, was a woman.

"Hold on tight, we're going to get you and these guys out of here." She motioned to the dog carrier. "Can you put your dog back in the carrier please? It will be easier to lift him."

Haley nodded and made her way to the carrier with Digger. Shielding her eyes from the whips of dust and dirt stirred up by the blades thwapping overhead, she turned in time to see Recon being lifted by her harness to the chopper.

The rescue worker motioned her over. "You're next." She reached out for the carrier, which Haley instinctively clutched to her chest. ''He'll be okay. He's riding up with me,'' the worker told her with a confident smile.

Haley forced a smile, thankful for her easygoing manner. As if this was no big deal, all in a day's work. Once again, it was brought home to her what amazing work people like Brett and this woman did. When it was all over, she'd make sure to thank them all personally. The woman motioned to the cable, which had been lowered again. She grabbed hold of it and unhooked the harness. ''Let's go,'' she shouted.

Haley looked up to see Brett all but dangling out of the side of the chopper, shooting her two thumbs-up. She shook her head and smiled... then strapped on the harness.

She kept her gaze locked on his the entire, hair-raising trip up to the chopper, never once looking down. Not so much because of a fear of heights—though dangling a hundred yards above the earth by a cable was not her idea of a fun time—but because she didn't want to see just how complete the devastation was below. She'd seen enough to know it would only make her more heartsick.

But as she was hauled into the chopper and released from her harness, she took one look at that cocky grin, that definite twinkle in his eyes, all there despite the pain he was in…and she had to wonder if she hadn't just escaped one life-threatening situation to land herself in another.

CHAPTER SIX

"You're supposed to be sitting with that ankle elevated."

Brett looked over his shoulder from where he was presently standing. Or sort of standing. Actually, he was balancing his weight on one foot, leaning the rest on the kitchen counter in his small Telegraph Hill home. "You're the guest, don't worry about me."

Haley leaned against the door frame and folded her arms. "I believe the deal was, you give me temporary shelter and I assuage my guilty conscience by nursing you back to health."

"I'm just making something to eat, then I promise—"

"Right, right. And last time it was just 'I have to get one thing from my room.' Or, 'I just want to get the Sunday paper, then I promise I'll be good.'"

Brett laughed, thinking if only she knew how

good he wanted to promise her he could be. Or how many times since she'd come home with him that he'd had to forcibly keep from yanking her into his arms and tasting that mouth of hers again.

Instead he enjoyed just looking at her, all neat and tidy in her fresh khakis and polo shirt. They'd liberated her luggage yesterday and to look at her now, you'd never guess she'd been banged up and suffered a near-death experience a day earlier. Circumstances notwithstanding, he'd liked her a bit messy and wild around the edges, but this Haley was just as arousing. Probably all those fantasies he harbored about getting her messy and wild all over again.

He wondered if she had any clue how much he enjoyed knowing she was in his kitchen, in his house, his home. Now if he could just stop thinking about having her in his bed, life would be much easier. But he didn't think that was going to happen anytime soon. She'd only been with him for two days, most of which had been spent in a whirl of talking with insurance adjusters, contacting various rescue and cleanup effort organizations and trying to determine how much, if any, of her home and belongings she was going to be able to recover. The second aftershock had not only destroyed the garage, but had caused structural damage to the foundation of her house. Neither appeared to be reparable. Not to mention that the road leading to her house was a total loss. The entire area had been declared a hazard and was off-limits for the time being.

He'd worried about Haley handling the whole ordeal, had made it clear he was there for her. But she'd taken charge of her destiny, as much as someone could given the circumstances, with hardly more than a ripple of emotion. He realized part of that was due to the fact that not only had she rescued Digger, but Brett had refused rescue until the chopper personnel had agreed to lift her small safe out of the garage, as well. She'd thanked him for both efforts so often he'd finally had to tell her to stop. It was his job. For her, it was all she had left. That and two suitcases.

Her house and land were probably worthless and she'd already decided she'd have to relocate. She hadn't said where, and he hadn't asked. But he knew if he wanted her in his life beyond the next couple of days, life-altering disaster or no, he was going to have to work fast. Because he wasn't going to just stand by and watch her walk out of his life again. She wasn't the only one whose life had been dramatically altered in one day. He felt as if his had been turned upside down. And he was enjoying the view just fine, thanks. So, as long as her life was being dramatically altered, she might as well alter it a bit more to include him.

"I'm waiting, and you're still standing," she said, tapping her fingers against her arm. But there was a smile lurking just behind that frown. He liked that it was always there, just below the surface. It encouraged him to coax it out of hiding. Something he'd discovered he enjoyed immensely.

"It's just a mild sprain. The doctor said—"

"I was there, remember? I know what he said, and you're not doing it."

"Nag, nag, nag," Brett muttered, but he was grinning when he said it.

Fighting her own smile, Haley picked up a wooden spoon and waved it at him. "Don't make me use this."

Brett laughed, then hopped away from her when she took a step forward. "Kitchen weaponry. One of the few wilderness skills I'm not trained in."

"It's a female thing," Haley informed him, taking another step, a fake scowl on her face. "We're born with it. Even us Brubakers, generations of whom have never set foot in a kitchen. But don't let that fool you.''

''No, uh-uh. I'd never underestimate a woman with a kitchen utensil in her hand.''

''Smart man. So don't make me teach you a lesson.'' She pointed to the door with the spoon. ''Go. Sit. Your own dog is ashamed of your disobedient behavior.''

Brett glanced at the door, where Recon sat observing the scene in front of her with avid interest. Usually that would be due to the fact that when Brett was in the kitchen, food might hit the floor at any time. But her attention was on the two humans in the room. She'd accepted the interlopers in her house with her usual exuberant joy and enthusiasm. Digger had initially annoyed her greatly with his endless inspections, until she figured out he could hold his own in a tug-of-war contest with her favorite knotted rag.

Haley had worried they'd break something with all their racing and ripping around, but Brett waved off her concern. After spending the past few months surrounded by destruction, it was wonderful and life affirming to have raucous happy noises fill his house. Even if they were canine in origin...and not Haley's moans of pleasure. He really had to stop picturing her naked, he decided. Even the wooden spoon couldn't deter him from a sudden tight fit to his shorts.

"Recon knows she won't get fed unless I get this done and on the floor."

Haley glanced at his food preparation and realized it was not intended for human consumption. "Oh." The spoon faltered. But only for a moment. "Fine, then," she announced, motioning to the small breakfast nook area that was part of the narrow kitchen. "Sit there, prop your foot up and tell me what to do."

"I begin to see the Brubaker strengths."

"We do run a tight ship. But, although my forebears might roll in their graves, not to mention the ones actually still breathing in the family mausoleum in Connecticut, the fact is, I'm handy enough in the kitchen. Just tell me what to do and I'll do it."

He was pretty sure she wasn't prepared for him to say, "Great, get naked and meet me in my bed in five minutes." Which was the time it would take him to hop there on one foot. *Yeah, totally smooth, Gannon. That'll have her drooling for you.*

He'd been wondering if he was the only one feeling the sexual tension lurking just below the surface of their platonic living arrangements. He wished now he hadn't told her about his teenage crush. She probably felt sorry for him. Or worse, still saw him as a too young contender. Which was ridiculous. It was one thing when he was sixteen and she nineteen, but now?

"So, what do I do with this stuff?"

"I really get to give orders now?" he said, grinning when she scowled at his smug smile. "Do Brubakers take orders as well as they give them?"

"Well, there is probably a reason why I work alone," she said with a grudging smile of her own. "Being my own boss doesn't give me anyone to order around. But then, I don't have anyone giving me commands, either."

He leaned over and snatched the wooden spoon she was still waving around as she spoke. It was all he could do not to reach for her, too. He tested the belly of the spoon against his palm, then leered comically at her. "Ah, the conniving cripple takes the upper hand away from the domineering damsel."

She feigned fright, clasping a hand dramatically to her chest. "Why, you wouldn't dare, sir."

He waggled his eyebrows and slapped the spoon hard in his palm, making her jump. And, oddly enough, arousing the hell out of him. Not that he wanted to use it on her, nor did he believe she wanted it used, but there was no mistaking that sexual spark that had just leaped between them. "Good thing I'm laid up with this bum ankle and dependent on your innate kindness and sympathy."

She merely rolled her eyes, then turned back to the counter. "So, what— Hey!"

She spun around, hands clasped to her very nicely rounded backside. The same backside he'd just leaned over and thwapped lightly with the spoon. He couldn't help himself, he who had never struck a woman, even in play. Sexual or otherwise. He didn't know why exactly he'd done it now, except he liked her better when she wasn't so perfectly contained. She had a sharp wit and he admired the fact that she wasn't a complete mess over this whole thing. She had held up almost too well during the entire ordeal. It made him wonder what all she'd been through that, despite the occasional smile and the under-lying foundation of good humor, she worked so hard to be in total control at all times. What was she afraid would happen if she just let go?

She rubbed her backside and gave him a look. "Do you want me to call your mother?"

Brett recoiled in mock horror, but he immediately put the spoon down. "I'll behave."

She smiled dryly. "That'll be the day."

God, did she have *any* idea what she was doing
to him? How badly he wanted them to misbe-
have? Together? Repeatedly and at great length?

Haley had once again turned back to the
counter. And his opportunity to act on his im-
pulses had once again safely passed. Damn it.

"Does she really eat all this stuff?" Haley
asked, nose wrinkled.

"Are you kidding? That's doggie gourmet cui-
sine. And after all she's been through, she de-
serves that and more."

Haley turned then, a thoughtful look on her
face. "I can't truly comprehend how hard it must
be for both of you, doing what you do. But I
think it's wonderful that you do it. And I know
I'm not speaking just for myself."

"Thank you," he said, humbled by her serious
comment.

"What made you get into this, anyway? Not
just the rescue part, the fire department, too. The
whole thing."

They'd talked in the car on the way to the airport yesterday morning and he'd told her about
how he'd spent the past couple of months. She'd

told him about the jewelry consignment contracts she'd just signed. But neither had talked much about how they'd ended up doing what they did.

"I volunteered at the fire department as part of a college course I was taking, for community service. I thought it would be interesting. And—well." He shrugged. "I guess you could say I found my calling. As for the SAR work, well, maybe that is my truer calling. I love working with the dogs, making a difference. It's incredible how smart they are. It started when I went with a friend of mine, who's a handler, to one of the competitions they regularly hold."

"Competitions? You mean, you compete against other handlers with their dogs?"

He nodded. "We have to continue training on a consistent basis, to be ready at any moment. This summer notwithstanding, disaster doesn't typically strike all that often. So we put together competitions to keep the dogs' interest up. They love it. It's all a big game to them anyway."

She raised an eyebrow. "Just the dogs see it that way, huh?"

He just smiled and shrugged.

"Well, game or no game, what you do is very selfless and I'm in awe of it."

For a moment, just a moment, he thought she

was going to touch him. Probably just a hug of
thanks or something, but the moment stretched,
expanded, became about more than simple appreciation. She looked so damn uncomfortable
about it, he couldn't act on it. So he did what he
always did. ''Aw, shucks, ma'am, it weren't
nothing,'' Brett drawled, making her laugh,
smoothing over the moment. Moments that were
springing up more and more often. He wasn't
sure how long he'd be able to tease them both
out of them.

Still smiling, Haley picked Recon's bowl up
off the floor and began scraping the meat and
veggie mixture into it.

''There's enough there for Digger, too,'' he
told her.

She cast him a look. ''And have him expect
me to cook for him like this once I get back home
again? I said I was handy in the kitchen, not Chef
Paul.'' She smiled, but he caught the flash of pain
in her eyes before she looked away. Most likely
because she'd been reminded again that she had
no home to return to.

He couldn't imagine what it was like, feeling
so alone and adrift. He'd made a life here, had
his work, his friends in the SAR and firefighting
community. But he knew that, if it all went to

hell somehow, he could always go home again. Back to Baton Rouge, to the loving, steady embrace of his family. He drew strength from that rock-solid foundation, and admired her all the more for thriving without having even the most flimsy of family safety nets to catch her if she fell.

"What did your folks say when you called?" He hadn't come right out and probed into her family history since they'd last seen each other, but it was obvious from the very stilted conversational tones when she'd contacted them to let them know she was okay that the Brubaker clan wasn't one big happy family. It killed him to think she didn't have any support network out there. And yet, she hadn't made any other calls. Other than to insurance adjusters and the like.

She shrugged now, but it was with a studied casualness he knew belied the real truth. And he wished he'd kept his trap shut and his nose out of her business.

"Glad to hear I hadn't been dashed against the rocks and swept out to sea," she said mildly. "Gave them a perfect opportunity to launch into their harangue about my lifestyle choices. Gave me the perfect chance to remember why I needed to relocate three thousand miles away. And we all hung up and resumed our separate lives, smug righteousness intact.''

"I'm sorry." She couldn't know the depth of his sorrow for her, and wouldn't appreciate knowing he felt it, either. Pity wouldn't sit well on those slender but oh, so sturdy shoulders of hers.

Shoulders she lifted in a light shrug now. "Yeah, well, we don't all have *Leave It to Beaver* families like yours." She immediately glanced over at him, contrite. "I'm sorry. That sounded really snarky and I didn't mean it that way. You have a wonderful family and—"

"I know I do. And I don't take them for granted, trust me." He found himself badly wishing his ankle would support his weight and hers so he could scoop her up in his arms and take her somewhere where she'd never again, even for a brief moment, look so lost and alone. But since that wasn't an option, he once again opted for the next best thing to lighten the sudden pall he'd brought into the room. He shot her his most cheeky grin. "But you'll notice that I moved about half that distance away myself. Even the best of families can be a bit stifling."

She smiled at him and he relaxed a little, seeing the humor reaching her eyes again. "Yes, well, you Gannons are an...exuberant bunch."

"And proud of it."

"Yes, I recall that, too."

He watched her bend with the dog bowls—she'd caved and fed Digger some of the mix, just as he'd known she would. Her oh, so in-control exterior might fool some people, but he knew it hid the softest of hearts. He just wondered who'd bruised it so badly. He suspected it was more than her stiff and unbending family tree. And despite the fact that this was probably the worst time to press his own case, he couldn't just let her suffer inside her own little bubble. Giving her a roof over her head, a calm center in the storm her life had become, was not enough. And this need wasn't based on his resurgent hormones, or getting her into bed, either. Well, not entirely, anyway.

With her back turned— and the kitchen utensils out of reach—he levered himself out of the chair. When she straightened and turned, he was right behind her. Before she could recover from the surprise, or reach for the nearest spatula, he levered himself up onto the counter, ignored the throb in his ankle and shot her a considering look.

"I don't want to stifle you," he started, then stopped. "I want—" He stopped again, shook his head with a little self-deprecating smile. For one of the first times in his life, words didn't spring easily to his glib tongue. "I want to be smooth here, but somehow, around you, I end up feeling like a sixteen-year-old, lust-crazed goober all over again."

That made her smile, despite the tension that was once again screaming between them. "Goober?"

He noted she didn't step away from his serious invasion into her personal space. Which he hoped was a good sign. Now he just had to not blow it. "At the very least," he said. He wanted to reach out, to touch her, to reassure her and, in a way, himself, as well. But he was pushing it pretty hard as it was, so he gripped the counter edge instead. For control, for dear life, he wasn't sure. "I know we haven't seen each other in a few years, and that I was basically on the fringe of your life way back then. But—" He shrugged, helpless for the right thing to say, to explain, so it wouldn't sound as though he was now a twenty-four-year-old, lust-crazed goober. Which he was, but they could get to that part later. What he wanted, needed, was to secure the fact that there could be a later.

She was watching him, confused and a bit wary.

He puffed out his cheeks, ran a hand through his hair and let out a long breath. Then he looked her square in the eyes and said, "I guess what I'm trying to mumble my way through here is, I still have an attraction to you. And I don't think it's any post-adolescent crush. I completely realize that your life is in total turmoil and my bringing this up now is probably one of the stupidest things I've ever done. And if I'm way off base here, I'll hate it if I've made you feel so uncomfortable you don't want to stay here, but—"

She did nothing more than raise her hand, but it was effective enough to shut him up. If he wasn't mentally kicking himself for his totally uncustomary lack of restraint—patience usually being a hallmark of his job—he'd have smiled at how coolly and efficiently she'd handled his rambling confession. She wore the Brubaker in her well. Very well. It was a damn shame her family wasn't proud of her. But he thought he might have enough pride in her to make up for the whole sorry lot of them.

She studied him consideringly. And he would have paid big money to know what was going through her mind.

"I'm attracted to you, too," she finally said. And so simply, too. And yet he was pretty sure he heard fireworks, a big marching band and a few rockets going off inside his head. He did, however, manage to keep from clapping in glee like a little kid.

Or ripping her into his arms and tasting her, taking her, right here on the kitchen counter if need be. Until neither of them could move more than their lips, and that would just be to sigh in deep contentment.

That would be wrong. Because, after all, this wasn't supposed to be about sex. Not entirely.

Still, she'd confessed attraction, so there was hope.

"But—" she went on.

He groaned before he could stop it. He hated "buts." They were never good news.

She made up a great deal for whatever blow she was about to deliver by smiling at his little outburst.

His dreams crumbling, he decided to spare her the delivery and him from having to hear her say it. "I know, I know. This is a bad time. You can't even consider thinking about a relationship with anyone. You have a life to rebuild, a future to relocate and I'm an idiot for even bringing this up now.'' He tried for the boyish smile, but deliberate charm was beyond even him at the moment. Suddenly this was serious. Terrifyingly, life-alteringly serious.

''Brett—''

Now it was his turn to raise his hand. ''Will you at least promise me, seeing as we have some basic chemistry here, that whenever you're ready...one month from now, a year, five years, ten—'' She laughed then and he said, ''Am I sounding too desperate here?''

''A little. It's good for my battered and bruised ego, though, so please, continue.''

''What, you and that soft heart of yours won't take pity on a guy with a bum ankle?''

''Me? Soft-hearted?''

''You thought you could bury it along with everything else?''

Now she looked at him with a great deal less humor and great deal more wariness.

''I should have stopped while I was only a little behind, huh?'' But his charm didn't work this time.

"What did you mean, 'bury it like everything else.' What do you think I'm burying?"

Hell. Now *he* sighed in disgust, only it was directed at himself. One shot and he'd already blown it. But what the hell, he was in it this far, might as well go ahead and detonate the rest of his one big chance at happiness. Which should have sounded melodramatic and blown all out of proportion. Only it didn't.

"Okay," he said, looking at her once again. "I could be totally wrong here, but I sense that you've been beaten up a bit. Not physically," he added when she tucked her beat-up hands behind her. "Emotionally. Your heart. I know your family is rough on you, always has been. And though you don't say much about them, that's as telling as anything. You do a really great job of holding it together, despite whatever is happening, even watching half your home disappear off the side of a mountain. And while I guess you probably got that core strength from your family, shored it up in order to get out from under their dominant ways…my guess is that tender heart tucked away there in the middle took a bit more of a personal beating."

She lifted her chin, a defiant gleam in her eye. "And I suppose you're the one who's going to make up for all the wounds and betrayals in my life? Is that it?''

It wasn't a direct answer, but the message was clear enough. Bull's-eye.

''I don't know. I'm admittedly not the greatest catch on the planet. My job mostly keeps me here, in one spot, but because of my SAR commitments, I do get called out on a moment's notice and can end up anywhere in the country for days and weeks at a time. Or overseas even. I put myself in danger as a regular course of business and asking anyone to share that type of emotional responsibility is something I don't take lightly and probably a large part of why I stay unattached.''

''But?''

He smiled despite himself, then it faded. ''But I look at you and I can't help thinking you're the one I let get away. Which is crazy, since I wasn't the one that had you in the first place. Only…now I feel like it's my turn. Our turn.'' He raked a hand through his hair. ''I know. It's insane. I'm insane. And it's not the painkillers, because I haven't taken them today.''

He gave her a smile that was more shaky than cocky, then took a breath and spit out the rest. ''But, as ridiculous as it sounds, given that our reunion has consisted of one terrifying day spent on a mountain that was crumbling beneath our feet, followed by two days packed with the mind-numbing realization of what you've lost, and what you still have to face, and all the myriad responsibilities that entails, I don't want to let you walk back out of my life. I want to help you, be there for you, not let you down. And I don't know if I can do all those things, be all those things, which is a bit terrifying when spelled out like that.''

''Brett—''

He held up his hand, stopping her from responding. He had to get it all out in the open. Or he might never get the chance. ''Terrifying or not, I'd at least like the chance to try. I mean, with everything the way it is, if we can muddle through all this and discover there might be something worthwhile hanging on to on the other side, then, well…why not go for it, right? Because one thing I've learned—and in the most elemental way—these past few months is, you can't wait around and hope for the perfect time to do what you want to do. Life doesn't always make that possible. So…so I guess, in addition to babbling like an idiot here, I'm grabbing for what I want now." He stopped, sighed, took a deep breath...and jumped. "And, Haley Brubaker, what I want, what I think I've always wanted, is you."

CHAPTER SEVEN

HALEY HAD NO WORDS to respond to his declaration. But it didn't matter. Her heart knew. And so did his.

She leaned into him at the same moment his hands came up to take her. She wasn't sure who moved first after that, but an instant later she was cradled between his strong thighs, wrapped in those hard arms and her mouth was crushed against his.

And there wasn't a single other place on earth she'd rather be.

Everything she'd thought she'd learned, every scrap of independence she'd fought so hard for…none of it mattered. Maybe it was because, for the first time in her life, she didn't need a man for anything. Which, if she hadn't been completely mindless with desire at the moment, would make her laugh, considering she was homeless, with nothing more than a dog and a handful of clothes to her name. But she'd survive without help, she knew that now. She'd be fine even without Brett's kindness, his generosity.

No, she didn't need Brett Gannon. Didn't need him to make her feel worthy, didn't need him to make her feel needed.

But, oh, how she wanted him. So much, she burned with it.

He let his mouth drift to her chin, which she lifted, allowing easier access to the tender skin of her throat. She sighed and pushed her fingers through his hair.

He winced, swallowed a little yelp, and she pulled back, instantly contrite. "I'm sorry. I forgot about the lump."

But he was already pulling her back, already putting his mouth on her. Apparently she wasn't the only one burning up.

"No pain, no gain," he murmured, making her laugh.

And that was another striking difference. In such a short time, and under the worst possible circumstances, Brett had brought laughter and spontaneity into her life. It was damn seductive. And she gave herself over to it. The thought of his charm and laughter spilling over into their lovemaking made her shiver. Love and laughter. Two things she hadn't had near enough of in her life. And to share that with Brett? The very idea made her instantly crave it.

She pulled his mouth from where it was making serious inroads inside the collar of her shirt, back to her mouth. Surely he wanted what she now had to have? He was all but consuming her. The very idea of which brought new waves of shuddering pleasure washing through her.

"Brett," she murmured against his mouth, "I—I—"

He slid his hands up her waist, along her spine and into her hair, holding her head so he could take her mouth again. And again. "Yeah," he finally said, breathing heavily. "I—I—too."

He slid off the counter and his body, hard—rigidly hard, in fact—slid down her body, making her tremble. They stood like that, pressed against each other, literally and figuratively wrapped up in each other, looking into each other's eyes, for what seemed like eternity. A deep, soul-satisfying eternity.

"With everything going on in your life, maybe this isn't the best—"

Haley silenced him with a kiss. It was tender, slow, and hopefully invested with all the burgeoning feelings he was bringing to life inside her. "You said yourself everything happens for a reason. I want this to happen."

Neither had to clarify what "this" was.

"But—"

She gave a mock groan. "I hate buts."

He grinned and began to draw lazy patterns on her back with blunt-tipped fingers. It sent shivers of delight all through her. And the frenzied need of moments ago settled into a banked, controlled desire.

They'd get there. She knew that now. And the journey was going to be as deliciously exciting as the destination.

"You're just seducing me to get me off my feet," he said. "A very ingenious method of getting your way, I might add."

She sighed. "You see right through my evil machinations." She began her own lazy exploration, careful to avoid the lump this time, and smiled into his beautiful, kind face. "We dominant damsels always win."

He wiggled his eyebrows, making her grin. "Dominant damsels. I'm beginning to see new potential here."

"Hey, who was the one wielding the spoon earlier? Speaking of which, now might be the time to tell me if you have any other kinky fetishes I should know about.''

''Well, as much as I hate to disappoint you, I generally don't employ kitchen utensils in my lovemaking. But, as my dog will tell you, I'm a willing student. Easily trained to fetch, cook, clean and—well, I think the possibilities are endless.''

She had to laugh.

He brought his hand up then, caressed her face, and the look in his eyes was so unbearably tender, it tugged a place deep inside her heart. ''I just want you,'' he said. ''However you'll let me have you.''

''Oh, Brett.'' She sighed. It shouldn't be this easy to dismiss all the defenses she'd worked so hard to erect. She could take the easy excuse, that she was already rocked to her foundation by what had happened over the past few days. But that wouldn't be true. Not entirely. Brett wasn't Glenn. Nor was he after her for her money. Which made her laugh. Hell, he couldn't be after her for anything but herself. She was all she had left.

''What's funny?'' he asked, tracing her lips with his fingertips.

"Well, before I let you have your way with me, I have one question."

"Ask me anything."

"You were right. Before. My heart does have its share of footprints on it. The last man I allowed to get this close to me ended up taking me for everything I had. And the theft of my pride and dignity hurt a lot worse than my empty bank account."

"Haley, I—"

She just kept talking. "So, I know you're not after my family money. And I know you're not after my worldly possessions, because, after all, I don't have any." She let a small smile curve her lips and realized just how freeing humor and laughter could be. How amazingly easy it was. With the right person. "But I do have one thing left, the one thing a man like you might covet."

"Haley, I don't want—"

"My dog," she finished.

Brett opened his mouth, then shut it again as he realized she was teasing him. He hooted with laughter.

"I think Digger and I are both a bit offended," she said as his laughter continued unabated. But then she was laughing, too. And he was kissing her.

And the time for slow and lazy was over.

"Any other time I'd sweep you off your feet," he said. "But if I tried that now, we'd pretty much have to make love right here on the kitchen floor. Do you think you can handle a man who has to hop instead of sweep?"

She kissed him on the tip of his nose and patted his shoulder. "Would it make you feel more manly if I hopped, too?"

He laughed, then kissed her hard and fast. "God, I l—" He broke off suddenly and she almost laughed at the comically horrified look on his face. She didn't know if he was horrified that he'd almost said the L-word, or horrified at what she might think if he did.

She wasn't sure. It was way too fast. Way too soon.

And yet her heart had foolishly leaped. And he'd only gotten as far as the *l*.

There would be time for declarations later. Whether it be a day, a month or a year from now. All she wanted, she decided, was the time with him to find out if there was a declaration to be made.

She linked her arm in his, pretending the moment hadn't happened, letting him recover without pressing. Or teasing. Though she found she wanted to do both. He made that such an easy element of their relationship.

Their relationship.

She should be terrified, thinking in those terms. And yet she'd just faced a close call with death and the destruction of her home, her dream, which had only made her realize just how tentative life could be. All her careful planning and independent strides were great, but something like this couldn't be planned. And she couldn't back away because the timing wasn't perfect. Brett brought her joy. More joy than she'd ever remembered feeling. And, in the midst of tragedy, that made it all the more precious to her.

So she let the joy in, without making any demands of it. It made her want to dance. Or, in this case, hop. She lifted up one foot and slung her arm around his waist. "Shall we?" she asked, balancing against him. "You know, if you'd gotten crutches like the doctor told you to, you'd—"

"Prove what a klutz I am? And ruin your impression of me as a larger-than-life rescue hero? No way."

They hopped through the living room. "Is that how you think I see you?"

"You mean, you don't see me as godlike and all-powerful?"

They stopped at the base of the stairs. She turned into him, meaning to tease him, taunt him a little, maybe drive him as wild as he was driving her. Instead she found herself cupping his face and speaking earnestly. "I see you as a kind, sexy, fun-loving man, who is dedicated to his job, to his dog, and risks his life to help others."

He actually blushed, and she felt her heartstrings tug even harder. "Okay, I guess that's a little godlike. You're too good to be true."

Then he waggled his eyebrows and made her laugh. "No, just too good."

She shrieked when he bent and swung her over his shoulder. "Brett! Put me down, you'll destroy your ankle. You'll—ooph."

"Sorry," he said, hopping up the stairs, one hand on the banister, the other across the back of her thighs. "You should conserve your breath." He bopped up to the first landing one-footed, then up to the next, as though she was nothing more than a backpack. "You'll be needing it later."

When he reached the top, she was too amazed to be upset. "How exactly do you guys train, anyway?'' she asked, noting she was the one who was breathless.

''You worried about my stamina?''

''No,'' she said quite frankly. ''I'm worried about mine.''

He laughed, then tugged her through the open doorway to his bedroom. She'd been sleeping up on the third floor, had passed this room the past two nights, unable to keep from imagining…well, this.

He popped the door shut behind her. ''I hope you don't mind, but as much as I love animals, I really don't need an audience.''

''No?''

He just gave her a look. ''Did you want to share some kinky fantasy?''

She shook her head, smiling. ''Not me. And I'm just as glad to avoid the possibility of a cold nose in the wrong place at the wrong time.''

Now Brett laughed. He tugged her to him and fell back on the bed.

She tried to keep from banging his ankle, but he'd already rolled her beneath him. ''Is this part of your stop, drop and roll fireman training?''

He pulled her down for a hard, fast kiss. ''How in the hell did Sean ever let you go?''

The words were out before she could think bet-

ter of it. "Maybe so I could be there for you.
When the time was right."

He stilled then. "Maybe," he said finally. He
kissed her again, gently this time. "It shouldn't
be the right time. Everything is upside down for
you. And…for me, too. I have some decisions to
make. About my career, about doing rescue." He
broke off and rolled his eyes. "And I can't believe I finally got you where I've been fantasizing
about having you for what seems like eons…and
I'm talking about my damn job."

"I'm not going anywhere," she said, trying
like hell not to squirm beneath him. He was
pressed intimately…right where she wanted him
pressed. Only they were wearing far too many
clothes. She almost rolled her eyes herself. Here
a man was trying to do the right thing, say all
the right things…and she was the one wanting to
say to hell with it all and go for it.

"We can talk about that later," he said, as if
reading her mind. "Right now, I have this powerful need to taste you. All of you."

She opened her mouth, then shut it. "Well,
then. What are you waiting for?"

"I have no idea." He dropped his mouth to
hers, then let it drift to her chin, then trailed his

tongue along her neck until her collar wouldn't let him explore any further.

"In the way," she managed to say, already a bit breathless.

"Definitely."

A moment later her shirt was gone. She started to peel off her bra, aching now to feel his mouth on her skin.

"Not so fast." He pulled her hands away and grinned. "This is Christmas morning and eight birthdays all rolled into one for me. I like to take my time unwrapping my presents."

Her body tightened in response to the promise she saw in his eyes. "As long as I get equal unwrapping time when it's my turn?"

His eyes went cobalt and she thought she might climax right then and there.

"I'll make sure of it," he said, his voice a little hoarse. Then he turned his attentions back to the lace trim of her bra. After a slow, torturous time spent peeling it back, inch by devastating inch, his mouth finally closed over the aching peak and she arched off the bed, hips grinding against him. "Brett," she gasped.

"I'm right here," he murmured. "Definitely not going anywhere." He shifted his weight off of her, swallowing her whimper of protest with his mouth. He toyed with first one nipple, then the other, while his hand moved to the waistband of her pants. He didn't take them off, merely slid the button free, then tugged the zipper down, so his curious fingers could continue their conquest. She arched again as he slid them first over the silk of her panties. "Wet for me," he all but groaned.

"Dying for you," she corrected, making him grin fiercely.

"Starving for you." He tugged her pants and panties away as he slid his body down to continue his leisurely exploration, this time with his tongue.

Pleasure ripped through her when he toyed, dipped and teased, then crested sharply as he pushed a finger inside her at the same time. She arched almost violently, pressing down on him, wanting more, needing— "Yes!" Her climax rocked her hard and continued as he refused to let up. He tugged her clothes free and all she could think was *Hurry, hurry,* but dimly, in the pleasure-fogged recesses of her mind, she seemed to recall demanding equal time.

Struggling, she managed to open her eyes, only to find Brett lifting his head from where he was presently kissing a trail back up over her abdomen. Eyes so warm, so full of desire and...other things far too soon to label. "How did I get so lucky?" It was only when his eyes widened that she realized she'd spoken out loud.

"Asks the woman who just lost almost everything she owns?"

"Tangible things," she said, lulled into such a blissful state nothing, not even harsh reality, could make her raise her walls again. He'd been honest with her, terrifyingly so. And it made her want to do the same. He deserved no less. And she realized with startling clarity that she could tell him anything. He'd slid past her defenses so easily, so quickly. And yet he was no stranger. She knew him. Knew he'd never knowingly do anything to hurt her. She knew where he came from, who he came from. And what she didn't know, she was dying to discover.

"You were right," she said softly. "Life makes no promises on tomorrow. You have to go after what you want today." And then it was her turn to grin, to marshal the remaining strength in her limp, pleasure-sated limbs, and push him to his back, lean over him and make a promise of her own.

"Sometimes I say the smartest things," he said, then groaned long and with deep pleasure as she slowly, inch by devastating inch, peeled his T-shirt off…with her teeth. Her hands slid beneath the soft, worn cotton…over hot, hard skin. He was a fascinating blend of supple muscle and unyielding steel. And he tasted like heaven.

She shifted over him, making them both gasp as her nipples rubbed across the light swirl of hair on his chest. She straddled him, marveling at her own playfulness, which despite her yearning to break free of her cloistered upbringing, had never come easily to her. But then, she'd never come quite so easily, or thoroughly, as she had under Brett's clever ministrations. And she was nothing if not a fair person. She only hoped she could come close to equaling—

He arched up as she settled her body across the now-screamingly taut fit of his gym shorts. And the expression on his face was her own present. One she planned to unwrap every chance she got.

"Shorts. Definitely need to go," he growled.

"Giving orders?"

He managed to open his eyes, but his hips still pushed up against her, making it almost impossible for her to not give in. She wanted him there every bit as desperately as he wanted to be there. Maybe even more, if that were possible.

"Never." He grinned, but it was tight and fierce, as if he was exerting major control. He jerked his chin. "Nightstand. Drawer."

She understood and stretched her body across his to reach for a condom, putting her nipples right in nipping range of his tongue. Which he naturally made full use of. Which she naturally let him.

And that was where she made her strategic mistake. Somehow, seconds later, she was flat on her back. But she couldn't argue. Hell, she couldn't speak. She was too busy trying not to swallow her tongue as she watched him shuck his shorts and roll the condom on himself. Talk about Christmas and birthday presents all in one!

"Next time can I do that?" she asked. She'd never even considered protection as part of foreplay. It was something done in the dark. For that matter, so was lovemaking. Or had been. But now... "I want to touch you."

"And I want that, too. Believe me. But one brush of your fingertips right now—"

He looked so primal, so fierce...and at the same time, just like Brett. Funny, sexy, patient. Her Brett. It was going to take some getting used to. This proprietary feeling he'd roused so swiftly, so strongly inside her.

And then he was moving over her. She spent a millisecond worrying about his ankle, but then he was settling his weight between her legs, and sliding the warm, hard, glorious length of himself inside her. And she couldn't think of anything. Anything but him.

And as he pulled her blissfully up to the edge…then ferociously over again, she realized it wasn't going to be all that difficult after all. Brett was inside her body but, more important, he'd found a way inside her heart. And she liked his warm, steadying presence there.

Now she only had to figure out a way to keep him there.

CHAPTER EIGHT

TWO WEEKS. Fourteen mornings spent waking up, finding her nestled next to him and remembering he'd won the lottery. The lottery of love. Brett rolled his eyes, but couldn't wipe the grin from his face. God, he was a goober in love. But he didn't care how corny his thoughts were. He looked at her and couldn't help his feelings. Didn't want to.

Brett traced lazy circles around Haley's navel with his fingertips. She made a soft, snoring noise and shifted in her sleep, but didn't push his hand away. Which was progress. He'd had her in his life, in his bed, in his arms, for days now. Nights. And though she gave herself to him with devastating openness when they made love; in her sleep, she was still putting up walls. But he was nothing if not patient. She'd had a hell of a lot longer to put up walls than he'd had to tear them down.

She'd told him everything now, about her family, about Glenn, the bankruptcy he'd forced her into. It amazed him she'd let him in as much as she had, and he was humbled by the faith she'd put in him, her trust.

And he planned to take tender, exquisite care of that gift, and her. God knows, she did the same with him.

It was almost as if she didn't trust the ease with which their lives had meshed. She was looking at places to move, still haggling with state and federal officials about retrieving what could be salvaged from her home and work studio. He didn't say anything, didn't beg her to stay with him. She was already with him. All he could hope was that when the time came and she found her new place…that it would feel empty without him. He knew he'd be lost without her. But he was trying not to push. Okay, push any harder. Because he already had more with her than he'd ever dreamed. They'd come together so swiftly, so completely, but he knew he had to let her find her own way. And if she thought she needed her own space while they found their way together, so be it.

But that didn't mean he wasn't going to try to influence the deal.

He replaced his fingertips with his tongue. And she woke up moaning, wet and ready for him. ''Christmas every day,'' he murmured.

She pushed his hands away when he peeled the condom from the wrapper, and took over, as she'd done every time since that mind-numbing first time that she—after informing him that while he liked to unwrap his presents, she enjoyed wrapping hers—had fumbled around sliding one over him. It was the worst kind of tease in the world…and the absolute best. Watching her, tongue caught between determined teeth, had been a highlight moment. He'd never had to fight so hard to keep from saying the words. Words he'd still yet to say, but that burned the tip of his tongue on an almost constant basis. Soon. First, he had to tell her something else.

But it could wait until after this.

He shifted his weight on top of her, knowing she wasn't as keen on being the wild one in the morning stream of sunlight that poured in his bedroom windows and sunroof. Patience, he knew, was the key there, too. At night, in the flickering shadows of candlelight, she was every wicked fantasy he'd ever had.

Which was really saying something.

Besides, he enjoyed dissolving her east-coast Brubaker shell. She was comfortable enough with her body, but still retained an overdeveloped sense of modesty. Which charmed him to no end…and nudged his more mischievous side. She nudged him right back. He was definitely in love.

They both sighed as he pushed inside her. Home. He sensed it, felt it, bone deep, every time. And knew he always would. He drove them there slowly…at least that was his intent. A lazy Saturday morning in bed. But Haley had other ideas.

And somehow, it was his resolve crumbling, his body being pulled beyond its will, until he was the one growling through his climax and she was the one smiling in delighted, smug pleasure.

"You're not the only one who learns fast."

He laughed, then noticed two sets of eyes peering over the bed. He motioned to them with his chin. "They're probably thinking we train well."

Haley laughed, then shrieked as both dogs bounded up onto the bed. Brett grabbed her hand and rolled her into his arms before Digger could land on her chest, then kept rolling until they were out of the bed entirely. "Come on, shower with me."

The dogs wrestled on the bed...and Brett and Haley wrestled in the shower.

It wasn't until they were downstairs in the breakfast nook, bowls of cereal and the weekend paper spread out between them, that he broached the subject that had kept him awake last night, long after she'd curled up next to him and drifted off.

"I got a call yesterday, while I was at work."

She pushed a stray curl from her face and looked over the edge of the paper at him. She was wearing his engine company T-shirt and panties, looking delightfully fresh scrubbed and well loved...and he wanted her all over again.

"You went out on a call? I thought you were still supposed to wait another—"

"No, I didn't go out on a call. I got a call. From a friend of mine. He runs one of the schools that help develop and train SAR dogs. It's one of the few in the country and he's really brought it a long way in a few short years. It's where I went—still go, in fact—to work with Recon."

"Is he the one that got you into SAR work?"

She saw the answer on his face even before he answered. "This is what you wanted to talk about before. About the career decision you had to make. He wants you to come work for him, doesn't he?"

Brett nodded. "We discussed it earlier this summer, but he hadn't made up his mind yet. And...well, it's more complicated than just changing jobs."

"Because of the time you've put in with the fire department, your retirement, the—"

He held up his hand. "I've thought all about that. Endlessly. But that's not it. Not really."

"Search and Rescue is what you really love." She didn't make it a question. She'd come to know him so well in such a short time. Better than anyone ever had.

"I love both things, but yes, if I had to specialize, this is definitely what I want to do. With the world being a changing place, and manmade disasters piling up alongside the natural ones... we don't have enough trained teams out there. I know we need to change that. Now I have an opportunity to do it."

"So...how far away is this place?"

"A couple hours from here. Up in the Sacramento Valley."

Her eyes widened. "That's a hell of a commute."

He reached out and covered her hand. "That's the complicated part I mentioned. Hank doesn't want me to come work for him. He wants to retire. Or, semi-retire anyway. He'll always be involved with SAR. His wife finally retired from her government job and they want to travel, spend time with their grandkids. But he doesn't want to leave the operation—"

"With someone who doesn't love it as much as he does," she finished softly.

"Yeah, well..."

"So, what? You buy him out, move the operation here, or—"

"You have to understand, this isn't the kind of place you drive to, to work. In addition to all the training facilities, there are dogs he finds, usually from humane societies and other breeders, that he personally brings in to train before placing with handlers. It's a full-time operation. Twenty-four seven."

"So he has kennels."

"Not exactly."

Her eyes widened. "He lives with all his train-ing dogs?"

"Basically, yes. You have to socialize them properly as pups, and they don't stay for long before either going to a handler or being placed as a pet if they can't make the grade." Brett stopped in mid-babble when the grin split her face.

"You've already decided, haven't you?" She squeezed his hand. "You want to move out there, take over the place."

Brett just looked at her, feeling like he was standing on the edge of his own giant precipice. "I want to, but—"

"You're perfect for this job, you know. He couldn't have found anyone better."

"Funny," he said quietly. "I look at you and think the same thing." He slid from his chair and tugged her from hers, until they were both stand-ing and she was in his arms. "I know it's a lot to ask, but will you come out there with me to-day? See the place with me? I want your input."

"My input?"

Brett wasted a second wondering if he wasn't ruining everything by pushing this on her so swiftly. Patience, he'd schooled himself a hundred times—a thousand—was the key to making their relationship work. It had started so abruptly, putting her under his roof, into his bed, literally overnight. And yet he felt as though she'd always been there, already couldn't imagine a roof without her under it.

"Yeah. You." He dropped a kiss on her nose. "I know you've been looking for a place here. And I've been trying really hard not to say anything."

She gave him a look.

"Key word being 'trying,'" he added with a sheepish grin.

She nodded, but looped her arms around his waist.

"I know rebuilding your life, your business, means a great deal to you," he said. "As it should. And I know my spare bedroom leaves a lot to be desired as a work studio. I also know how important your independence is to you and I understand that completely."

"Brett—"

"Wait," he said, feeling suddenly overwhelmed by how important this was, and how badly he was probably going to screw it up. "Let me say this. I shouldn't probably, should be more patient, but—''

''When you have to be, you're the most patient man I know. I've watched you work with Recon. And I know how you are with me. You're kind, loving and generous to a fault. You're also the sexiest, most fun, most trustworthy man I've ever known.''

He opened his mouth, then closed it again, completely unprepared for her heartfelt words.

''I've been falling more deeply in love with you every second of every day,'' she said. ''I tell myself it's nuts. I tell myself it's insane. And yet I look at you and my heart swells.''

''But the house-hunting—''

''I wasn't house-hunting. I just wanted you to think I was, because I didn't want you to think that just because you brought a stray home, I was going to stick around until you were forced to throw me out when the time came to end this thing.''

He panicked. ''But I don't want to end—''

''I know,'' she said, then grinned suddenly. ''Isn't it incredibly amazing?''

His heart was pounding so hard he could barely hear. In all his planned speeches, this was never how it went. He was going to be so careful, careful not to pressure her, not to be too overwhelming in revealing how deep his emotions ran, promise her he'd go as slow as she wanted. Only—

"I was searching for a storefront," she explained. "Along with all the other revelations I've had in my life, I've come to realize that maybe instead of hiding in my little studio and sending my pieces all over the country for someone else to sell...it was time for me to sell them myself. In my own place. It's what I've always wanted...but after things went so bad, I guess I crawled more deeply into an emotional cave than I thought." She leaned in, hugged him tightly. "You make me want to come out of that cave. Back into the sunlight, back into the world. But it's a world I really don't want to be in without you." She grinned. "Or Recon, or all of Hank's dogs, and all the ones to come along after them."

He hugged her hard, pressing her tightly against him, his eyes suddenly burning with unshed tears. The ferocity of his emotions almost left him speechless. "What did I do to deserve you?" he choked.

She leaned back, looked up into his eyes.

"Funny, that's what I think every time I look at you." She kissed him again. And this time it was a kiss full of promise, full of hope. "So, let's go see this new menagerie of yours. And, who knows, maybe afterward we can check out the local storefront properties out there."

"Haley—" He didn't know what to say. His heart was full to almost bursting.

She laughed. "My God, I've done it. I've actually managed to leave you speechless."

He laughed, too, then tugged her back tightly into his arms. "Almost, but not quite," he said. With her eyes still sparkling with laughter, he realized the right moment to speak his heart was any moment he wanted to. "I love you, Haley Brubaker."

She caught her breath, and now it was her eyes that had a suspicious sheen of moisture. "I didn't know how wonderful that was going to sound."

"I'll be more than happy to say it again. Every day. For years." He kissed her, intending soft and sweet, but somehow it turned primal and demanding. His emotions were running so swift and strong, he thought he could explode with it. "I do love you," he murmured against the soft skin of her neck. "It awes me how much you've come to mean to me." He lifted his head. "We both have a lot of changes, and I swear I want to take them one at a time—"

She was already grinning.

He couldn't help it, he shrugged. "I can try to take them one at a time."

"We'll leap together."

He sighed in amazement. "The lottery of love."

"What?"

"It's a goober thing."

"Ah." She smoothed a hand down his face. "As it happens, I love goobers."

His smile faded. "Do you?"

She nodded.

His heart stopped.

"I love you, Brett Gannon."

"Did you feel that," he whispered.

"What?"

"I'm pretty sure the earth just moved." He swung her around, making her squeal in surprise. "Or maybe it was just my heart rocking."

"No," she told him. "You've been rocking my world since the moment you stepped back into it."

He grinned. "Now those are the kind of aftershocks I'll never get tired of.'' He put her down just as the dogs raced, barking wildly, through the kitchen and back around into the living room. Digger in the lead, dragging the bedsheet behind him.

''How many dogs did you say we'd be living with again?'' Haley asked.

He opened his mouth, shut it again, then finally judiciously asked, ''How many is my limit?''

She burst out laughing. ''As many as you can con me into.''

''I love you, Haley.''

''I love you, too, Brett.'' She grabbed his hand and headed up the stairs. ''Come on, we have a drive to make.''

He scooted in behind her and flipped her neatly around and over his shoulder.

''You really have to stop hauling me around.''

''Fireman drills. Consider it keeping me trained and ready.''

''Oh. Well, then. Trained and ready is good.''

He slid her to her feet on the first landing, and backed her up against the wall. ''Wanna play damsel in distress?'' he teased, dropping kisses here and there.

"Fire, fire," she deadpanned, grinning. "Help."

He pushed her T-shirt up. She shoved his shorts down.

"Officer fireman, sir," she panted against his neck. "I think I'm going to burn alive."

He lifted her up against the wall. "Hold on tight. I'll save you."

She wrapped her arms and legs around him as he slid deep inside her with one long thrust. "Yes," she groaned, holding him tight. "You can. Only you."

And the earth moved. Again.

* * * * *

Look for Sean Gannon's story,
part of the
AMERICAN HEROES
Temptation miniseries.

SEAN,

Temptation #934, coming in July 2003.

STRANDED!

Jill Shalvis

CHAPTER ONE

IT WAS A RARE DAY all around. First, there was the storm, which with its raging winds and slashing rain made working on the house a definite challenge.

Then there was the reason Matt Walker was able to work on the house in the first place—he actually had the day off.

That in itself was so unusual, he almost hadn't known what to do with himself, but he'd figured it out pretty quick. Being an emergency room doctor had taught him nothing if not how to prioritize.

He stood in the middle of what he could loosely call his heritage, a falling-down-on-its-axis, three-story house on the gulf coast of Texas, left to him by his grandfather.

He'd been given the place, while his brother Luke had been left the big, fat bank account, when the truth was neither of them, both doctors and well-established, needed anything. Still, the money seemed a hell of a lot easier on a guy than this house.

Good thing he loved his brother, the lucky jerk.

So why had the house and the neglected, over-grown one hundred and fifty acres surrounding it, come to him? He didn't need it, he didn't need anything. Or anyone, for that matter.

And what was he, a man without a spare moment to call his own, supposed to do with it? His job was all-consuming, and he liked it that way. He put in a minimum of eighty hours a week at the hospital where he headed the emergency department, saving people twenty-four seven. If he wasn't treating others, he was planning the treatment of others.

Or, during the rare few hours in a row he had to himself, sleeping.

True enough, he worked with his hands, but this renovation project was so far beyond his abilities it was laughable. And yet here he stood in jeans, a T-shirt and work boots, music blaring out of his portable radio, contemplating the mess around him as though he knew what he was doing.

The foyer stretched out, opening into a living room bigger than his entire apartment. But his apartment didn't have rotting carpet, drywall nails coming through the walls and a ceiling turning yellow from leaks.

He was going to have to do something about all of it, but hell if he knew what exactly.

The music stopped abruptly and a deejay cut in. "Sorry, folks, but we've got something more important than vintage Van Halen at the moment. We're talking about that storm out there, the one that's wasting your spring veggies."

Matt craned his head and looked out the window. What had started out as a pretty pathetic offering of a few sprinkles had upgraded itself with a vengeance. He could hardly see for the slashing rain and incredible wind.

"It's upgraded itself from pesky to downright dangerous," the deejay continued. "Coming in off the Gulf, and basically, if you're anywhere near the coast of Texas or Louisiana, you're in for it."

Well that solved the problem of what to do with himself today. If the storm was that bad, he'd be back in Houston, in scrubs soon enough, treating injuries and worse.

The house would be on its own.

It was a hundred years old, it could handle it; if it held through that storm, that is. Matt didn't care either way, his parents had seen to it he didn't have a sentimental bone in his body. They'd traveled extensively, and exclusively.

Exclusively meaning no children invited.

Which meant that more often than not, he and his brother had landed here. Grandfather had pretty much let them run wild and, Matt had to admit, they'd spent some impressionable months here, he and Luke, racing through the fields, swimming in the creek behind the house, dodging grandfather's ire over their antics...

Funny how he'd forgotten that when he'd learned the house was his. All he'd felt was resentment at having to care for something other than his patients.

But now as he stepped past the living room, the formal dining room, the den, the kitchen, all fading from their former glory, memories slammed into him like a two-fisted punch.

From outside came the sound of the howling wind. The rain drummed the walls, the roof. Matt had seen lots of storms in his thirty-two years, and this was going to be a whopper. Overgrown bushes outside the windows scraped against the glass, hitting with such force he winced.

"Yes, sirree," he heard the radio announcer say from the radio in the foyer. "Batten down the hatches and get the heck out of Dodge, everyone. Don't be a hero.''

From where Matt stood in the lanai, an enclosed porch he'd camped out on too many times to count, he could hear creaking and groaning above him. The supports and rafters were straining.

Not good.

The house had been built in 1902. It'd been in the family all these years, passed down from generation to generation, skipping his father of course, a man far too busy for such things.

Only a few moments ago Matt would have said the same thing, which left a bitter taste in his mouth.

He didn't want to think like his father.

This house was the only thing he had in the way of a past worth remembering, and suddenly he didn't want to see it destroyed.

"Get out those flashlights, folks." This from the radio announcer. "Be careful, be smart, and be safe—"

The radio died as the power went out.

With a sigh, Matt moved toward the scant daylight the clouds hadn't choked out. He wasn't a hero, not today. He knew enough to leave. But first he turned in a slow circle to take a good long look around him.

He could almost hear himself as a kid, chasing Luke down the hallways, frogs in their pockets, running like hell from their enraged grandfather.

Oh, yeah, those had been good times. He felt bad that Luke, older by two years and working himself into an early grave as head surgeon in Los Angeles, wouldn't get to see this place one last time.

No matter really, Luke was even less sentimental than Matt.

"Hold on," he said out loud to the empty rooms. "You've made it this long, you can stand strong against a silly little storm."

Around him the creaks and groans increased. The drumming of the downpour against the windowpanes was so loud he could hardly hear himself think. It wasn't going to be a pleasant run for his car, but he needed to get out now before the long dirt driveway washed away.

He'd go straight to the hospital, he figured, because he could only imagine the injuries piling up.

As he turned and caught a glance out the window, he tensed. The creek that ran through the east and west fields was about to overflow its banks.

Not good.

Twice in the past hundred years it had flooded the house; it might yet again if the storm didn't let up.

But that's not what made Matt step closer to the window. He'd seen a flash of blue in all that wild, stormy gray. There, on the shore of the swollen creek....

Unbelievable.

The field had once been farmed, but not in the past twenty years. It was now just an open, overgrown space dotted with bush and trees and divided by the creek. Valuable, given the offers he'd been sent since his grandfather's death, but neglected just the same.

There was another flash of blue, but with the rain and wind distorting his view he couldn't tell what it was. A blanket? A truck? Even a person? And then he watched. It moved again. Matt's stomach fell. Whatever was out there, it was alive.

A child, he thought grimly. What if it was a child?

He hoped not, but with the mind-blowing wind, anything could have happened. There could have been an accident on the main road, someone could have been blown off of it, become completely lost.

Well, hell. He couldn't leave without finding out.

Hero complex, he could hear Luke scoffing. But his brother was a fine one to talk. Luke had the king of hero complexes. Whether it came from practically raising themselves, or the fact that as a result, they preferred to be needed rather than needy, Matt had no idea. He didn't care.

But he couldn't leave until he checked out the field.

The windows on the back door rattled. Instead of stepping back, Matt headed directly for it. On a hook hung yellow rain gear that looked as if it might have been there since the First World War. The pants were too short and the poncho too wide, but it had a hood. A hood was good.

Grabbing a spare poncho, as well, he opened the door. The wind nearly sucked the life right out of him. In fact, it sucked his body right off the porch. To balance himself, he took two running steps forward, and nearly plowed face-first into the wooden porch swing.

He wrapped his arms around it and held on through the gust. As unbelievable as it was, in

just the past few moments the winds had dou-
bled. Tripled. The rain slashed across his vision,
pelting him, stinging his face.

Pulling the neck of his T-shirt up, he was able
to at least cover his jaw. Holding on to the extra
poncho, he let go of the swing and stepped off
the porch. With the gale force hitting him in the
chest, walking was nearly impossible, but he
staggered forward.

He couldn't see any blue now. But someone
was out there, he could feel it, and his instincts
were rarely wrong. And if there *was* someone out
there, they had to be in trouble.

His ears were ringing and the stinging-cold
rain hurt his eyes, but at least, thanks to his shirt
over his mouth and nose, he could breathe. He
was also thankful for the neglected field because
he used the occasional bush and tree to propel
him forward.

With little to no visibility, he was wondering
how he thought he was going to make his way
back in when the flash of blue popped up again,
much closer now.

The unrelenting wind gusts helped propel him
forward, practically lifting him off the ground,
wanting to toss his body through the air as if he
were nothing more than a rag doll.

Having no choice but to run to keep his legs beneath him, he ended up far too close to the edge of the creek, which had turned itself into a wild, level-five rapid. Scanning the area, he found the blue. It was clinging to a small tree by the edge of the water, and it wasn't a blanket.

Not a truck.

Not a child.

But a woman.

CHAPTER TWO

MOLLY HELD ON TO THE TREE for dear life. Getting caught in a storm hadn't been in her electronic organizer under Planned Activities For Today.

But then again, Professor Molly Stanton usually forgot to enter anything into the contraption in the first place, so she couldn't complain.

How had this happened? All she'd wanted to do was to collect some soil from the edge of a natural creek for her students at the university. They were studying the effects of the past few storms on the land, and she'd been out in the field, thoroughly engaged in her work. So engaged, she'd missed the signs of a storm going bad.

Nothing new. She'd been missing signs for some time now, including any signs of a personal life for herself. But work was so much more interesting than anything going on in her own life, so it'd been easy enough to bury herself in it.

That had been before the winds had picked her up, body and clipboard and nearby resting bike, and as casual as she pleased, slammed her into the tree she now clung to.

Stunned at first, she'd lain where she'd landed, dazed and utterly shocked at how much it had hurt to hit a tree. God only knew where her bike had ended up. With the velocity of the wind, it could be in Oklahoma by now.

Actually, she should consider herself lucky. Two more feet and she'd have hit the creek, and certainly been swept away by the roaring water.

Absentminded professor, she could hear her students saying. *Noticing nothing but her studies again.*

Well, she noticed her surroundings now, thank you very much, only this time, those surroundings just might get her killed. She was wet, cold, and felt as if she'd been steamrolled.

And she was out in the middle of nowhere, being pelted by the elements, all alone, with nothing but her trusty clipboard—

Nope, not even her clipboard, she realized, patting the ground around her. Even that had blown away.

Oh, boy, wasn't this a fine mess. Given the way her vision kept fading and the pain radiating through her body, she'd definitely done it this time. Even as she thought it, the wind somehow managed to kick up another notch and she could feel her body being pulled away from the tree.

Panicked, she wrapped her arms around the trunk that had knocked her so silly only a moment before. But when she pressed up against it, little black spots danced in front of her eyes. Crying out, she fell back to the ground.

On the one hand, she'd located the pain center. It was in her ribs.

On the other hand, she was still breathing—mostly water and wind—but breathing was good. *Alive* was good. She decided right then and there to make more of being alive the moment she got herself out of this mess.

Assuming she got herself out of it.

Her teeth were clicking together so hard, her jaw ached. Her head felt as if it might fall right off. The driving rain made seeing more than a few inches in front of her impossible.

But she really wanted to live. She wanted a life.

"I'll get a cat," she yelled into Mother Nature's face. "I'll join a bowling league." *Just don't let me die.*

Again the wind threatened to pick her up and

toss her into the water, so she crawled back to the tree, the only stationary thing around her, and carefully, very carefully, plastered herself to it. Whimpering a bit pathetically, she put her cheek to the trunk and closed her eyes.

"I'm on a beach," she whispered, heart pumping as she felt the tree sway. "In the Bahamas. It's ninety degrees." Oh, yes, that worked. She was sitting in a chair facing the calm, quiet surf—

A terrible crack nearly split her eardrum, dissipating the beach image in a heartbeat. The crack came from her tree, which now swayed violently, assuring her it was only a matter of time before it was ripped the rest of the way from its roots, leaving her with nothing solid to cling to.

This was bad, very bad. "Sand beneath my toes," she whispered desperately, but it didn't work now. Nothing could take her away from her horrid reality.

She had no idea how long she sat there, huddled to the loosening tree, doing her damnedest to pretend she really was on some fab beach vacation, when something made her open her eyes.

A face appeared in front of hers, so suddenly that she let out a cry of surprise and shrank back against the trunk that had become her entire life.

Fear was as insidious as the pain invading her body. Sometime between hitting the tree and bathing on a beach, her thoughts had become fuzzy, but one thing remained clear: she was going to die.

The monster's face swimming in front of her was surrounded by yellow.

Yellow plastic.

Wait. She blinked the rain out of her eyes and tried to focus. No. Not a monster. A man. A man who was completely covered in rain gear, only his eyes showing. Those eyes were midnight-blue and leveled right on her.

Her fear didn't ease. How could it? No one knew where she was. Why? Because she'd reduced her world to just work, damn it. No one would even know she was missing until she didn't show up for classes tomorrow.

By then she'd be fish bait.

The man in yellow lifted a hand and pulled something away from his face, revealing his mouth, which made her realize his mouth was moving.

Funny, she couldn't hear his voice.

In fact, she couldn't hear anything. She shook her head—big mistake as her dizziness turned to nausea—but nope, still no hearing. Given the way the trees around her were still straining, and the clear and obvious rain still drumming down, it was the oddest thing.

The man hunkered down in front of her, his mouth still moving. It was a grim-looking mouth, and not a particularly happy-looking face, but wow, his eyes were the most unusual shade of blue she'd ever seen. They mesmerized her, those eyes, and she locked her gaze on them, wondering if she'd died and this was her guardian angel.

Yes. And he was going to take her to heaven.

No. An angel wouldn't look so fierce, so intense, nor be so big. She could tell he was well over six foot, though with his huge, bulky rain gear she couldn't discern anything else about his physique. In any case, he was far too big for an angel. And anyway, an angel would be smiling. He'd have a soft voice, a sweet, kind—

"Give me your hand," he said, his voice rough and serrated suddenly breaking through the silence.

The voice of sin personified. Oh, no! She wasn't going to heaven, she was going to h-e-double-hockey-sticks—

"Damn it, that tree is going to give and you're going to end up in the creek!" Dropping his outstretched hand he moved in closer, towering over her, and put his hands on her body.

Okay, she wasn't dead, because as he gripped her waist, his fingers hitting her ribs, pain shot through her like a knife. It overrode her exhaustion and fear and confusion, and, reacting, she plowed an elbow into his belly.

Had she wondered about his physique? Well, he wasn't fat, her elbow nearly bounced off the rock-hard surface of his midsection. Still, the wind was on her side and, propelled by both, he fell backward.

At the same moment, with an ear-splitting crack, the trunk of her tree split. As luck would have it, the half she held on to ripped free.

The next thing she knew, she was hanging over the roaring creek, her fingers digging into a branch that seemed far too fragile for her weight. "Ohmigod. *Ohmigod.*"

"Hold on!" The man leaped to his feet, wavered for a moment when a gust hit him full in the chest. Then, without an apparent care for his own safety, he waded into the rushing water, his gaze intent on hers. "I'm coming!"

He was coming. Good. That was good.

Except her branch cracked again. And before she could open her mouth to let out a scream, the thing gave, crashing it and her into the tumultuous, wild water below.

SHE VANISHED before Matt's very eyes. Horrified, he shouted after her, eyes glued to the water as he surged forward, nearly losing footing himself.

The branch she'd been holding rushed away, and he backed up and out of the water so he could run downstream, keeping the branch in sight because she had to be close. She had to be. He couldn't have lost her.

Though she had short, curly blond hair that should have stuck out in the dark, dim world around him, he didn't see her, and his stomach dropped. ''Come on, come on,'' he prayed as he ran along as best he could, tripping over his own frozen feet, the wind making breathing all but impossible.

Finally, a very long moment later, he caught sight of her and nearly fell to his knees in gratitude. She'd grabbed on to a pile of debris at the edge of the rushing creek, about a hundred yards down from where she'd fallen in. Her hold seemed tenuous, as she was being whipped by the driving rain and wind, not to mention being pummeled by the rising water.

"Hang on," he yelled, cupping his mouth to make the sound of his voice travel farther, his pulse kicking up a notch when whatever it was she gripped for dear life slipped and she nearly lost her hold.

Amazingly enough, she lifted her head and landed her moss-green eyes right on him. Her pupils were dilated, her breathing rough. She had blood oozing from a cut on her head and God only knew how many other injuries. He had no idea how long she could hold on, but he wasn't going to lose her now.

She wasn't quite close enough that he could stay on the edge and reach her. Of course not. So he stepped into the creek again, the icy water hitting his knees and sucking the air from his lungs. By the time he made his way closer the water was at his thighs, threatening to carry them both downstream.

The debris she clung to looked to be a stack of wood. Could have been a boat, a shed, anything, but whatever it was, it had almost completely broken up. The power of the water was beyond comprehension, and if she let go, she'd be broken up, as well.

Then the entire pile slipped. Icy fear had him diving toward her. "No!"

With a scream, she whipped her head his way just as the debris broke entirely free of the shore.

"Here!" he shouted. Digging his feet into the sand beneath him, he reached out at the same time she reached toward him.

By some miracle he snagged her wrist, latching on to her with a death grip stronger than a vise. "Got you!"

For one long, horrifying second the wind and water fought him for her, but with the most utter determination he'd ever seen she battled the current and managed to lift her other arm, which he also grabbed.

Hauling her to him, he took a step backward, toward the shore behind them.

Twice he lost his footing and they nearly went down, but then he was sitting with hard, wet ground beneath him, cradling her in his lap.

For another long moment they stayed just like that, panting, gasping…holding on for dear life while the storm continued to beat on them with sharp, stinging, torrential rain and a wind so strong he could hardly take a breath.

Knowing she was injured, and knowing he had no idea how badly, he kept his hands light on her, but it was difficult because he had the oddest urge to haul her close and hug her tight.

He, who never had the urge to cling and hug anyone tight. Not that he didn't like women. He loved women. Tall, short, thin, chunky, dark, light…he didn't care, he loved them all to such a degree Luke often called him a hound dog, but in his life women had their place and priority.

They were more important than say, going grocery shopping, but not as important as work or sleep. Not particularly flattering, but there it was.

If there'd been a woman who mattered lately, she'd been a patient. A case. When he'd healed her, he'd moved on.

He had no doubt this woman needed his medical skills, but holding her soggy, wet, cold body against his, he wasn't exactly thinking like a doctor. He couldn't help it, whatever the hell she wore was thin and filmy and had long ago plastered itself to her very petite, very nicely curved body.

A body he had against his. A body he'd slid his hands over several times now. A body—

Lifting her head, she looked into his eyes. "I've been wondering…are you from heaven or hell?" she asked before her eyes rolled into the back of her head.

CHAPTER THREE

OKAY, yes, Molly was confused. But damn it, she wasn't *that* confused. She knew the huge, fierce-looking man holding her wasn't from heaven or hell, she knew she hadn't left good old planet earth yet, so why had she asked him such a thing?

It must be the bump she could feeling growing on her head. Or her need to change her life.

But she'd been living this way, this careful, staid way, for so long. It came from being an only child of divorced parents. From being moved around a lot because of her mother's career. From wanting nothing more than security and stability.

But suddenly the two big S's weren't enough.

The man's hands, gentle but firm, started to glide over her body, and though she was greatly weakened, she lifted her hands to smack his away, until she realized he was checking her for broken bones.

Closing her eyes against the dizziness, she realized she couldn't hear a thing again except for a funny ringing in her ears and the wild wind.

In fact, with her eyes closed, she could go back to the beach fantasy now…a nice, *warm* beach—

But then his strong, probing fingers made their way to her ribs, and she nearly jerked out of her own skin.

"Shh," he said in her ear, his voice still low and rough. A small part of her foggy brain marveled at his voice cutting through the ringing. "I have to make sure…"

She had a moment to feel as if her entire world shrank to that stabbing pain before she realized she was back in his arms, cradled against his chest in a way that made her feel small and defenseless. Cared for.

How long had it been since she'd allowed someone to care for her? Hmm…she'd never let anyone care for her.

Then they were moving. Or maybe just her head was still spinning, she had no idea. "I hope heaven is warmer than this," she said on a sigh.

"Hey, stop it. You're not dead yet." He hunched over her, putting his mouth close to her ear so she could hear him. He was protecting her from the rain and wind with his own body, she realized, and something sort of warm and fuzzy happened inside her belly.

Much as she was a millennium woman who could take care of herself—which she'd always told herself was important—it was nice to know he wasn't going to let anything happen to her.

Anything else, that is. "Thank you." She opened her eyes. "For saving me. And I know I'm not dead. I'd just hoped I was having a nightmare." Had she really thought his eyes cold? They crackled with life now. "But if I was just dreaming, you'd be in a bathing suit. We're at the beach," she said when he shot her a look of concern. "It's a distraction technique."

His mouth pulled into a frown.

"I'm okay," she told him. "Really."

"We'll see." He was breathless, and fighting his way over the rough ground. Around them the wind kicked it up a notch higher, if that was even possible, and Molly figured he should be grateful she'd eaten those two donuts this morning. She'd done her part to anchor them, that's for certain.

Still, the going wasn't easy; he struggled to put each foot forward. She could feel the muscles in his arms and chest strain against the wind and rain with every passing second.

"I can walk," she tried to tell him, but he just pulled her a little closer and shook his head.

She could feel his arm beneath the backs of her thighs. His other arm banded beneath her shoulder blades, his hand high on her side so that his fingers curled just below her breast.

Such an intimate embrace and yet they were utter strangers. It was the oddest sensation, being held against a tall, strong, warm man she didn't even know. Odd and…inexplicably arousing.

Definitely, she'd hit her head too hard, she decided and, fighting dizziness, just closed her eyes and held on. Mmm, yeah, that was nice…she felt as if she was floating…

Oh, his arms were wonderful. She thought about telling him so but it would be such an effort to make herself heard and she was tired, very tired.

He stopped once to hitch her up and closer, and for the briefest, most heart-stopping of moments, her face slid to his. Jaw to jaw. His was slightly rough from a day's growth of beard, and it made her shiver.

Mistaking that for a chill, he made a noise deep in his throat and pulled her even closer. Ooh, that was nice, too, he had such warmth emanating from his body. She still had her eyes closed but she could feel the puff of his labored breathing against her cheek and knew with the slightest of movement, she could bring her mouth to his.

That she even wanted to was a rather unwelcome reminder of how long it had been since she'd felt the touch of a man's mouth to hers. "You're hot," she said without thinking. A common ailment of hers, talking without thinking.

Another reason she didn't have anyone in her life, she supposed.

She felt his startled stare on her face and in spite of her freezing, she felt her face flush. "I mean...you have n-nice body heat."

"Uh...good," he said, and she tried not to wince at what an idiot she was.

And then suddenly she realized the rain was no longer hitting her face. Opening her eyes just as he set her down, any words she might have offered backed up in her throat when he slid an arm around her hips, careful not to touch her ribs, supporting her while he fought with a door.

They stood in front of the magnificent old house she'd so admired whenever she'd driven through here. It was a three-story plantation style far past its glory days, but there was such a wealth of character and charm to it she never failed to stop and just stare. "This place is yours?"

She didn't think he'd heard her in the deafening noise of the storm, but he yelled back, "It is now." He went back to concentrating on opening the door.

She had a thousand questions. What was his name? What did he do for a living…? How wonderful was it to live in this house?

But the wind was brutal here beneath the covered porch, whipping through, creating a wind tunnel of flying debris and dirt, nearly knocking them both down. She could no longer control her shivering, nor hardly keep her eyes open, but she forced herself to watch as he wrestled the front door open.

"Come on," he yelled, pushing her in ahead of him, turning to fight it shut while she sank to the foyer's cold tile.

God, she was tired, so very tired. Leaning her head back against the wall, she tried to keep her eyes open as he strained with all his might to shut the door. But she couldn't. The laws of gravity pulled her eyelids down against her will.

What might have been a minute or an hour later, she felt him drop a blanket over her. Then his hands were on her face as he tipped it up.

"Open your eyes," he commanded. "I want to see your pupils."

She tried, she really did, but couldn't he see she just wanted to sleep?

Apparently not, as he simply pried one eye open, stared into it, then did the same with the other. His fingers probed the bump and cut on her head until she hissed at him.

"I don't think you're concussed," he finally said. "But you have a nasty bump and God knows how many other injuries. I'll get you to the hospital. Wait here."

Before she could open her mouth, he was gone.

Good. Giving in to the exhaustion, Molly tipped over on her good side. "Warm sand beneath me," she whispered to herself, and tried to believe it. She was halfway there when he was back again—damn him—lightly shaking her.

"We can't get out."

She opened one eye to find him hunkered in front of her, still entirely covered in yellow except for his eyes, nose and mouth, which was even more grim now. "My car won't start and there's no one else around. Think you can make it to the storm basement?" He pulled off his hood and looked at her.

"Um..." She blinked, but yep, she was indeed seeing his entire head and face for the first time, and yep, she'd lost her ability to think. Short, dark hair clung to his scalp, and those startling blue eyes were full of worry. For her. And his mouth, good Lord, she'd already come to the conclusion it was made for sin.

But it was frowning, that mouth, and waiting for an answer.

"Um..." She was educated and highly intelligent. And registered an idiot by him revealing his face. Definitely too long since she'd been with a man. She promptly added that to her mental list of must-dos.

"We can't stay here," he repeated. "The porch we just stood on? Gone. So is the back decking." A spasm of emotion flickered across his face. "The roof is going to go next, and then we're dust."

He was going to lose his house, this glorious house. "Oh, no," she whispered, reaching out, putting her hands on his upper arms. "Isn't there something we can do?"

"Not unless you know Mother Nature personally."

He spoke lightly enough but she could see unsettled and complicated emotions in his gaze, and it made her heart tip on its side. "I'm so sorry—"

He surged to his feet, apparently not wanting her pity. He bent to pull her back into his arms, but she held up a hand. "I can walk."

He had a backpack on his shoulders; he must have gotten that from his car. "Are you sure?" he asked, watching her very carefully.

Was she sure? No. She wanted to whimper pathetically and crawl into bed for a week, but he'd been so strong, so gallant, when he had everything at stake. She couldn't let him think her nothing more than a helpless little mouse. "I'm sure."

He took her hand in his. It was a big hand, warm and strong and sure. A stranger's hand; one who'd risked his own life for her to be here. She stared at his fingers entwined with hers and felt an inexplicable lump in her throat. She'd make the most of this second chance. *She would.*

But above them the roof groaned and creaked and made so much noise her conviction to do so wavered.

"Come on," he said, more urgently now, glancing up as he tugged her down a hallway, through a kitchen and to a back door. Before he opened it, he carefully tucked her against him. "Don't let go."

Molly's arm slid around his waist. He felt good and solid, and beneath the yellow poncho his big body radiated warmth.

No, she wouldn't be letting go.

He opened the door. Whatever daylight there had been earlier had started to fade, reminding her it would be dark soon.

She hated the dark.

And though she'd already been in the storm, the force of it startled her anew, but he didn't let her hesitate. With his arm around her, he propelled them right into it.

GETTING TO THE BASEMENT was yet another adventure. The woman huddled against him was shivering and injured. And also far too silent.

In his experiences, women weren't silent. "Almost there," he shouted, heading them around to the side of the house, to the entrance to the storm basement. Once, when he'd been ten years old, Luke had locked him in, then promptly forgotten about him until his grandfather had come looking for him himself.

It had been dark, damp and musty, but if Matt remembered correctly, also filled with supplies, and since he'd personally eaten the entire stash of candy bars only to puke them up, he was fairly certain he remembered correctly. He didn't hold out much hope that his grandfather had re-stocked, but at least he had his medical bag and a flashlight from his car.

They'd be okay to ride out the storm, he fig-ured, assuming he could treat her injuries here.

But God help him if the storm lasted a few days because he was positive he couldn't manage to be polite company for long, locked away with a woman who'd in all likelihood expect him to talk.

The rain and wind hadn't slowed any, and he had to sit her down to wrestle open the storm door. She looked small and defenseless, and when he turned back for her, she was sitting with her head on her knees, still and silent as the storm pelted her.

Damn, but if that didn't tear at him, when he really didn't want to be torn at.

What he *did* want should have been so simple. Maybe a damn day off without any pressure. Maybe not having to think. Maybe having some-one tend to *him* for a change.

Yeah, right.

"Okay," he said, and reached for her.

With a surprised cry, she jerked back, then grimaced in pain from her quick movement.

"Just me," he said lightly while his heart kicked hard. She had no idea who he was, but at least his voice seemed to soothe her because her shoulders relaxed a bit when he stroked a hand down her wet hair.

"I'm sorry, I—"

"It's okay. Come on, now."

She made a gallant effort, despite her obvious exhaustion. He wondered why that got to him because as a doctor, he considered himself fairly jaded against such things.

He was a man who did his absolute best in the best of environments—that being the hospital— and then after the crisis, moved on.

But he wasn't at his best now, not even close. If something happened to this woman here, with him, he didn't think he'd be able to be so blasé about it.

That disturbed him. Deeply.

He must be far more tired than he'd thought. A good enough reason right there to get the hell out of this storm, to get as far away from this oddly touching female as humanly possible.

As soon as humanly possible.

The storm nearly blew them away as he guided

her into the dark, dank basement. He was chilled straight to the bone, and knew she had to be, too. Exhaustion made movement difficult, but he was already thinking about how he could get them both out of here and to the hospital as he flipped on the flashlight and turned back to the door, just as the wind slammed it shut on his face.

Shutting them both inside.

CHAPTER FOUR

WHEN THE STORM DOOR slammed, Molly was very grateful her rescuer had already turned on his flashlight. She'd always had a fear of the dark, and though for the most part she'd outgrown it, she could feel her chest tightening at the thought of being shut away down here for an extended period of time.

How long could this really last? she wondered, looking around her a bit frantically, already feeling a bit closed in. Added to that was the fact her body had gone alien on her, starting to shake so violently her teeth chattered.

"Hey. Hey, it's okay."

She blinked his face into view. He'd shed his poncho and held her shoulders in his big, capable hands, peering intensely into her face, making her realize she'd let out a pathetically needy little whimper.

"Here, it's shock. Take this." Holding out a muscular arm lightly dusted with dark hair, he handed her the flashlight. Then he gripped the blanket she'd been clutching around her and spread it open to look at her body.

She knew her gauzy skirt and shirt had been a bad idea. Dry, they'd created an easy-to-wear, lightweight, flexible garment she could do anything in, from go to the beach to an elegant dinner.

Not that she had an invitation from anyone to go to an elegant dinner.

Wet, however, the skirt and blouse had become a different garment entirely. Wet, it had become as sheer as lace. Wet, it clung to her every curve and nuance. Wet, it left next to nothing to the imagination.

Her trembling increased, though she had no idea if it was from being frozen solid or from her being very aware of him looking at her.

Without a word, he put his hands very gently on her face, probing the bump and gash over her eye, wincing when she hissed out a breath. "Dizzy?" he asked, his breath puffing her hair.

Yeah, but she had the feeling it was his proximity and nothing more.

He tipped her face to his and waited until she spoke. "A little," she admitted.

"Nauseous?"

"When I move too fast."

His hands slid to her waist. "I've been worried about these." His voice was low and a little gruff as he traced her ribs with his fingers until he came to the spot that made her suck in her breath hard.

"Not cracked, I don't think," he said, eyes furrowed with concentration as he touched her so intimately.

With his head bent, his face very close to her, his hair brushed her breasts. The touch caused some sort of electrical malfunction in her every sensory nerve, shooting a bolt of lightning right between her legs.

Then he lifted that head and locked his gaze on hers. "I can wrap them, that will make it easier to move around." While he said this, he left his hands on her. As though they belonged there. She could barely take a breath and it had nothing, nothing at all to do with her aches and pains.

"You're cold. Before we get you out of your wet things, what else hurts?"

Before we get her out of her wet things? That brought reality back pretty quickly, and she blinked. "I—"

When the violent shiver racked her, he swore and rescued the flashlight before she dropped it and it broke, then pulled the blanket, wet on the outside but still dry on the inside, closer around her. "Okay, one thing at a time." Rising to his feet, he nearly hit his head on the ceiling. With a low oath, he hunched over a little, looking around them.

They were in a room larger than she'd thought at first. It had been finished, with shelves lining one wall. Plastic storage bins lined those shelves. Along the other wall was a narrow cot, bare of bedding, but it looked so inviting she nearly whimpered again. There was yet another door, and when he noticed her looking, he said, "Toilet."

Well, thank God for small favors.

He started pulling down boxes, muttering to himself until he found what he was looking for—candles, which he set on the floor and lit with quick precision. While the wind and rain continued to rage above them, he dove into another box and came up with blankets, which he spread over the narrow cot.

Above them came a large crash and he winced. "Hopefully not the roof," he said to her frightened upward gaze.

He said this lightly but he didn't fool her, not

when his eyes were filled with things she imagined he didn't want her to see. Regret. Worry.

"It'll hold," she said, wanting it to be so for him.

He lifted a shoulder, then came back for her. He pulled the wet blanket off and Molly to her feet. Holding on to her when she wavered, he said, "You're going to have to lose the wet clothes."

Uh…pretty much over her dead body. Just because he was gorgeous and had the sensual touch she'd been craving didn't mean—

"Here. They're my grandfather's, from God knows which decade, but they'll keep you warm." He thrust a bundle into her hands and steered her toward the bathroom, which was barely big enough for one person to stand in. There was no power so he took a candle and set it on the back of the small commode, which was the only other thing in the room. He eyeballed her shivering body with unease. "Do you need help?"

Okay, so she'd only imagined the heat in his eyes a few moments ago. Understandable, really, as she'd hit the tree pretty hard. Plus she'd been thinking of how to change her life, which meant maybe having sex more than once every few years. "I'll be okay." Behind her back she gripped the door handle because in spite of her bravado, she really did feel dizzy.

"I don't think—"

"I'll be fine."

He didn't look convinced but he didn't press. "Call if you need me."

After she shut the door, she promptly sat on the closed toilet and put her head between her knees, but that seemed to make the vertigo worse so she sat back up. Her shivering had increased and she knew he was right. She had to get out of her wet things.

No problem. With shaking fingers she unbuttoned her blouse while she listened to the storm ravage the house above her. But for the quick thinking and compassion of the man outside the bathroom door, she could still be out in that weather, injured. Or worse.

Peeling the blouse away from her cold, clammy skin seemed to drain whatever energy she had left. She debated whether to lose her bra, but it was soaked through and uncomfortable. It took another moment of fumbling before she managed to unhook it.

"You okay?" came a very male voice at the

door, startling her so that she fell right off the seat.

The door flew open so fast the candle went out, which was just as well really, because she was stuck face-first between the wall and commode, with no top on and her wet skirt falling over her head.

She heard swearing, then squinted her eyes as the flashlight flickered over her. She tried to put herself back on a nice, warm sandy beach, but she couldn't do it. Not when she knew exactly how she looked hanging upside down. Half-naked.

Not to mention she was quite sure her head was going to fall off.

"Jesus." Big, warm hands snagged her hips and tugged. Uprighted her. Now she had one of those hands low on her belly, the other curled around her back to just beneath her bare breast. In fact, the way she'd slouched over, that breast was pretty much resting against his fingers. The realization made her sit straight up, which shot an arrow of pain right through her ribs.

"Sit still," he demanded when she let out a soft cry. "What the hell were you doing?"

"T-tr—" It was the oddest thing, her teeth chattered so wildly she couldn't talk, and when she tried to cross her arms over her chest, she popped him in the nose.

"Damn it." And then she was back in his arms, her own pinned to her sides. Above them the storm berated the house with such strength the place shook, while right here, he berated her, as well. "You could have bumped your head again. Or upgraded your bruised ribs to broken. What were you thinking?"

Dizziness mixed with humiliation as he moved, so she closed her eyes and pretended she couldn't hear him.

"All you had to do was call for me." He carried her out of the bathroom into the main room of the basement, where the storm was even louder, if that were possible. Thanks to the candles, light flickered over the walls that were vibrating from the force of the wind. "You should have let me help you." He set her on the cot in what she supposed was a gentle manner for a giant of a man. It still hurt like hell. "But you had to be stubborn." And then he not so gently tugged off her skirt, leaving her in nothing but a pair of plain white serviceable panties.

He stopped talking.

She squinted her eyes closed tighter and told

herself *some* men liked short, slightly too rounded women.

For a long moment there was nothing but the sound of the wind destroying all that was above them. Then a blanket drifted down over her body, and then another one. She opened her eyes when a weight sank at her hip.

"I'm a doctor," he said gruffly. "I, uh…"

"See stupid naked women all the time?"

The corner of his mouth twitched, despite the fact that he looked less than thrilled to be holed up here with her.

"I'm sorry," she said in a whisper because it hurt her head to talk any louder. With her eyes closed, she said, "I'll be quiet and stay out of your way until we can leave."

"Okay," he said so gratefully that she would have laughed if she could.

Men. The not-so-mysterious species.

She drifted on that thought for a few moments, but then nearly leaped off the bed when something cold was set to her temple.

Her hero again. He had an opened medical bag at his side. He was studying her face intently as he cleaned the cut by her eye, and another on her chin she hadn't even realized she had. "I'm going to wake you every few hours,'' he said. ''Fair warning.''

''My name is Molly.'' When he frowned, she tried to smile. ''You know, in case you wanted to know.''

''Molly,'' he repeated, and at the sound of her name on his very sexy lips, she shivered.

His frown deepened and he went into the bathroom, coming back with the things she'd dropped when she'd taken her embarrassing tumble. He shook out the first item, a man's button-down flannel shirt. Before she could say a word, he'd tugged the blanket off her, gently pulled her to a sitting position and held out the shirt for her to slip into.

Molly closed her eyes to the view she was presenting him with and jammed her arms into the shirt. As she reached up to pull the thing closed, her hands bumped into his.

Her eyes flew open again to lock gazes with his, which was no longer quite so calm. ''I can do it myself,'' she said, her voice awfully husky.

''Are you s—''

''Positive.'' She even managed a smile as her overly sensitized nipples scraped against the old, soft flannel. They wanted more. They wanted him. They wanted… She felt hysterical laughter bubble up as she buttoned the shirt. She tried to keep her mouth shut, but it just wouldn't stay that way. When she was nervous, as she was right this very minute, her mouth tended to run off with both her brain and good sense. "I'm a scientist." She hauled the blanket up to her chin. "And a professor at the university. I was in your field studying the effects of the last storm on the land."

"You might have waited for *this* storm to be over first."

"Yes, I should have." She licked her dry lips. "I don't know how to thank you for—"

"Don't thank me."

"But I have to. I want to. I…" She stared down at her hands. "I'm incredibly grateful. Look, I know I don't pay too much attention to what's going on around me when I'm working. That's what everyone tells me, anyway—everyone being my students. I'm not married," she added inanely, wanting him to know, wanting to know about him.

But he didn't say anything. He just shook out a pair of sweatpants and held them out to her. "Here."

He clearly didn't want to talk. Just as he clearly expected her to lose the blanket and expose herself again. It was shocking how much she suddenly wanted to do just that, and have him reach for her. Hold her. Touch her.

It hadn't missed her notice that this could be fate. After all, she'd been rescued by an enigmatic, beautiful, strong-minded, strong-willed man who could possibly give her part of what she'd been missing. An adventure. A decent orgasm.

So why hadn't she worn exciting panties?

Because she didn't own any.

"My life is going to change," she said, bicycling the blanket down with her legs, wondering if she turned him on at all. She watched him carefully but he was equally careful and didn't look at her. "I decided that when I was locked on to that tree," she said, telling him even though he obviously didn't want to hear her story. *Look at me.* "My life is too dull. It needs a facelift." She stuck her feet into the sweat bottoms. "Did you know I still don't know your name?"

"Matt," he said, and if she wasn't mistaken, he said it from between his clenched teeth as he carefully studied the wall above her.

He didn't want to look at her.

Interesting. "Well, Matt, I need more from life. I need to let people in." She wriggled the sweats to her knees. "I haven't done much of that…especially men."

His gaze flew to hers and she let out a nervous laugh. "I'm not a virgin or anything, I just…I've…never been much interested. Not that I don't like men," she added quickly. "I do. I think I do, I just…"

"The sweats." He swallowed hard. "Pull them up."

Because he could, or couldn't, resist her? She wished she knew. "I need something new. A cat. Or to learn to ski. Do you ski, Matt?"

"Please," he said again, sounding a bit desperate. "You need to finish. You need to warm up."

"Yeah." She tried to sit up. Instead she sucked in a breath, paled from the dart of pain, and closed her eyes.

He was there in a second, putting a big hand on her belly. The other reached for the pants at her knees. As he pulled them over her legs, the backs of his fingers touched the bare skin of her knees…her thighs.

"It was the storm," she said, her eyes closed, her breathing ragged. "I thought I was going to die. That's when I made the promise to myself, that if I lived, I wouldn't ever just let life pass me by again.''

Matt let out a slow breath and told himself he was a professional. He was not, absolutely not, attracted to this woman who was hurt and talking too damn much. He was not aroused, not at all—

She lifted her hips so he could pull the sweats past her thighs.

His knuckles brushed against the heat of her.

Her eyes flew to his and she stopped breathing.

So did he.

Instead of jerking his hand back, he watched his own finger trace a path over her quivering belly.

''Tell me you're not married,'' she whispered. ''Pretty please, tell me that you're single. Available.''

''I'm not married,'' he whispered back.

''Okay, good.''

''I'm single.''

''Thank God.''

''But as for available, I'm—''

''Shh.'' Then she pulled him down and put her soft, warm mouth to his.

CHAPTER FIVE

FOR A HEART-STOPPING moment her lips clung to Matt's, and he let them. He let her kiss him until he couldn't remember why he shouldn't.

Then finally apparently taking mercy on him, she slowly pulled back. "Thank you," she whispered.

"Molly—"

"You can see why I want to get a cat." The lips that had so thoroughly kissed him let out a little laugh. "And learn to ski. I want to live, Matt. But mostly I want..."

No. Don't ask. Don't even look at her, but damn... Her hair had started to dry, tightening into blond curls, one of which fell over the softest, most amazingly expressive eyes he'd ever seen. She lay there, open and beautiful, wanting him.

How long had it been since he'd allowed a woman to look at him that way? Since he'd reciprocated?

Too long. But this wasn't the place or the time, it wasn't—

"Mostly I want a man," she whispered, still holding his gaze. "Not permanently, nothing like that. Just…just to show me what I've been missing, if only for a night."

Ah, hell. Because he was a man.

And he had a free night. "You need sleep." He lifted the flexible wrap he wanted to put around her ribs. "After I put this on, you'll be more comfortable." And sleepy, he hoped. Very sleepy.

Eyes on his, she reached up and unbuttoned his grandfather's flannel shirt. "I guess you have patients who throw themselves at you all the time."

"No." When he helped her sit up, the shirt fell away from her a little, playing peekaboo with her incredible body.

"No?" She tipped her head, then winced and carefully straightened it. "How can that be?"

"I'm not exactly known for my bedside manner." He unraveled a long stretch of wrap.

"How come? You don't like people?"

"Not especially." He took a deep breath and spread the material of the shirt away from her so he could work.

Beneath was nothing but a creamy expanse of belly and two perfect, full breasts tipped with rose-colored nipples his mouth was suddenly watering for.

And a left side already bruising so badly his stomach dropped. "God. You got it good." Forcing his gaze to what he was doing, he wrapped her as gently as he could, experiencing the oddest sensation. Compassion and empathy, if he wasn't mistaken. It wasn't that he didn't care about his other patients, he did, he most certainly did, but he had been working too hard, had become too jaded.

But damn it, that's what this house was supposed to do for him, slow him down, give him something to focus on besides work. And yet chances were that the house wasn't going to make it.

Leaving him back at square one. His fingers brushed Molly's sides and she sucked in a breath. "Cold fingers," she whispered.

"I'm sorry," he whispered back. He leaned over her, bringing the wrap from her back to her front, his knuckles brushing against the very bottom curve of her left breast.

Her nipples hardened, and so did his body. He'd done this countless times before and had never, ever, felt aroused. He couldn't say that right now. Then he realized he wasn't breathing, and neither was she.

"I'm nearly done," he said, not wanting to look into her eyes, not wanting to look at her body, and failing at both. When he finished, he slowly reached out and tugged the material of her shirt closed. His fingers were shaking.

She put her hands over his. "It's okay if you don't want me. It's happened before."

He stared at her in shock. Obviously she'd missed the erection threatening the buttons on his Levi's.

"They call me the absentminded professor, did you know that?" Her vulnerable smile broke his heart. "I'd forget my own head if it wasn't attached. Men, intelligent men, don't like that."

"Molly. I want you."

"You...do?" Her gaze searched his with a hopeful hunger that made him groan.

"Yes. But—"

"Uh-oh. The but."

"It's just that you're hurt. You're vulnerable. I can't, won't, take advantage of that."

"I'm not that hurt."

"Really? Because you're green, which means

you're nauseous. Dizzy. You need to rest, Molly.''

"Yeah." Her eyes closed, her expression too tight with pain for his comfort. "Matt?"

He swept her hair from her face, shocking her with the gentleness of his touch. "Yeah?"

"If you're not going to kiss away the pain, could you talk to me?"

His fingers went still on her. "What?"

"I rambled on about me, it's your turn. Talk to me. Tell me about this house, your job. You."

"I don't like to talk about myself."

"Please?" Carefully scooting back, she made room for him, looking up at him with eyes hurting and more than half braced for rejection.

Ah, hell. With great care he lay on his side, facing her, and very gently brought her still shivering body against his. Then he closed his eyes as a wave of unexpected tenderness and need rolled over him.

She'd hit his weak button dead-on. He couldn't stand to see anything or anyone hurting. It was as if she knew he'd never willingly open up, but because she was in pain and he was programmed to try to alleviate that pain, he'd do as she'd asked.

But to actually do it, talk about himself...
"Well...you asked about this house."

"Yes." Eyes still closed, she put her cheek to his chest and smiled. "It's a lovely house."

"It was my grandfather's. He—" A vicious wind whistled through the basement, followed by the sounds of wood straining, cracking.

Had he only a few hours ago been whining to himself about the work the house needed? Now, with all his heart, he wanted to be able to do that work. "He left it to me."

"What about your parents?"

"They died in a plane crash on vacation in the West Indies three years ago."

"Oh, my God. I'm so sorry. Were you close?"

"No." He'd expected her hair, with its wild curls, to be rough to the touch, but it was soft and silky. Irresistible. "My parents...they weren't really meant to have children." Damn, where the hell had that come from? "We didn't spend much time with them, my brother and I."

"But you had your brother."

"Yeah. Luke."

"You're close?"

"As close as we can be living one thousand miles apart. He's in L.A."

"And you had your grandfather." She opened her eyes and studied his face.

He wondered what she saw when she looked at him like that. "So to speak. He was pretty much stuck with us."

"But he left you the house. What a lovely legacy."

"I didn't want it."

Beneath his touch, she sighed and closed her eyes again. The tension lines around her mouth eased a bit. "Why?"

"It needs what I can't give. Time. I don't know why he did it, I don't need the legacy."

Her fingers rested over his heart. "Everyone needs something from their past. It's what you build your future on. I don't have much because we moved around a lot, but I have pictures and my old Barbie dolls. And postcards from my dad from wherever he was."

And because she was sentimental—something he was not—these things obviously meant a lot to her. "My parents didn't save anything."

"No pictures, nothing?"

"Nope."

"Surely your grandfather kept something of your childhood?"

"Just the house. Which I don't need, not when I spend my time in Houston in the E.R."

"Ah. You work too much."

He looked down into her face and stroked at the remaining tension in her temples. "Like you, apparently."

"Like me," she agreed. "But past tense only."

"Yeah, well, I don't feel the need for a cat and I already know how to ski."

As he'd hoped, a ghost of a smile touched her lips.

"And this house…" He looked around the damp basement. "It just seemed like too much work. Until…"

Eyes still closed, she squeezed his fingers. "Until what, Matt?"

He'd never heard her say his name before, and on her lips it sounded so…intimate. "Until I got here." He took a deep breath and tipped his head back to study the ceiling, wondering what was happening above, if there was anything left. "I spent summers here. I didn't remember until today, when I was walking down the empty hallways, that the time I spent here, with my brother and grandfather…those times were the best times of my life."

"And now that you remember? Are you okay with taking over the care of the house?"

"There probably won't be a house left to care for, not after this storm."

Now she opened her green, green eyes. Brought his hand to her mouth, brushing her lips over his knuckles lightly. "Do you believe in fate, Matt?"

Slowly he shook his head, mesmerized in spite of himself by her lovely eyes, by the feel of her lips on his skin. He should pull away, should take his hands off her, but he couldn't. "No, I don't believe in fate. We make our own destiny."

"If that's true, then this will work out, because you'll make it work out. Right?"

An image came to him. It was summer, he was on a ladder painting the house, bringing it back to its former glory.

On a ladder next to him was another painter, back turned. But then she faced him. Molly. Smiling and working with him side by side.

His heart skipped a beat and he surged abruptly to his feet.

"Matt?"

How had he let that happen? How had he managed to spill his guts? Managed to get himself good and attracted to a woman he knew little about and was never going to see again after this? "I'm...still wet." He turned and pawed through the box for more clothes.

She let out a sound of regret. "My God, you are, I'm so sorry, I forgot. How could I have? Here, take one of the blankets—"

"No," he said a little too harshly when she struggled to rise. "There's more here." He gentled his voice, hardened his emotions. He was a doctor. He was her doctor. "Go to sleep. I'll wake you soon enough."

She wasn't buying his sudden retreat. "Matt? What's the matter?"

What was the matter? Other than she'd somehow coaxed him to talk about himself when he never did that? "You need rest."

"And I scared you. Was it because you opened up? Or because you want me as much as I want you?"

"Molly."

She let out another ghost of a smile. "It's unnerving, isn't it? This...this instant connection we have?"

"Go to sleep." His voice sounded terribly desperate, even to his own ears.

"I will. If you come back." When he just looked at her, she let out a low laugh. "To keep me warm.'' Her voice had it all—patience, worry, affection. Fear.

It was the last that really got him. Fool that he was, he climbed back onto that cot and wrapped his arms around her small, hurting and, God help him, hot body. And when her breathing was deep and steady, he stared down at her, wondering what it was about her that reached to the very depths of his soul, as no one else ever had.

SHE DUG HER FINGERS into the branch and whimpered. She hung over the roaring river, which rose with every second. It hit her toes, her calves...her thighs.

Her life flashed in front of her eyes; her boring, staid, sexless life.

No, she refused to die like this. With all her might she held on to the branch, but the vicious water swirled around her waist now, dragging her down. If she fell, the current would sweep her away.

Then the branch cracked. Terrified, she stared up at it, watching as it fell away from the tree in slow motion.

Screaming, she fell toward the swirling depths of the water—

"It's just a dream, Molly. Come on now, it's okay, you're safe. Molly?"

She jerked awake to find Matt holding her close, his face hovering above hers.

"That's it," he murmured, his big hand cupping her jaw. "You're awake now. You're fine."

Frantically, she patted herself, amazed to find her body dry. "I'm...not wet."

"Do you remember where you are, Molly?"

He seemed worried about her head injury, was looking into her eyes very intently. Closing her eyes, she sighed. "I remember. It just seemed so real." A shiver racked her, and with a deep sound of regret, he tucked her closer.

Brought her in full contact with his long, deliciously built, warm body. She moaned softly as he skimmed a hand down her spine. When he feathered his lips over her temple, the tip of her nose, she lifted her face, wanting more, wanting him to come down on top of her, nestling his weight between her thighs.

Yearning and burning, she shifted, wrapping a leg around his hip. She felt his erection, felt him sigh into her hair. "Matt..."

A husky groan tore from his lungs and he lifted his head, his eyes hot and heavy. "You need to go back to sleep." His fingers skimmed over her cheek. The sensation was so delicious she wanted him to stroke the rest of her, too, and when he would have retreated, she grabbed his hands.

"Stay with me."

"I am." He cupped her face, looked down at her, letting out an agonized groan when she arched to him, telling her without words he didn't intend to stretch out over her, link their fingers and drop a kiss on her waiting mouth.

So when he did just that, her heart nearly over-filled. The tension left her body, and she sank into the kiss.

Oh, yes, this is what she wanted, needed. His kiss, his touch. She wanted more. "Matt."

His kiss deepened and her bones just melted away. But he wasn't close enough, not yet…she shifted in fumbling haste…and gasped in pain.

He let out an answering moan and pulled back. "God, I lost my mind for a minute. Molly—"

"I'm fine, I'm hardly hurting anymore at all."

"No. You need rest." Gentling his hands on her, he put his forehead to hers. "Not another body touching your hurting one."

"Yeah." But that's exactly what she wanted as she drifted off again, held close to the body that took over her dreams.

CHAPTER SIX

SOMETIME LATER, Molly jerked awake. Her senses kicked in first. She was seeped in warmth, wrapped tight to the source. Above her the shrieking wind howled. Candlelight flickered over the dark, musty room, and as she blinked the cot, the wall lined with shelves into focus, she remembered.

The storm. The rescue.

Her hero.

Oh, yeah, her hero. They were spooned together, her back to his front. She was using one of his arms as a pillow, the other was draped over her, his fingers curled around her hip.

His legs were much longer than hers, which left his bare feet sticking out of the blanket. Not that it affected the heat radiating off his big body, which, given how she'd cuddled up to him in her sleep, she'd been grateful for.

As she lay there marveling over how lovely it

felt to have a man holding her, he stretched and groaned, then went still again.

But not her heart, which had started pumping at the flood of realizations. With the storm still raging, she remembered him waking her several times in the night, his low, husky voice murmuring questions. Feeling better each time, she'd hoped for more.

There had been no more.

Gallant, her hero was. But she didn't want gallant. She wanted passion and heat, all of which she'd seen in his eyes. She wanted to know she was alive, and that she'd stay that way.

His breathing was deep, even. He was lost in slumber while she lay here smoldering. Couldn't have that, so she stretched, wondering how he'd react to her arching like a cat against him.

"Mmm," came from deep in his chest, but he remained perfectly still, his breathing still deep and even.

One hard thigh lay against the back of hers. It took little to shift that powerful leg between hers. Little to rock her hips back so that there wasn't an inch between them.

Oh, yes, he was aroused, and it wrenched a helpless little murmur from her throat.

Suddenly, instantly awake, Matt sat straight

up. She imagined years in the E.R. had taught him how to do that.

"Molly?" The blanket fell away from him as he surged up and leaned over her. He put a hand on her forehead as he frowned down into her face. "What's the matter? You hurting?"

Oh, yeah, she was hurting. Just looking at him. His dark hair had rioted in his sleep, falling over his forehead. He had a shadow of growth along his jaw. His eyes were deep and full of concern. And his chest…good Lord, his chest was bare, his every muscle perfectly defined, and lit by the soft glow of candlelight as he was, he looked like a pagan god.

"Molly?"

"I'm…good."

"Your head? Your ribs?"

"Better." Unable to help herself, she tipped her head down the expanse of his flat, hard belly, trying to see the rest of him, but her own body thwarted her view.

When she struggled to sit up, he slid his hands beneath her to help, one getting caught in the material of his grandfather's shirt so that his fingers touched her bare spine.

Her gaze flew to his just as he practically leaped off the cot.

He wore a pair of sweats, low-slung on his hips and untied. ''I…'' He looked around him as if he desperately needed something to do, and if she hadn't wanted him to touch her again so badly she might have laughed.

''I remember there being a box of dried foods,'' he said quickly. ''I'll…find us some breakfast.''

Interesting. They could be close only when he was the caregiver, she the patient. When she became a flesh-and-blood woman, he went for distance.

Carefully holding her ribs, she sat up. She put her feet to the floor and tested her equilibrium. Pretty good, considering, so she stood. She wobbled for a moment, but held her own, even when the sweats she wore threatened to fall off her hips. Smiling, she held them up and shook her head at the man who'd done nothing but take care of her. ''It's my turn now.''

He looked adorably wary. ''Your turn to what?''

She made her way to him. Her head didn't quite reach his wide shoulders. Up close and personal like this, with all her wits about her for the first time, it wasn't easy to tear her gaze off his body, but she figured, given the volume of the storm still raging outside, she'd have all day to look her fill. ''It's my turn to take care of you. I'll make breakfast.''

He stared down at her as if no one had ever offered to do anything for him before. Which only stirred up a lot more than lust within her. She moved past him on her way to the boxes and, quite accidentally, her arm brushed his. Just that light touch brought her to a level of awareness she didn't know exactly what to do with.

Especially since it suddenly was more than just his body she wanted. That was a first for her, too.

She found that by moving slow, her ribs didn't hurt too much. In the storage bins there were granola bars and dried fruit, bottles of water, more candles and a radio and batteries.

She held up the bounty and smiled. ''Breakfast and news is served.'' Her smiled faltered when he came close with an intent expression on his face. Then it was her heart that faltered as he cupped her face, tilted it up and put his mouth on hers.

''What was that for?'' she asked shakily.

''I'm not sure.'' He looked shaky, too, as he spread a blanket on the floor. ''But it felt right.''

That it most definitely did. So right, she wanted another. And another.

Instead they sat leaning against the wall, their legs out in front of them, because sitting any other way was uncomfortable for Molly's aching ribs. They shared the food and listened to the radio tell them what they already knew.

The storm hadn't abated. The damage was extensive and reports of injuries and deaths had started rolling in.

Molly watched Matt's face grow more and more somber. "There's nothing you can do," she said gently, putting a hand on his forearm, feeling the muscles jump beneath her touch.

"I should be at the hospital."

"You will be. Soon as you can get there."

"Yes, but—"

"If you'd been there already instead of looking out the window of the house when the storm broke out..." She lifted a shoulder. "Let's just say I wouldn't be here, all warm and toasty. I'd be..."

He grimaced, reaching out for her hand. "Molly."

"I'm glad you were there," she said fiercely, clutching his hand to her heart. "I wasn't ready to die—"

"You wouldn't have—"

"I would have. If not for you."

The wind roared. The house above them groaned. Cracked. Beside her, Matt's eyes darkened with worry.

To take his mind off the house and the very good possibility he was losing it, Molly rose to look through the other boxes. She found one that didn't have supplies, but a teddy bear, a cap gun and a photo album. On the front of the album was a picture of two smiling little boys' faces, their arms tossed around each other, each missing their front teeth.

"What did you find—" Coming up behind her, Matt peered over her shoulder and let out a slow, shaky breath.

"You?" She pointed to the boy with piercing eyes filled with wit and humor.

He ran a finger over the teddy bear and the cap gun, then picked up the album. "Yeah. And Luke. I had no idea..." He slowly turned the pages.

Molly wondered if he had any idea how stunned he looked, how touched.

"I didn't know Grandpa kept anything. I thought..."

"That it didn't matter?" she wondered softly. Oh, yes, he was moved. Unbearably so if the working of his throat and warmth in his eyes meant anything. And so was she that it meant so much to him. "Want to look through the rest together?"

He started, as if he'd forgotten she was there.

"Come on." She backed him to the cot and carefully sat, patting the spot next to her. "Sit."

Wearing nothing more than sweat bottoms, he did. He put a hand behind her so that she was settled into the crook of his arm. When she tipped her head to see his face, he let out a half smile and she nearly melted because truly, he was the most thrilling, intense, sexiest man she'd ever met. "Is the teddy bear yours?"

Lifting it, with its missing eyes and ripped arm, he grinned. "This was my best friend. Max."

"Did Max keep all your secrets?"

"He did." His smile faded slowly and he shook his head, his eyes dark with memories. "My grandfather wasn't a sentimental man. Nor an affectionate one. He took care of us because my parents dumped us on him. In fact, he'd been thrilled when we were too old to come and destroy his world. Or that's what I used to think…"

"Would a man who wanted you out of his life have kept these things?"

Matt stared down at a picture of himself sitting

in front of a bonfire, roasting marshmallows. His grandfather stood beside him, guiding the stick into the fire, watching him with love and pride while Matt just grinned at the camera. He couldn't tear his eyes away.

"When was the last time you smiled like that?"

Turning his head, Matt met Molly's gaze and slowly shook his head. "I look pretty happy there, don't I?"

She never took her eyes off him. "Yeah," she said softly. "You look pretty happy."

When she'd been standing, he'd noticed she'd needed one hand to hold up the too big sweats. He'd wondered what would happen if she let them fall, but she hadn't.

Now, sitting, her hands were free and she ran a finger over his lower lip, a touch that went straight to his groin. "I meant right now, when you were smiling as you looked at the picture. You looked happy."

When he looked at her in surprise, she cupped his jaw. "It's a good look for you."

How long *had* it been since he'd felt that content? Carefree? That he couldn't remember didn't seem good enough.

And yet in spite of the storm, in spite of possibly losing the house, and not being at the hospital where he needed to be, he did. He felt…content. Happy.

She did that for him. He had no idea how that was possible, when for years and years he'd avoided any emotional attachments. But in a matter of twenty-four hours she'd found her way past those barriers.

Taking her hand in his, in a gesture he didn't know he had in him, he brought her fingers to his lips. "Thank you," he said a little hoarsely.

She looked a little stunned. "You saved my life. What are you thanking me for?"

"For being here with me."

Her lips curved in confusion. "But you know I didn't have a choice."

"Yeah, but if I had to be stuck in a basement during the storm from hell…" He set down the album. Slid a hand into her hair, his thumb lightly tracing the bruise on her temple. "I can't think of anyone else I'd rather have with me."

She went still, searching his gaze with that heart-stopping vulnerability he'd seen before.

Then a horrifying crash sounded above them, and another. Then yet another, and he instinctively reached for her when she cringed. "It's okay," he said, knowing it wasn't. Knowing that above them everything he knew and loved might just have been torn off its very axis.

"You don't have to be strong for me," she said, her face pressed into his neck. "You don't."

The noise above them was incredible. It was terrifying.

Or it would have been if he'd been alone.

But he wasn't. There was Molly, holding him as tightly as he was holding her, looking at him with so much trust in her eyes it hurt.

"Matt…"

When he met her gaze, she kissed him. Just another of her sweet, unbearably arousing kisses, but this time apparently it wasn't enough for her.

Hell, it wasn't enough for him, but…

She nibbled at the corner of his mouth, tearing a groan from his throat. "Molly. This isn't—"

"Shh." Cupping his face, holding it still, she nibbled at the other corner of his mouth. "Let me do this," she whispered. "Let me be there for you for a change."

He didn't need that. He never would.

"Don't hold back, Matt. Not with me."

He gripped her hips and rocked them to his so that she couldn't possibly mistake the throbbing bulge behind his insubstantial sweat bottoms. "Does this feel like I'm holding back?"

Her chest rose and fell with her rapid breathing. The pulse at the base of her neck had rioted. And she kept her wide, wild eyes on his as she purposely slid the neediest part of her over the neediest part of him. "But you *are* holding back. Please, Matt…"

"We'll be out of here by tomorrow morning at the latest," he said with his last vestige of control. "You're going back to your life and I'm going back to mine."

"I'm not going back to the same life."

"But I am."

She made a sound of regret. A sound of sorrow.

"I am, Molly." His fingers traced her jaw. "My life is full, I don't have time or room for anything else."

"Or anyone?"

Fingers still on her, he swallowed hard and fought with the need to pacify. But he never said anything less than the truth. Ever. "No," he said softly.

"Well, then." Her eyes were bright as she sank her fingers into his hair. "We'll just have to make the most of this time, won't we?"

"Moll—"

Her tongue outlined his lower lip.

With a rough groan, he hauled her close and surrendered. "God, Molly, what is it about you?"

She lifted her face, smiled a smile that reached straight through and grabbed his heart and squeezed. And this time when their mouths met, he knew. When she touched him, when she kissed him, she soothed a part of him that no one had ever touched or soothed before.

She needed this, she needed him, and for right now he could be what she needed.

After this, they were still going back to their lives, their very separate lives. He didn't have time or the heart for anyone in his, so he could do no less.

Yet right now, with her arms around him, with her body arching against his, and her tongue in his mouth, he was hers.

Just as when he was with her like this, she was his.

As simple and devastating as that.

CHAPTER SEVEN

As THAT SHOCKING realization came to Matt, he stood. Molly stood, too, her mouth wet from his, her eyes half hopeful, half resigned.

"Is that it?" she whispered, holding the ridiculously too large sweats up. "Is that all you'll let me give you?"

He'd thought this was about her, and what he could do for her. Take her mind off the storm. Keep her safe. Keep her comforted.

But he'd been fooling himself, it wasn't about that at all. From the moment they'd ended up in this basement, *she'd* been keeping *his* mind off the storm. She'd been keeping him safe. Keeping him comforted. "We can't."

"Why not? We're both consenting adults."

Yeah, Matt, why not? "We don't have protection."

"I'm...on the pill." She looked away. "I, um, like the regularity."

"The pill isn't protection against—"

"I haven't...done this in a long time." Her voice dropped to a low whisper. "A very long time."

His heart took yet another stumble, and he cupped her soft cheek in his hand. "Me neither."

Her gaze flew up to his. "You...haven't?"

"No."

"Then let me—"

"No. Let *me*."

Her breath caught when he trailed his fingers down her cheek, caressing her jaw. He'd never in his entire life touched a woman this way, this slow, purposeful memorizing of features. But Molly put a craving deep inside him he'd never felt before, a need he'd never felt before. His mouth skimmed over hers, once. Then again.

She made a whimpering sound in her throat and pressed closer, and the kisses turned wild and wet and deep, as necessary as air. Everything about her attracted him; her touch, her scent, her smile. He didn't know how he could get enough of her in just this one heavenly interlude, but he would try.

Cupping her breasts, he rasped his thumbs over the nipples that were already hard for him.

"Matt." Her sigh came thick and husky, and

made him want more. She lifted her hands and held them to the backs of his.

As she did, taking her hands off the too big sweats she wore, the material slipped off her hips. Past her knees.

Puddled around her ankles.

With a gasp, she would have bent and reached for them, but Matt held her still with one arm very carefully hooked around her waist, lower than her bruised ribs. The other toyed with the hem of the shirt that covered her to mid-thigh.

Dressed only in the shirt now, with the sweats still pooled at her feet, it took nothing more than a slight touch here, a button undone there, and the shirt floated down as well, leaving her soft and pale and gleaming by candlelight.

With a dreamy smile she reached out and untied his own bottoms, then added a shove of her hands until they both stood there bathed in the flicker of candlelight and anticipation.

Supporting her weight, he worshiped her breasts one at a time until her breath came in hard pants, her hands clutching and unclutching his shoulders, his name on her lips.

Taking care with her bound ribs, he laid her on the cot, but he didn't get on it with her.

Eyes opaque with desire, she blinked. "Matt?"

Kneeling on the floor at her hip, he turned the other way and kissed the very top of her big right toe.

"Matt?"

With a glance over his shoulder, he sent her an innocent smile. "Hasn't anyone ever kissed your toe before?"

"No." She was looking at him with a heart-melting mixture of shameless need and wariness. Then her breath sucked in hard when he trailed his tongue up her calf.

"How about there?" he asked.

"Uh—" She broke off with a strangled gasp when he took a foot in each hand and spread her legs so he could kiss the inside of her knee.

Then above that knee, eliciting another gasp.

"Or here, I take it?" he murmured, dotting openmouthed kisses over the tender skin inside her thigh.

"N-no."

"Hmm." Slowly, ever so slowly, he moved his hands up her legs until his fingers met, and then he kissed her there, *there,* light feathery kisses that tasted like pure heaven.

She cried out, her breath coming in little gasps

while her fingers fisted themselves in his hair. "Ohmi—"

"Good?"

"Oh, yeah." The low, rough sounds she made as he pleasured her nearly undid him. "*Please,* Matt…"

"Come." With slow, knowing care, he took her into his mouth. "I want you to."

Watching her, touching her, tasting her as she did just that was everything. He used his fingers, his mouth, and then she was arching back, shuddering, shuddering, shuddering, sobbing out his name while he slowly brought her back to earth.

"Hold on to me," he whispered, shifting between her legs, careful to keep his weight off her ribs as he slowly sank into her. "Oh, baby, you feel good."

She opened her eyes on his, her own bright and shimmering and full of unspeakable emotion as she gripped his upper arms and lifted her hips, desperately seeking the same thing he was, burying her tongue in his mouth when he lowered himself over her.

Desperately afraid he was looking into his future, his heart, he closed his eyes and thrust home. She was hot and wet, and his. *His.* He felt release coming too hard, too fast, from his body and his heart, and he tried to hold back, to regain some control.

''No,'' she murmured, reaching down, gripping his hips in her hands, urging him on, urging him to match the flex and pull of her movements. Then they were reaching together, for something he'd thought impossible...

The moment, when it came, was shockingly powerful. And together their breathing, their bodies, became one.

When it was over and they lay panting in each other's arms, Matt held her, overwhelmed by an emotion he had no defense against. It would fade now, any second, he told himself. She'd sated him physically. It was over.

But her arms still clung to him, and he waited for the inevitable claustrophobic feeling he always felt when a woman clung.

He waited.

And waited.

Then, with a low, sexy purr that started his engines again, Molly kissed his ear.

And still, Matt waited. Yeah, any moment now. The glowing emotions would fade away, leaving him back the way he'd been before.

But Molly turned her head, lined up their mouths.

His body was already hard again when they made love a second time. And then a third.

And still, the emotions never faded.

"DO YOU HEAR THAT?" Molly asked. They were sitting on the floor, Matt pretending they hadn't just shattered each other while making love over and over, and Molly pretending it didn't matter what he thought.

Matt set down his bottled water and got to his feet. Turning away from her, he studied the door they'd crawled through sometime yesterday. "I don't hear anything."

"Exactly."

He whipped back toward her, his mouth dropping. "My God. You're right. It's…over."

Yeah. And he was climbing the walls to get out there and on to his work. His life.

It wasn't easy for Molly to admit she'd hoped the storm would never end, but she did. She'd come to life here in Matt's arms, as she never had before.

Because of it, she now knew what people meant when they spoke of love, just as she now knew exactly what she'd been missing.

"Yeah, it's over," she whispered, but she was talking to his bare, sleek back because he'd

368   STRANDED!

turned toward the door and was trying to pry it open.

"Don't you want to get dressed back into your clothes first?" Anything to postpone the inevitable. Anything to have a few more moments.

He turned back, his chest heaving from the exertion. "Yeah, good idea."

He headed toward the back shelving unit where they'd spread out their drenched clothes. Without any of the hesitation currently stabbing her heart, he collected their things.

Handing hers to her, he grimaced. "They're not dried all the way through, so they're probably going to be cold and damp."

"Better than nothing," she said, clutching her stuff to her chest, trying not to stare as he unselfconsciously dropped the sweats from his hips, leaving him gloriously nude for one moment before he stepped into his clothes.

Then, realizing she wasn't doing the same, he cocked his head in concern. "You okay? Your head hurting again? You dizzy, or—"

"I'm fine." And she would be. Even if it killed her.

Which it might.

Her clothes were indeed still damp. And cold. And her heart hurt. So did her ribs. But hell if she was going to say a word about any of that while he walked right out of her life.

Nope, she was going to hold her head up and watch him go.

But she didn't expect him to come close. To take her clothes from her suddenly cold fingers. Didn't expect him to smile a smile that reached her chilled heart as he stripped her out of his grandfather's spare clothes.

"You're beautiful," he whispered, his breath catching as she let go of the shirt and held out her arms for her own, causing her breasts to sway inches from his face. "So beautiful."

Her nipples hardened. Not because she was cold, but because of him. For him. "Matt…"

His expression shuttered, and he turned away. Got to his feet. "I need to see the house."

"I know." She buttoned herself up and came up behind him, staring at his stiff shoulders, knowing he was already lost to her, already out there and moving on.

Then he muscled the door open and reached back for her hand. "Ready?"

No.

"Molly?"

"Yes." She forced a smile. "I'm ready."

CHAPTER EIGHT

MATT CLIMBED OUT of the storm cellar, his heart in his throat as he reached back to help Molly. Around him the rain was still coming down, only gently now. The wind had died, leaving them in a world of eerie silences.

He didn't let himself register the south wall of the house, or the west wall as they walked around without talking, their feet sinking into inches of mud.

But as they came around to the front and he could see, he let out the deep breath he hadn't realized he'd been holding.

The house still stood.

Half the windows were gone, as was the porch and the veranda, and a good portion of the upstairs roof, but the foundation had held.

He still had the legacy that suddenly meant more to him than he could have imagined.

Or maybe not so suddenly, he thought as Molly reached for his hand, also staring in won-

der at the house. "Wow." She smiled at him
through her exhaustion and lingering injuries and
all they'd shared. "It's still here."

"Yeah."

"I'm so glad, Matt." Turning to him, she
slipped her arms around him and hugged gently.
His arms wrapped around her and for a moment
he buried his face in her hair and wondered what
it would be like to hold her like this every single
day for the rest of his life.

Then he remembered he didn't do forever.

"I'm so glad for you," she said, clinging as
hard as she could without hurting her ribs. "Your
life will be the same, just as you wanted."

Yeah. Just what he'd wanted.

So why couldn't he let her go?

A honk startled them both. Coming down the
washed-out driveway was a truck, driven by a
high school kid Matt instantly recognized. He
couldn't remember the boy's name but he was
part of a volunteer group at the hospital.

"Dr. Walker," he yelled out the window, waving his free hand. "You're here!" He hopped out
of the truck, sank into the mud up to his ankles
and grinned in relief. "Dr. Salenski sent me out
here looking for you, thinking maybe you were

stranded. I'm sorry, Doc, but you're needed at the hospital, pronto.''

Good. Great. He was needed at the hospital. By Dr. Salenski no less, his friend and boss. The only man who'd think to find him here because he was the only one at work who even knew about the house. ''We need a lift,'' he said, and when he felt Molly take a step back, he grabbed her hand.

''You've got to go.'' She stared down at their joined hands, hiding her expression from him when her curls fell into her face. ''So…goodbye.'' She tried to tug free but he wouldn't, couldn't, let her go.

''Molly.'' Suddenly he could hardly take a breath. ''Where do you think you're going to go?''

''Home.''

He didn't know where that was. Panic flared, and he held up a finger to the kid, who nodded. Then he grabbed Molly's other hand and pulled her toward him.

They weren't touching except for their fingers; he couldn't touch her again because that would be continuing this amazing interlude beyond what they'd both wanted.

Wouldn't it?

"I want you to come with me," he said quietly. "I want you checked out."

"I'm fine, Matt."

"You're coming. She's coming," he said to the kid, and before she could pull her hands free, he'd opened the truck door.

She ground her heels in and gave him a look that made him sigh.

She was going to be stubborn. Fine. She couldn't wait to get out of his life, but damn it, he apparently needed more time. "Moll, there is no electricity, not to mention there isn't a phone for miles. I'm not leaving you here. Don't ask me to."

For a long heartbeat she just stared at him, and he wished he could read her mind, but then she got into the truck.

The ride to the hospital was long. Cramped. Her thigh was pressed to his thigh, her arm against his side. The shocking devastation of the storm should have sidetracked him from that connection he had with her, but it didn't.

Wanting more, he lifted his arm so that at the next turn she sort of fell into him. He liked that, or he would have if she hadn't held herself so stiffly, clearly not wanting to be touching him at all.

When they got to the hospital, his staff practically jumped him, overwhelmed with the crowd, the demands of the storm and the injured. Matt wanted to treat Molly himself, check her out thoroughly, but before he could, one of the nurses gently pulled her away.

By the time he'd delegated as much of the crisis as he could, and run to the cubicle he knew they'd put her in, it was empty.

If he thought he'd felt panic before, it took over his body now. His heart pumped, his mouth dry. "Where is she?" he demanded of a nurse in such a raw tone she blinked in surprise. "The woman being treated in this cubicle," he repeated. "Where did she go?"

"Uh…" She consulted her clipboard. "Molly Stanton?"

Stanton. Thank God, there would be records. He'd be able to find her if he was too late—

"She just left—"

Before the nurse could finish the sentence, he took off, dodging nurses and patients as he headed toward the exit, searching for that blond mop of curls. "Molly," he said with huge relief, turning her around—

"Sorry," the woman who wasn't Molly said with a regretful smile. "But—"

Matt kept running.

He'd thought he'd needed out of that storm cellar; he'd thought he'd needed to get back to his own life. But as the hours had passed, and Molly had brought him to life in a way he hadn't expected, he realized the truth.

He hadn't saved her.

She saved *him*.

It was true. While the world had raged above them, in her arms he'd discovered heaven.

He skidded to a halt at the double glass doors, searching right and left. She couldn't have gone far, not yet, he assured himself. Not when he'd just come to understand something else.

Now he understood exactly what he'd been missing all his life, something he just might have found in the most unbelievable storm of his life…

"Molly." He nearly collapsed in gratitude when he saw her petite form waving down a cab. He ran up to her, then was so out of breath he had to bend over and put his hands on his knees. He, who ran five miles every other day. "I…"

"It's okay, Matt," she said softly, opening the door of the cab. "I know."

"You…know what?"

"This is goodbye." She touched his face. "I'll never forget you. Ever."

"No." He grabbed her hand when she would have slid into the cab.

"No...what?"

"No. I don't want it to be goodbye."

She went utterly still. "What are you saying?"

He'd given speeches. Classes. Lectures. He'd been barking orders all his life, so why now did his tongue suddenly tie up on the most important speech of his life?

"Look, I know you wanted an adventure. You wanted to restart your life. I know these past few days gave you the courage to do that, but I don't want to just be the catalyst, Molly. I want..."

Her gaze searched his. "You want..."

What? What exactly did he want? Tell her!

Her eyes went a little sad when he couldn't spit out the words, and she patted his shoulder. "Thank you," she whispered. "Thank you for saving my life."

She slid into the cab.

He grabbed the door, held it open. "You saved me. *I'm* thanking *you*."

"Matt—"

"And now I want you to save me every day for the rest of my life. I love you, Molly."

Her eyes widened. She swiveled, looked at the cabdriver, then stared at Matt again. Slowly she got back out of the cab. Shut the door. "Could...could you repeat that?"

"I want you to save me—"

"The last part please," she said very shakily. "Just that last part."

Feeling the fist around his heart loosen, he pulled her close and buried his face in her neck, inhaling her scent, knowing now he would never, ever, get tired of saying it. Lifting his head, he smiled down into her face. "I love you. Now could you say you might possibly feel the same way about me someday in the near future so I can breathe again?"

"I might possibly feel the same about you in the very near future," she repeated obediently, then threw her arms around his neck. "Matt... how does now sound? How about, I love you now?"

All his tension dissipated and he grinned. "Now sounds just about perfect."

EPILOGUE

"SO YOU WERE SAVED by a woman."

Matt put the cell phone to his shoulder, which freed up his hands to hold Molly close. "You're taking that out of context, Luke."

"Oh, excuse me. You're the big hero. You're strong. You're rough and tough enough to haul her out of the creek—"

"It was a raging river!"

"And you kissed her cut all better."

"It was more than a cut," Matt protested, even knowing Luke was teasing him.

"Bottom line, *she* saved *you,* big guy. Admit it."

Matt looked over at Molly, and felt his heart swell. "Yeah." They were being driven home by that same volunteer kid Matt now knew was Tim. Molly had stayed at the hospital under observation for her head injury while Matt had worked a very long shift, and as he still wasn't ready to let her go, he was taking her home to his condo.

If he had his way, he'd never let her go.

Luke, who'd been frantically calling Matt ever since the storm had hit to make sure he was okay, sighed. "So I guess you're going to marry the only woman who's ever tamed you."

Matt never took his eyes off Molly, and it wasn't panic but hope that made his heart catch. "I just might."

"What a sad, sad day for single women everywhere. But at least they still have me."

"Until you're saved by love, as well, big brother. Watch out, it comes when you're least expecting it."

"I'm not expecting it at all."

"Then it's probably already on its way." Leaning over, Matt put a soft kiss to Molly's lips. "I just hope it's as good for you as it is for me."

* * * * *

Don't miss Luke Walker's story,
part of the
AMERICAN HEROES
miniseries in Temptation. Catch
LUKE,
Temptation #938, coming in August 2003.

Don't miss the sequel to
Men of Courage. **Here's your chance**
to save $1.00 off the purchase
of any one of the following
AMERICAN HEROES titles:

Riley by Lori Foster
(June 2003)
Sean by Donna Kauffman
(July 2003)
Luke by Jill Shalvis
(August 2003)

These men are heroes—
strong, fearless…and impossible to resist!

SAVE $1.00

off the purchase of any one of the following
AMERICAN HEROES titles: *Riley, Sean* or *Luke.*

Coupon expires September 30, 2003.
Valid at retail outlets in the U.S. only.
Limit one coupon per purchase.

110520

5 65373 00076 2   (8100) 0 11052

Don't miss the sequel to
Men of Courage. Here's your chance
to save $1.00 off the purchase
of any one of the following
AMERICAN HEROES titles:

Riley by Lori Foster
(June 2003)
Sean by Donna Kauffman
(July 2003)
Luke by Jill Shalvis
(August 2003)

**These men are heroes—
strong, fearless…and impossible to resist!**

SAVE $1.00

off the purchase of any one of the following
AMERICAN HEROES titles: *Riley, Sean* or *Luke*.

RETAILER: Harlequin Enterprises Ltd. will pay the face value of this coupon plus
10.25¢ if submitted by customer for this product only. Any other use constitutes fraud.
Coupon is nonassignable. Void if taxed, prohibited or restricted by law. Void if copied.
Consumer must pay any government taxes. Nielson Clearing House customers submit
coupons and proof of sales to: Harlequin Enterprises Ltd., 661 Millidge Avenue, P.O.
Box 639, Saint John, N.B. E2L 4A5. Non NCH retailer—for reimbursement submit
coupons and proof of sales directly to: Harlequin Enterprises Ltd., Retail Marketing
Department, 225 Duncan Mill Rd., Don Mills, Ontario M3B 3K9, Canada. Valid in
Canada only.

Coupon expires September 30, 2003.
Valid at retail outlets in Canada only.
Limit one coupon per purchase.

52604371

Visit us at www.eHarlequin.com   HTCOUPAHCAN
© 2003 Harlequin Enterprises Ltd.

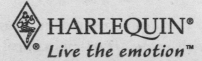